All Things in Time

A Time Equation Novel

Eric S. Martell

Second Initiative Press

This book is dedicated to loyal readers of my Time Equation books. Thank you for taking the *time* to read!

Thanks to Kelley York of SleepyFox Covers for the great cover art and design.

True Love is Precious

But, what if the two lovers cannot possibly make their relationship work?

The two grew up together. Each often knows what the other is thinking. They get along perfectly. Unfortunately, they belong to different sentient species. There is no chance for them as a couple. How can she compete with a beautiful but twisted female of his own kind?

Each needs a mate of their own species, but finding a suitable life partner can be problematic. There will almost always be missteps, sometimes even fatal mistakes.

There is no such thing as an impossibility in the infinity of years available throughout eternity. The laws of probability imply that given enough time, any event, no matter how improbable, has a chance of happening.

The ability to jump through time and space can make things easier or more difficult. It also attracts those who will kill to get the secret for themselves.

When all of infinity is available to search for a mate, will it be necessary to go beyond death to find success?

This is the fifth story in the Time-Equation Series.

Contents

Introduction

I usually don't write introductions to my stories, but I decided to write one in this case.

A Time for All Things is the fifth novel in the Time Equation Series, and most of the characters have previous roles in the earlier books. Their personalities are established, and they have a history in common.

While I worked to make this novel understandable and enjoyable to readers who have not read the previous books, there are references to events prior to those in the story. In general, that will not be confusing, although it may raise a question about the previous event in the reader's mind.

Rest assured that the story makes sense because the characters develop as the plot progresses and no previous knowledge is required.

Chapter One

The Pleistocene

She knew from experience that she was almost invisible in the dappling of shade and sun shining through the canopy of leaves. She waited there for prey. As she waited, her mind refused to come to grips with her problem no matter how much she wanted a resolution.

Lola had concealed herself in a mixture of trees and the thicker growth near the edge of the hilltop copse. Her brilliant colored feathers paradoxically blended into the various shades of russet and sun-splashed green.

In confirmation, she glanced over her shoulder and flexed her arm, causing the trailing feathers to reflect a bit of the sunlight that was filtering through the leaves overhead.

Not too bad, she thought. I'm pretty. I know I'm pretty. He loves me, it's true, but...her train of thought changed. The self-admiration tinged with an undercurrent of insecurity and sadness slid into the back of her mind as she tried to analyze what she'd just seen.

What was it? There had been a brief movement below her on the far side of the open area. Whatever it was, it hadn't exposed itself, only moved a few leaves as it passed. The movement wasn't due to the non-existent breeze. It was unusually still for an autumn day in this northern latitude.

It was hot, and the lack of wind made it hotter. It wasn't an ideal time to hunt, but she was hungry, and the small group of grass eaters that had been drifting toward the cool of the trees from out on the plains should pass within attack range.

Her hunting prowess was high, but she had limitations. She was considerably smaller than her Aunt Fancy. Her deceased Aunt Belle had been even larger. She sighed quietly, remembering how beautiful Belle had been and how much smaller and bedraggled she'd looked with a killing bullet hole through her breast.

———◦○◦———

Lola took after her mother. Lolita was the runt of the three deinonychus sisters brought forward from the Cretaceous by Jason Gridley. Lola was small, too. The last time she had stepped on the scales, Kathleen had told her she was right at ninety-eight pounds.

That was just about right as far as she was concerned. She fit neatly into Cole's arms when he was sitting. The thought of snuggling with him gave her a warm feeling inside. She considered it. It was similar to snuggling with her mother or Kathleen, but there was a trembling undercurrent of strange emotion, too.

She was easily old enough to have a mate. Her mother encouraged her to seek one, but the motivation had never been strong. She sighed again, louder. The problem was evident to her, although she tried to hide it from everyone else in their small group of humans, wolves, and deinonychus.

She'd grown up with Cadeyrin and Kathleen's son, Cole, and had been with him so long that they had bonded emotionally in some powerful sense. She'd never questioned their friendship or even the fact that human language came so quickly to her. She was more fluent than her mother, who spoke somewhat broken English, and much more fluent than her Aunt Fancy. It was only in the last year that she'd begun to view their relationship differently. She wanted more from him, but she had difficulty with what that meant.

The terrible fact that Cole was human and she was a deinonychus created an impassable barrier between her desire and reality. She shook her head in an imitation of human negativity. Lola wanted to have a family. She was old enough. Past old enough.

Her mother had encouraged her to find a mate. It was easy enough. One of the humans, Kathleen, or perhaps even Cole, would transport her back through time to the Cretaceous period. Her mother had suffered bad luck with her first two mates. One had been killed fighting a government raid on Kathleen's house, and the second had died from a respiratory illness. The third was a good male but wild in his ways. Lolita had taken him off, far away from the human settlement, hoping that he would learn to control himself. Humans weren't safe around him.

She looked down at her toes, flexed her killing claws, then raised her head. The wind was stirring, and a distinct odor of carrion was wafting across the open area. Whatever was in the trees over there was definitely not a grass eater. It probably was looking for the same prey she was attempting to ambush. She made a soft, irritated noise. It'd better not interfere with her kill.

Her mind went back to Cole, and from him, she moved to the nature of humans. It was true that humans were not well endowed with natural weapons. They had no claws and no real ability to bite. Their strong points were in other abilities. They had a wide variety of knives and firearms that were better than claws and teeth. Cadeyrin even used his bow and was deadly with arrows out at a range beyond her sprinting ability.

She considered that for a moment. The clearing below her was perhaps a hundred meters wide. Cadeyrin could kill a deer with an arrow at that distance. On the other hand, she would be hard put to get close enough for a kill. Her muscular thighs were good for instant acceleration to a fast sprint, but she slowed down after forty meters or so. It wasn't that she got out of breath. Her lungs were excellent, but her thigh muscles would always begin to burn and tire after a relatively short period of total exertion. Because of that limitation, she had learned from Lolita and the other flock members to choose her ambushes carefully.

In the present case, the valley floor narrowed to a bottleneck off to her right. She had intended to startle the oncoming grass-eaters so that they would run toward the opening. It was just at the farthest extent of her sprint distance, and she thought she'd have an opportunity to close with one before the prey could escape.

She raised her head, listened, and smelled the wind. The meat-eater's odor had disappeared, and there was no sign of prey. Maybe the grass-eaters had turned away from the clearing. She would wait a little longer, then move a kilometer to a hillside for a better view.

Cole came back into her mind. He wasn't like her, but he wasn't exactly like the other humans, either. He was tall and muscular like Cadeyrin, yet there was some of Kathleen's look to his face. He was considerate and kind, and he treated her as an equal. More than an equal. She was totally at ease with him, confident that he would always treat her gently and never hurt her, either physically or mentally. He hadn't a cruel spot in him.

They had grown up together, played, ate, and cuddled together. How was she to blame if she'd imprinted on him rather than her own kind? Was he as attached to her as she to him? She made a distressed, soft sound from deep in her throat. She didn't know what to do, but her body told her that she needed a mate.

Meanwhile, Cole was off at someplace that Kathleen said was a special school, a college. It was a place that would teach him advanced knowledge. Lola snorted, completely forgetting her ambush. Cole hunted perfectly well with her and used his bow almost as well as his father. He could shoot a rifle better, in fact. Together they could survive anywhere in the Pleistocene wilderness. What other kind of knowledge was necessary?

The deer hadn't shown up. She was still hungry, and it was getting later in the day. She decided to move to the hill. It was closer to the stone house and other buildings, but it offered a good view of the hunting range. She might meet some of her kind or maybe some of the humans near there. They all used it as a look-out point. Besides, she thought, Cole would be showing up reasonably soon.

His ability to travel in time using his mother's discovery and natural ability distressed her a little. It was so easy to lose someone in all of the moments available. Cole had promised her that he would always return. Moreover, he was extremely careful to ensure that the duration of the time he spent in the future was equal to the duration of time he was away from the past.

That was a little confusing to her mind, but she understood it to mean that he and she would always be the same relative age. The potential offered by time-travel was such that he could spend years away from her but return a minute after he had left. They had both agreed that would be unfair, and Cole had said he feared it would change their relationship irrevocably.

A wave of distress overwhelmed her. She made another soft squawking sound. What relationship? The wolves considered themselves to be members of the human pack. The humans showed the wolves affection but treated them as less than equals. Kathleen had explained to her that humans and deinonychs had no natural business living together. Without time-travel, there was no chance the two species would ever come into contact.

Kathleen had said that the fact the deinonychus sisters had proven capable of learning to speak had stunned all of the humans. In the time where Kathleen had originated, African Grey Parrots could master possibly a thousand words and often used them appropriately. Still, they were not considered sentient in the fashion of humans.

What was sentient anyway? She thought, planned, felt emotions, and had desires for her future. She understood gentleness and cruelty...and, she hesitated before putting a word to the feeling: love.

Distracted, she had moved out of the trees as her mind pondered her problem and was halfway across the valley floor. A tremendous roar brought her sharply out of her mental fog.

The carrion odor was suddenly more pungent. The leaves on the far side of the clearing broke open, and a bear charged out, coming directly for her, its jaws gaping in a snarl. She instinctively dropped her head and spread her wing-arms, claws outstretched in the deinonychus attack posture. The bear was probably five times her weight, one of the smaller kind with a short muzzle. Still, it could easily outrun her in a long-distance race. She screamed her battle cry.

There would be no escaping a fight.

Chapter Two

Battle

Lola circled to the right. The bear had charged forward, then slowed and stood on its hind feet. It moved its head back and forth indecisively. Lola continued to circle, realizing the animal didn't know what she was and was undecided about completing its attack.

Abruptly, the bear snarled and dropped to all fours, then charged at her. She sped up, and it turned, trying to keep up with her. The circling strategy wouldn't delay the creature for long. She'd get tired, and it would figure out how to anticipate her movement.

She slammed on the brakes, spreading her wings and flipping her outspread tail feathers to help change direction. The dust rose under her feet, obscuring the dry, short grass. The bear tried to turn as quickly, but she had headed back to the left. She swerved and jumped high to kick at the animal's side as it passed. The killing claw of her right foot dug deep between the bear's short ribs, but her other foot missed its hold. She kicked hard and bounced back and to the left. The bear bawled in anger and spun so quickly it went down, rolling over twice before it came back to its feet.

Lola stood, head low, her arms outspread with her clawed fingers ready to grab. The bear sprang forward, and she slashed with her fingers at its eyes as she ducked under its jaws. A blow from the bear's forearm sent her careening away, but she kept her feet and turned her movement into a curving run back to the right.

The bear's tongue lolled out, and a trickle of blood dripped down its flank. Her claw had hooked deep, but, perhaps, not deeply enough. It snarled again and trotted forward, intent on closing with her but not falling into a blind charge.

She took three steps left, then turned and ran past the bear. This time, it spun quickly enough that she could not get past its opened jaws. She leaped over its muzzle and slashed downward with her fingers. The bear howled, its eye a ruin of torn flesh.

Lola turned to run away, but a heavy paw slapped her leg, knocking her down. She staggered to her feet and looked up. The creature loomed over her, slaver flying from its teeth.

There was a sudden flat slapping sound, and the bear grunted, looked puzzled, then its hindquarters collapsed. Delayed slightly, the sound of a rifle came booming in from the south end of the valley.

Limping, Lola moved away to a safe distance. When she judged she was far enough away, she stopped and turned to look. The bear had its remaining eye fixed on her. It could not get its hindquarters to work correctly, but it dragged itself after her with its front paws.

A second shot echoed down the open space, and the bear grunted again. It paused, then a gush of blood came out of its mouth, and it slowly laid its head on the ground. Lola watched from where she was. Even though her blood was up and she was angry that the beast had managed to hurt her leg, it would be stupid to approach it closely.

It wasn't finished yet, and a dying blow from a paw could still do immense damage. After a moment, she realized that it wasn't going to get back up. She turned and looked across the grass to see Cole heading toward her at his best running speed, a rifle in his hands.

Relief flooded her. She screeched in excitement, took two steps, and collapsed. Her bruised thigh muscles had locked in an excruciating cramp. She rolled over in agony and tried to straighten her leg, but it refused to move.

The pain made her vision haze, but she could see Cole getting closer. He came pounding up, breathing heavily.

"You little idiot! You could have been killed." He knelt and touched her leg. It hurt, and she hissed reflexively.

"It's alright, Cole. You're here now, and that bear is dead. I was going to kill it anyway, so maybe we get some meat and go home, huh?"

He leaned close and hugged her. She put her arms around him and rested her muzzle in the hollow at the base of his neck. It was a vulnerable position for him. Her jaws were well-armed with sharp teeth, but he showed no fear. That was one of the things that made him special to her; his complete trust.

"What hurts?" He pulled back and looked at her leg again.

"Bear hit me. My leg cramped, and my muscles are too tight. I can't walk right now."

"You shouldn't have let it hit you. It's too big and too fast to take on by yourself. You know that, Lola. Can't I trust you not to get in trouble?"

He was angry. She clicked her teeth together in agitation, then said, "It didn't give me any choice about it. I just wanted a deer, but I got a bear. Bad luck, huh?"

"Yes. Bad luck." He looked down, and she realized that he was trying not to show his anxiety for her. She nuzzled his neck again. After a moment, Cole began to feel her thigh muscle with his blunt fingers. She often marveled at his fingers. No claws, but he made up for their lack with amazing dexterity. Ahh, his fingers had found the knotted muscle and were gently probing around the area.

"Hurt?"

She hissed softly in pain. "Yesssss. Don't stop. It hurts, but the muscle is relaxing, maybe."

He began to work on the cramped thigh, massaging the knotted muscle deeply. It hurt, but she could tell the knot was loosening. She made a low humming from deep in her chest. It felt good. His attention always made her happy, even though her leg was still cramping. His fingers and nearness made the pain seem distant and disconnected from her.

"I can't go off to class for even a day without you getting in trouble. I'm going to have to stay here with you and give up learning, just to make sure you don't get hurt." He grinned as he spoke. "And, don't keep making your happy sound. I know you're hurt. You shouldn't be happy."

That was better. She'd been afraid that he would be angry with her, but he was going to forgive her. They had always gotten over things with each other quickly, and she didn't like to think that he was angry.

His fingers worked, and her mind floated in a haze of gradually lessening pain mixed with the peaceful feeling that being near him engendered.

No deinonychus could do what he was doing. How could she survive without Cole by her side? Her mind drifted to a scene in a bright meadow. She approached Cole, and he bobbed his head. She returned the gesture, realizing as she did that it was the beginning move of her kind's courtship dance. He looked over his shoulder, then bent down. She watched critically. He was not as graceful as a male of her species, in some ways, but he was perfect in his own way. She moved closer, breathing quickly.

The sky over the meadow darkened, and Cole's likeness morphed to a male deinonychus. Lola's instinct told her what to do. They walked slowly side by side, then she lowered herself and he—a bolt of lightning flashed overhead followed by thunder. She jerked out of her fugue and almost snapped at Cole's hands but caught herself in time.

He pulled back. "Did I hurt you?"

Lola felt sick. Her sadness was nearly too much to bear. She thought about it, then decided. Cole was her best friend. They'd always shared their feelings, but this was difficult for her to discuss.

"My leg is getting better. Maybe. You'll rub more of the pain out of it?"

He resumed the slow massage.

"Cole?"

"Yes?"

"I...we are not the same kind." Words failed her, and she looked around, trying to find a way to express what she felt.

He seemed to understand. He looked away as he spoke. "No, Lola, we are physically not the same, but we are soul-mates. We've been together from the time that I could barely walk. You know we often think the same thing at about the same time. You can't fool me. I have a good idea of what you're thinking. We can be together, hunt together, live in the same place, but we will both have to find mates of our own kind."

She moaned softly. "That's...that makes me sad. I have a pain in here." She indicated her breast with a graceful movement of her clawed hand. "It hurts."

He stopped rubbing her cramped muscle and placed a hand flat on her breast muscles. It felt firm and cool. His normal body temperature was lower than hers. She awkwardly grasped his hand with her claws, taking care not to scratch.

"It's right there. The pain, but it doesn't feel so bad with your hand there."

He sighed. "Lola, I'm sad, too. Grid told me that you were old enough to start a family. He said I should take you back to the Cretaceous and help you find a suitable mate. I guess I'm selfish. I wanted all your attention for me, but now I'm studying in college in the future. I have to spend a lot of my energy on that. It's not fair to you for me to hold you back." His voice grew thick and sounded choked.

She made another distressed sound, then shook her head. "I will stand up now." She moved, careful not to pull the muscle tight again. Cole lifted and helped steady her. Once on her feet, she moved forward slowly, testing each step.

"My leg is better. I cannot run, but I can walk. Let's get some bear meat and go back to the stone house. Maybe we can talk more on the way." She thought frantically, trying to come up with something, anything that would distract her from the painful topic. "I saw a horse earlier. It was by itself. Do you think it's lost from its herd?"

He glanced at her, then responded, playing along. "They sometimes get driven out of their herd. Horses have problems too. It might have been alone."

Her mind circled wildly, coming back to the problem in a rush. "Cole, I don't want to be alone! I want to be with you, but we can't have...we just can't."

He stroked her neck, ruffling the fine feathers as his hand trailed along the side. She leaned toward him. That was a pleasureful feeling.

"Lola, I know what you're trying to say. If I were one of your kind, I would be your mate in all ways. I'm your soul-mate, your friend. I think we will always be friends. I can't think of what it would be like for me if you were not here. I was afraid that bear had seriously injured you. You

have to be more careful. I, uh, I couldn't stand it if you were gone."

They continued walking, but he paused in his speech, apparently thinking of what he wanted to say. She contrived to walk closer so that their bodies brushed together.

Cole stopped in mid-stride, then put his hand on her neck. Their eyes met, and he stepped back, then dropped to a sitting position. She moved forward, lowering her body to rest on his legs. Their arms wound around each other's body, and she placed her head next to his neck.

"Lola, I love you. You are dear to me. You know that."

"Yes, Cole. I do. I know more. I know that we have to find a way to stay together but still fulfill our natures. I'm willing to try to find a mate in the past if you help me choose. Will you?"

He laughed somewhat shakily. "I will, but I'm not as good a judge of male deinonychs as you or your mother."

She snorted. "Mom is not a real good judge. She's picked two males that died and a third who is too wild. Maybe I'd better get Aunt Fancy to help me. She's got a good mate. He hunts well, too."

His hands scratched along her neck and softly under her arm, then across her breast muscles. She made a pleased cooing sound.

"No male deinonychus could do that as well as you do, Cole."

He pulled her close and shut his eyes. After a minute, he said, "We'd better get on back to the house. They'll be wondering where we are."

She rose, careful not to hook his legs with her claws. "Okay. I think my leg is well enough to get there."

He smiled at her. It was an expression that she understood intellectually, but not instinctively. She had little ability to express herself with her face, aside from a jaws open snarl of anger. Her lips wouldn't move in that way. She bobbed her head in acknowledgment. Her body movements showed her emotions better than her face.

"I think I'd better move us through space-time rather than have you walk." Without waiting, he pulled her close, then transitioned into the strange environment that his mother had first described with equations, but which his honorary aunt, Serensaa, traveled through naturally.

Lola closed her eyes. It nearly always made her dizzy. After a moment, he released her, and she opened them. They were in the center of the yard. The barns were to the left, and the main house was directly in front. She limped toward the stone steps, moving slowly and feeling as heavy as the rocks that made up the body of the house.

Despite her intentions, she still wanted Cole, but there was so much physical difference between them. She wanted, no, needed to raise a family, just as Lolita had raised her. She'd need a mate of her own kind, regardless of how her heart pulled toward the human male at her side.

She climbed the steps, her feathered crest lower than usual.

At the top step, Cole took a deep breath and said, "It will be alright, Lola. I want the best for you, and I'm going to see that you're happy."

In her ears, it sounded like a rejection rather than a pleasant promise.

Chapter Three

Mom

"Give it here." Kathleen pointed to the pack of bear meat that Cole had haggled off the deceased animal. "I don't need it right now, but it will keep in the icebox for a day or so. I'll probably mix it in with some venison stew. The bear fat will make it taste better and will help with our nutrition needs also."

Cole shrugged. His mother was sometimes too pedantic. She held a doctorate in particle physics, after all, and she'd taught before she had discovered time travel. He grinned to himself. He would like to know precisely how his father had found her and under what circumstances. She was probably near death, he thought. The Pleistocene Ice Age was not safe for an academic girl from 2015.

He watched her turn to the solar-powered appliance to stow the meat. She moved gracefully, although he knew that she had once had such bad scars that she had limped nearly everywhere. Credit was due to his dad's so-called primitive medical skills. Cadeyrin was amazingly knowledgeable when it came to survival skills. Languages and time-travel, too. His mother had been saved from a Smilodon by probably the only poly-math genius of the Clovis people in North America.

He grinned to himself again. Speaking of luck, he had his own share conferred by his parents. He had inherited their mental acuity, his mother's grace, and his father's physique. Living as they did, in the inter-glacial period, there were plenty of opportunities to hunt, and he had developed a significant percentage of his father's strength.
Hunting with the Deinonychus clan, and always with Lola, had sharpened his senses to their maximum. He wasn't at Lola's level when hunting, but he suspected that few humans could match his ability.

"Mom?"

"What is it, Cole? Did you have trouble with your classes today?"

He was attending the University of Michigan in the future. It was funny.
With all time and space to select from, his mother had insisted that he go to
that school in 2016. He'd argued that, rightfully, he should attend the during
the most recent year to which he could jump. That hadn't met with her
approval. She'd explained that 2020
was about the last point that he could avoid a lot of political and social
danger. He could graduate before that whole problem came to what she
surmised would be its inevitable disastrous conclusion.

He'd worried about it, but a quick jump with her to 2022 had allowed him to
investigate the news stories. Academic society had become focused on
politically-driven social issues and had seemingly forgotten about the simple
concept of meritocracy. He guessed she had a point. His current classes were
rigorous but fun. Then there was the societal madness about some flu-like
disease. He didn't worry about that sort of thing. His immune system was
more than potent enough to fend off that kind of illness.

She had purchased a small house for him that was just off-campus. That
allowed him privacy to jump back and forth. He kept modern clothes there.
Sometimes he'd arrive
dressed in buckskins. His father insisted on wearing animal skins that he had
tanned himself and, in point of fact, they were comfortable and more
durable than so-called modern clothing. Anyway, it wouldn't do to have
fellow students see him dressed in deer-skins. That would have attracted too
much attention.

Mom had explained that attention was not desirable, so he maintained a low
profile on campus. The government and several shadowy entities desperately
wanted her time-travel formula, and, she said, they would stop at nothing to
get it. If he were to become a news story in 2016, the limited time-travel
available to the government would allow them to send a squad of operatives
after him. If he were captured, she'd be in danger – something that he didn't
want. He knew she could fight and more than hold her own against those
people, but sometimes luck ran out. He knew that from hunting, and he also
knew just how easy it was to get severely injured.

"Not classes, Mom. It's just that Lola seems to really miss me when I'm
gone." He wasn't sure how to describe the problem he had with Lola. They

had been raised together and had been more than close for years. He trusted the brilliant little Deinonychus with his life, and he would do anything to avoid hurting her, but he couldn't see how to cope with what was becoming a real problem for them both.

Kathleen stopped rinsing the cutting board and turned to look at him. He gazed back, subconsciously proud of her. It wasn't everyone who had a mother that beautiful and intelligent.

"You're not telling me the whole problem, Cole, but I suspect I understand more than you know. Lola needs to be encouraged to find a mate of her own kind." She
held up her hand, stopping him as he opened his mouth. "I know. I know you don't want to share her with anyone, and you think that she'd leave you if she had a mate."

She paused, thinking. Then her face broke into a smile. "She would, too, when she had a chick. There's something about children that takes a mother's attention. The male has to learn to share her affection. He has to bond with the children, also. If nature works as it should, both parents find that loving their child also strengthens the bond
between them, their love for each other."

He started to speak again but stopped as she continued. "You have your own needs. Have you met any cute girls at school?"

He blushed. Of course, he had. "Well, yes, and no, I guess."

"What's that mean?"

"They are cute, but they're affected. Uh, maybe artificial is a better description. They are so caught up in their friends, parties, looking for boyfriends, athletics, social media
status, and so on, that they don't seem very real to me."

"So, they're not down-to-earth enough for you? Is that what you're saying?"

"I guess that's it. It's not that they aren't interested in me. At least, I think they are. It seems like there is always one or more of them that kind of hang around or follow me when I leave class. Is that because they're interested? I'm not sure."

She laughed, a full-throated but highly feminine sound. "Oh, Cole! You really don't know." She paused, then added, "Of course, they're interested in you. You're handsome, strong, and smart. Plus, you have an attitude of wisdom and calmness beyond your years. Young women like that. They're looking, perhaps subconsciously, for a suitable mate, and a suitable mate is one that will be able to provide for them and a family. I know that doesn't fit in with the cultural attitude on campus, but it's true, nonetheless. There's one other thing that they probably like about you. You are self-sufficient with enough money to have your own house."

He frowned. She was probably right. Sometimes he didn't want to admit it, but she usually was. Having a Ph.D. in physics didn't mean that was all she knew. In his experience, Mom was amazingly insightful.

"Well. Maybe that's all true. I could try out for some athletic team. Maybe that would attract more attention from girls. If more of them knew me, perhaps I'd have a chance to meet one that was less, uh, flighty." He finished with an embarrassed shrug.

Kathleen turned back to her work, then glanced at him out of the corners of her eyes. "Not a good idea. You'd compete too well. You may not realize it, but you're probably at least twice as strong as most modern humans. Your father's genetics and lots of exercise in this time and place give you an advantage no future man has. If you played football, you'd be in the national press, and researchers from the future would find out. Then we'd have trouble. I don't want them kidnapping you. It's too hard to get people out of that kind of situation. Your father and I have been fortunate in the past. Right now, no one up there knows when and where we are, and I'd like to keep it that way."

He shrugged again. "If you say so." The idea of future danger didn't seem real. He rephrased his objections to the women he'd met. "I just haven't met a female human who keeps my interest very long. Maybe I won't ever find one."

She nodded. "I understand how you feel. I never met anyone who could match your father. If I hadn't accidentally ended up in his path when I did, I might still be limping around campus and teaching first-year students."

He brightened. "Yes, but Lola is –"

Kathleen turned abruptly. "Stop! Cole, dearest son, listen to me. You cannot be an adequate mate for Lola. You two might be the best match mentally, but there is an unbridgeable difference physically. She needs, and it's a built-in biological requirement, to have her own family. The only way she can do that is if you love her enough to help her find a suitable male."

He nodded unhappily. "I know you're right, but it makes me feel bad inside, just thinking about it."

"You're going to have to mature out of that. She'll still care for you, even if she has ten chicks. Now, straighten up. It's time for you to show her that you care in return. Help her find a mate. We'll get your father and go back to the Cretaceous to find one."

He nodded again. "Think Grid would like to come?"

"Yes. I think Jason would probably be interested, and so would Lolita. She's confided in me that she's worried about you and Lola, too."

He laughed. "Even a killer raptor has more sense than I do. Is that it?"

She nodded. "Lolita is one shrewd little predator. She can see that you two need help as well as I can."

If Lolita felt he was too close to her chick, he had better listen. While smaller than all of the other Deinonychus clan, Lolita made up for her lack of size with a furious level of activity and, when needed, intense aggression. She'd been the first of Jason Gridley's adopted babies to begin to speak, and she was still the most human-oriented one of the group, aside from Lola.

"Okay. Maybe we can make it an expedition. I want to go back there. I've always wanted to see what it's like. Your stories and Jason's make it sound like a lot of fun."

She shook her head, although she was still smiling. "My goofy son you are. It's terrifying back there. Not fun. We'll need heavy weapons, and we'll also need to be prepared to jump out if the going gets tough. There is a significant amount of danger. That's why we've never let you go on your own."

He nodded. He had been taught advanced math at an early age and had long understood her time-equation. However, he'd learned more from his father. Cadeyrin had instinctively comprehended Serensaa's ability to walk through inter-dimensional space and time. His dad could use the time-equation but found that the spiritual approach worked better for him. Cole had learned that technique from both his father and Serensaa.

Serensaa was Logan Walker's Clovis culture wife. He'd met her when he accidentally slipped into the Pleistocene in Florida. It was funny that the two Clovis people were better attuned to spiritual life than the more modern humans. But then again, maybe it was not. There was a vast difference in life as he understood it and living in the future. He was much more, now that he thought about it, fully grounded than the people he'd met in the future. It had something to do with facing immediate consequences for your actions and realizing that a mistake could mean the difference between life and death. He'd never considered going through time to places not permitted by his parents. There was, after all, time enough for him to go where he wanted once he'd learned more.

Chapter Four

Lolita

Lola hadn't followed Cole into the house. She wandered slowly to the end of the porch and leaned against the rail, looking vacantly at the distant hills.

She was unhappy and confused. It didn't seem right that she couldn't have Cole the way she wanted, although she wasn't sure what that would entail exactly. He wasn't going to give her a chick, that was certain, but the other male Deinonychus weren't attractive to her. They were already mated, for the most part, but the four eligible males of her generation didn't attract her. She knew that they were interested in her. Two of them had made overtures, but she'd rather rudely ignored them.

Now, they ignored her, too, unless they were hunting as a pack. Not that that happened much. She usually hunted exclusively with Cole. The two of them worked like a highly efficient killing machine.

There was a 'whuf,' and she turned. It was BW, one of Shewanee's cubs. The wolves were the other main partners of the humans. Cole's mother had found Ulfsaa even before Cadeyrin had found her. The big gray wolf had lived a long and happy life but had reached the end of his trail two years ago. Still, he'd left a legacy. There were twenty-one wolves living near the settlement, and of them, twelve had picked humans as their primary companions.

BW, short for Black Wolf, was Serensaa's close companion. He was one of the lower-ranking males of the pack. When he wasn't with Serensaa, he often followed Lola around. She didn't mind. He was company when Cole was absent, even though he couldn't talk.

"You come to see me, huh, boy?" she asked.

He wagged and opened his mouth. Knowing the wolf form of greeting, she bent low and allowed him to place his jaws gently on her muzzle. He released her, and she took his muzzle in her mouth just as carefully.

Now that the formalities were over, he sat down beside her, arranging himself so that their flanks were touching. She leaned toward him, grateful for the contact and the distraction. He whined in response.

"You know that I'm sad, don't you?" she asked, not expecting an answer.

He whuffed again and wagged his tail. He was good company, she thought, and even better to hunt with, as long as Cole wasn't around.

There was a clicking sound made by claws tapping across the stone porch.

Lolita moved up and sat on her other side, sandwiching her between the wolf and herself.

"Lola. I see you sad, and I got to say that you have to quit this. You old enough for a family, but to get a family, you gots get a mate, a nice male, and Cole is not who you need."

Lola felt a surge of resentment. Her mother should know how perfect Cole was. She hissed softly in frustration.

Lolita chucked from deep in her chest. "Yeech. Yeech. I know that Cole your friend. You two been close since both chicks. Still, Cole a human. He not a raptor like you. We gots find you a male, then everything be right. You see, just wait. All will be clear to you. You still gots Cole. I gots a mate and still gots humans I love. You do same. All be better." She paused, then added, "'sides, I wants grandchicks to play with. You gots to provide. I gots no one else."

Lola sighed. Lolita was amazingly intelligent and undoubtedly correct despite her less than perfect English. Her mother had been unlucky with mates, losing her first two, and then she had banished her third a year ago. Lolita had only one child, and Lola felt the burden of all her mother's hopes on her. She needed to produce a chick.

The vision of a small fledgling standing between her and her mother gave her a warm feeling in her middle. As Cole would say, it warmed her heart.

The vision partly made up for the sick feeling when she thought of Cole finding a mate of his own. It was a previously unrealized insight. Part of her pain was based on the idea of him finding someone else to love besides her. Would he still care for her then?

Lolita clucked comfortingly. "You got to share Cole, too. He share you. You share him. All be one happy family. Not need to lose Cole. He love you always. I know that. But, just like you, he need a mate of his own kind."

That was just the problem. They both needed one of their own kind. That was clear. Even so, it didn't help the pain in her heart.

------◦------

Lolita had gone to see about some of the other females. Even though she was the smallest, she was nominally the one that all of the others sought for advice and judgments on complex issues. Lola was proud of her mother, even though it would be nice if Lolita would use better English.

Lola had left the porch and wandered up the hill. Cole was still busy inside with something that required his full attention. School, she thought, disgustedly. Whatever that was, it took too much time.

She hadn't gone to school. She learned human speech from humans, just like her mother had. Lolita had her own style and did not spend the effort to speak correctly. She settled for shortcuts as long as people understood her.

Lola snorted disparagingly at Lolita's English as she climbed the hill. It was a matter of her own self-esteem. She'd go to any length to ensure that Cole never thought poorly of her.

The hillcrest was ahead, and she looked back, gazing down over the buildings and the distant river. Everything looked peaceful and home-like. A warm feeling flowed over her. True, she was a raptor, but she knew ever so much more than her kind back in the Cretaceous. She was mentally the equal of the humans, possibly with certain exceptions. It was true that she couldn't travel in time the way they could. She'd never studied math the way Kathleen had. She knew math involved complex numbers, but it didn't seem necessary to her in her life.

The time jumps she had experienced were all in the company of one or more humans. Most lately, she had only traveled with Cole. He had taken to time-travel effortlessly and had no difficulty moving in the odd in-between environment that led to every location in time and physical space. It had made her dizzy at first, but lately, she was able to stand without putting her head against Cole's side.

She turned to look at the treeline at the crest of the hill. An arm of the riverside woods had marched up the backside of the hill, and here it lightly brushed the crest. She stiffened and stopped. There was a familiar scent.

Lola glanced back at the houses, indecisively scuffing her foot in the dust. The scent was that of the Forest Giants, those large hominoids that Kathleen called Sasquatches. Lola was familiar with the creatures, as were all the Deinonychus, even though the Squatchies, as Lolita called them, weren't common. She thought that was because they ranged effortlessly through time.

Lolita had told her that she had seen them in the Cretaceous before being brought forward by Kathleen when she rescued Jason Gridley. Lola had never approached one closely, but now the scent was strengthening. A shadow in the treeline darkened, attracting her eyes. As she looked, a form gradually appeared. She couldn't tell if it had walked closer to her or if it had faded in through time, but regardless, it was there, and it was looking directly at her.

Cadeyrin had told Cole that the Giants were not enemies but also that they had their own motives and were not to be wholly trusted. The old one of the tribe that sometimes appeared near the human habitation had been friendly to the extent that he had given Cadeyrin the formula for the miraculous red paste that extended human life and vitality.

Since the humans had been given that gift, they had apparently ceased aging. Kathleen and Cadeyrin both looked as they had when she was just a chick. Cole had not been allowed to take the compound as yet. Lola understood that he needed to attain his total growth before the paste essentially froze his development. According to his mother, he was still a few years from that point.

The paste worked on the Deinonychs, too, but it was more difficult to judge how much of an impact it had. It seemed to allow them to prolong their vitality, but that didn't necessarily mean they would live longer. Her kind didn't appear to age until they were much closer to death than was typical for humans. It was possible that she would die long before Cole began to age. Feathers remained bright and facial skin didn't sag the way human skin did. That thought made her feel a brief wash of sadness as she remembered their differences. Her face was not the same as Cole's. He could make innumerable expressions. Her skin was tight over her skull, and she could not make small expressions. It was just another thing that emphasized their difference.

The Squatchie was beckoning to her now. This was unprecedented. She walked forward slowly, unafraid. The creature was taller than the tallest human and probably weighed as much as a full-grown grizzly bear, but her natural armament gave her a level of confidence that a human could never match.

She stopped in front of the large creature, looking up. It didn't speak, but she felt it was communicating with her. She understood that it meant no harm. It held out a hand, and she carefully laid her clawed fingers against the giant palm. The creature's fingers closed over hers, burying her hand in its grip.

Abruptly, they were in the in-between world, the spiritual space that connected all parts of reality. The Forest Giant spoke to her now.

"You are a child of the deep past, but you've never been there. You are close to the humans, and I see that your mental processes are in alignment with theirs." It paused, bent down, and looked closely into her eyes.

"Ah. You have a problem. You are confused with your desires. Your mind is too close to human, yet your body is that of your kind. The simplest solution is to change."

She tried to speak, but no words formed. She wanted to ask what it meant by 'change,' but the in-between space began to swirl, and she recognized that they were

traveling in time. After a moment, the movement ceased, and she became aware that they were on a high rise of ground overlooking a strange area. There were innumerable tall rectangular structures with glass. She suddenly recognized windows in the nearest rectangle. Her recognition resolved the view into a city. She'd seen some pictures in a book, but never the actual thing.

The Squatchie spoke to her mind. "This is the environment of the humans in the future. It is not friendly to your kind. Humans made it for humans. There is no place to hunt and no peace. It is not friendly to modern humans either, but they are only beginning to realize that. They have a sickness in their approach to life. It is possible they will not recover from it."

She shivered and thought, "Why did you bring me here?"

Rather than answer, the Squatchie pulled her hand, and they were back in the in-between. After a brief moment that might have been an instant or an infinity, they were out, standing on another hill.

This time there were trees in front of her. The smell was jungle-like, redolent of living green things and animals. There was a massive creature in the near distance stripping branches of a tree and chewing. It was a plant-eater, one that was too large for her to view as prey.

"This is the environment in which that your kind belongs. The man and the female human with the bright hair took your mother and her sisters from here. We, The People, were against that action at first, but it has proven successful. We have seen that some humans from the future and your kind from the past can form an alliance. You have fused to become one tribe, a thing we hadn't predicted or even thought possible."

She stiffened, looking past the Giant. A group of her own kind was openly stalking the huge plant-eater. As she watched, it raised its head in alarm and began to move away from the trees. The distant Deinonychs dashed in and clambered over the herbivore's sides, kicking with their killing claws. It bellowed in response and continued to move forward at its best speed.

One of the Deinonychs reached the base of the herbivore's neck, clung with teeth and front claws, and kicked with both feet. A bloody gash opened across the side of the plant eater's neck. A second kick and suddenly a massive gout of blood shot out. The herbivore bellowed again and sped up.

The other Deinonychs dropped off and followed the creature while the one on its neck clung where it was. After a hundred meters or so, the enormous creature slowed, then stood, its head drooping as it gasped deeply. It took two steps, then went down on its knees. After a minute, it rolled to its side. The killers moved closely and proceeded to rip at the underbelly. She heard a tearing sound even from the distance at which she was standing, and then a massive flood of entrails spilled out. The Deinonychs began to feed, snapping and snarling at each other as they did.

Lola looked down. She was both ashamed and yet thrilled. This was her true nature. She looked again, then turned away. No. It was not. Yes, she was a huntress, but she was also part of the human clan. While they killed to eat, they also shared the kill equally, taking pleasure in ensuring that all had enough.

The Forest Giant twitched, and they were back in the in-between. "You are different. I see that now. You are part of the human group, but they have become part of your group, too. They have learned to live with your kind. You will find it difficult to change in the way I thought you should."

She had nothing to say. The space roiled around her as if it were composed of clouds, some black and some multi-colored. She felt helpless and confused.

The Giant spoke again. "Your original kind cannot travel through the inter-space, but you are no longer entirely one of them. Here. Accept this gift."

Something happened in her head. It wasn't quite painful, but it was uncomfortable. The discomfort grew more intense until there was a snapping sensation behind her eyes. The clouds that had been roiling took on another look. They were now ordered in a strange way, one that she could comprehend.

There was a clear path back to Cole. That was what she saw and what she wanted.

The Giant spoke. "Travel is by desire and thought. When you want to be there, you are. Now, take us where you want."

She stepped forward, into and through the colorful clouds. She was back on the hillside overlooking her home. The Squatchie was nowhere to be seen. She spun, looking, but there was no sign of him, no scent either. It was as if she had been dreaming the entire time.

Confused, she looked back at the house and saw BW trotting up the hill toward her. She walked slowly to greet him.

"Come on, boy. Let's go and find Cole. I have to talk to him."

Chapter Five

Lost Time

Some crows were flying over the hill. She had been conscious of their cawing since she'd arrived back at her home time. Now, one swooped down and flew past her head to land in a small tree part-way down the hill. It looked at her and BW with its beady eyes, then made an inquisitive caw.

She imitated the sound, and the crow, as if answered, took wing and climbed the air back to its friends. BW looked up, wagging his tail in a puzzled manner.

She was embarrassed. She couldn't communicate with crows, but she sometimes emulated their sounds. It was surprisingly easy. It was another example of how different she was from mammals. The thought depressed her. She was more closely related to birds than Cole. Her mind circled the problem.

Perhaps if she considered her intellect rather than her physical aspect, she'd find more justification for her feelings. That seemed to offer some consolation. She was intelligent in a way that was closer to humans than not.

The two arrived back on the porch, and the black wolf went to lie down in the shade, his tongue lolling to one side. Lola watched, her head turned critically, then mentally shrugged. She pushed the heavy door open and went inside, looking for Cole.

He was not in the main room where she'd expected to find him. He had a habit of curling up to read in an oversized, comfortable chair located to one side of the fireplace. His scent was there, but it was faint. It occurred to her that he hadn't been using the chair in the past weeks.

That had started when he began attending classes in the future. It was his favorite place to read, and he had spent many hours there in the past. She sighed discontentedly. There was something in the future beyond her reach that seemed to have taken the place of the chair. She hesitated, then thought it, and her place, too.

The thought came with a painful feeling in her breast. If she could go there, perhaps...but, but she could! The Forest Giant had conferred that ability upon her. With that thought, she straightened decisively. She'd go and find him right now.

After a second, she slumped again. That was the human environment she'd seen. She would have no clue how to navigate the world she found. Besides, there would be no Deinonychs there. The humans would be frightened, and that would be dangerous.

A sudden thought struck her. Kathleen had taken Lolita and others of their group to the future numerous times. She should ask her mother about the human world. There was no excuse not to take the time to learn all about it.

Kathleen walked into the room at that point.

"Hello, Sweetie! What are you thinking about? You look like you're lost."

Lola jumped. She'd been staring at the fireplace. The odor of cold ash had reminded her of happy winter evenings when the hearth was hot, and the flames warmed everyone in the room. Now the smell of old stone and wood smoke was faint and depressing.

"I was..." She stopped. What was she doing? She'd decided to change, but her mind kept coming back to the issue. Surely she had more control of herself than that. "I was thinking about Cole. Wondering what he was learning in the college. The human college."

Kathleen stopped and looked concerned. "Lola. I understand what you mean. You're not really interested in the knowledge he's acquiring, are you?"

Was she? Was there some jealousy? Did it bother her that he was learning things that she had no opportunity to learn for herself?

"Maybe. I don't know. I think I'd like to learn more. I know how to talk human language, and I know how to hunt. I don't know why or how about a lot of things. Is that what he's learning? Why and how?"

"Mmmm. You could say that. I'm sorry, Lola. I didn't think you would be interested. You see, as far as human knowledge goes, a deinonychus is a predator that lived in the distant past. Humans have no experience in living with your kind. Our best experts would probably say that you just mimic human speech without really understanding the meaning." Kathleen frowned. "Of course, they'd be wrong. How wrong, I'm just beginning to grasp myself."

She placed her hand along Lola's jaw, trailing her fingers through the fine down and across the smaller feathers of her neck. Lola shivered. It felt nice, but it did little to help her mental state.

"You mean that humans think I'm not able to think? I am, though. I'm confused about myself. The others, well, they hunt and are happy with each other. I think there is more than that. How do I find out about such things? Cole has told me a lot. You have told me about things that a deinonychus would never encounter in the past. So have the others. Grid, Annie, Cadeyrin, Logan..." Her voice trailed off.

Kathleen straightened, having come to a decision. "Lola, I'm going to teach you to read. We have a library here and, once you can read, you can pick the books and things you want to find out about."

"I know books. Cole reads. He's read some to me, and I always listened to you read to him when I could." Kathleen had read stories to all of the children when they were younger. The deinonychus chicks had participated, listening in to the human stories. It was a good memory, the entire group sitting in front of the fire, listening to a story. At first, it seemed like Kathleen was telling something that had actually happened to her, then Lola had thought that she was making up a story from imagination, but she'd rather quickly come to understand that someone else, in some other location and time, had made up the story. Kathleen was somehow seeing it in the book she held.

Books had become magical objects to her after that. They carried information from long ago and far away, yet it was always available. "Please. I'd like to read things. Maybe then I'd understand better. I think I'd like to go to college, too."

Kathleen looked serious. "Lola, dear. I don't think that would be advisable. You'd frighten the students, and the authorities would want to capture you and do all sorts of unpleasant experiments. They don't have any idea that you are more than just a curiosity, an animal they can study. They might feel threatened and shoot you, too. That's a possibility. It's lucky you can't travel in time by yourself. It keeps you safe."

But she could. She started to tell Kathleen, then hesitated. Perhaps Kathleen would disapprove and, even if she didn't, it would worry her. She'd think that Lola would get in trouble. It would be just like Cole's mother to worry. Her own mother often expressed worry about Cole.

She had a flash of amusement. Deinonychus or human, mothers were always the same. They worried. She wondered if she would be similar if she had a family. She suspected she would. Chicks and baby humans were to be protected—even baby wolves. The wolf pups were cute and funny, but they grew quickly. Humans, not so much. Her own kind grew faster than humans. They were physically able to hunt at an earlier age, but, from her own experience, she and Cole had matured at about the same rate when it came to mental ability and attitudes.

Kathleen was looking at her curiously, probably wondering what mischief she was planning. She rushed to say, "I'd like to learn to read. If I want to read about something and it isn't in a book we have, though, how will I find out about it?"

That did it. Kathleen's concern was forestalled. "Oh. That's no problem, dear. Cole or I can easily bring a book or books back to you. Don't worry about that. Let's just see how well you take to reading first, though."

She could see that Cole's mother wasn't sure she would be able to learn at all. She resolved to prove her wrong in that respect. "When will you teach me? Oh, and where is Cole now?" she asked.

"Cole's gone back to the future to meet with a group of students. They were going to get together and study for a test they're taking tomorrow. He said to tell you he'd see you around noon tomorrow."

That was something they had worked out between themselves. Cole could jump through time, spend days or even years on his personal timeline, and then jump back to a second or two after he had left her. The problem was, they would then age at different rates. Besides, he was afraid that their interests would change. It would be hard for him to go off for what appeared to be a long time in his frame. Then come back and take up where she had every right to expect him to be, since, to her, he'd just left for a moment.

Kathleen continued. "As for reading. I've got some time right now. Let's go to the library and select an easy book. I'll show you. Speech is made up of words, and words are made up of sounds. The sounds are represented by symbols. Letters, we call them. You say a word, and you know what it means. If you know the letters and the sounds they represent, you can put the sounds together in your mind and understand the word. When you become proficient, you can look at each group of letters and automatically know what the word is. Combine lots of words, and you have thoughts. Combine lots of thoughts, and you have a story or information about any number of things."

"It doesn't sound simple. Are you sure you can teach me?"

"Uh. Well, I've taught physics, and it's lots more difficult. I think I can teach reading. I taught Cole to a certain extent. Annie Gridley taught for longer than me, though."

"I know. I was present part of the time. But, why didn't anyone try to teach us? We were part of the group."

Kathleen flushed. "I'm sorry, Lola. It was a lack of understanding on our part. Humans are used to thinking they are superior to animals. I guess, even knowing how smart your mother is, I still didn't think you would be interested or could learn. I'll make it up to you. I promise."

That would be good. If she could read, perhaps she could hold Cole's interest. She followed Kathleen to the library. It was across the entrance hall from the gun room, but it was a larger space with windows and comfortable chairs. They were large enough for her to curl up in and rest against the arms. She'd taken naps there many times. Now, she was interested in finding out how books actually worked.

Chapter Six

Power

Winston Passway was rich. Not just wealthy, but rich beyond most common people's ability to grasp. His father had been incredibly wealthy, and Winston had inherited it all when his mother had died. Winston had been a senior in college majoring in finance law at the time, and his education was immediately put to use taking control over the family fortune.

Winston's father was a mystery. His mother wouldn't speak of him, but apparently, he had disappeared shortly after Winston was conceived. For all his mother would say, Winston's male parent might have been a casual encounter. In fact, there was no record of her ever getting married. The strange part was that she had somehow taken control of billions of dollars without apparently ever working or knowing anything about finance. While there were those who questioned the situation, the sheer volume of wealth provided adequate insulation from inquiries. There had also been some suspicious deaths among those who had exhibited too much curiosity. His mother denied involvement, but she had access to plenty of people who could arrange such things.

After she died, Winston had used the money to make his mark in the world of finance with a series of mega-real estate deals. Not long after closing on his largest purchase, a package of three huge casinos in Las Vegas, he turned his focus to the industry in which his mother had invested much of the fortune.

Now he had fingers in both digital hardware and software with an increasing thrust towards developing Artificial Intelligence. He knew, on a gut level, that AI was the key to something he lusted for, but refused to name.

He meant to keep his goal of world domination totally secret until he had progressed in his plans to the point that the plans were unstoppable. He had expanded into military applications – the new military was almost totally dependent on AI in terms of planning, battle data flow, and command linkage.

In addition, Passway was developing a wide range of autonomous killer packages. These ranged from mini-hunter drones of hummingbird size to large flying hunter-killers. He had introduced inexpensive stealth robots, the size of small dogs, that could infiltrate enemy lines and then lie camouflaged until the opportunity to strike at an enemy soldier arose.

Most lately, he had conceived the idea of a squirrel-sized killer that could hide in trees to deliver either a grenade-sized explosive or a load of fast-acting nerve poison in the midst of an enemy squad. This last system was still in development. The Killer Squirrels were a little too small to carry enough power to make them usable for more than a few hours. Passway now had his best engineers working on new battery concepts as a result. With a better power storage system, he could miniaturize the weapons to the size of a mouse.

A better power system would also benefit the mini-hunter drones. As they currently existed, they would only operate for a period of ten minutes. This necessitated a larger mother drone to deliver the small ones to the battlefield. Passway viewed the larger drone as a weakness. It was too big and too easy to notice.

He was a busy man and found little time for a personal life, but he was happy. His life was oriented towards his goal, and that was almost all he needed.

When his mother had left the fortune to him, he'd had a brief fling with an international fashion model. It had been fun, but his habit of sleeping only two hours per night, then working, had made her crazy. They'd gotten married – he now thought of that as a childish error – and the marriage had resulted in the birth of the one person he actually cared about: his daughter Devonette. His ex-wife had expressed no interest in the child.

Still, despite his love for the child, he was a busy man, and he'd farmed off her care to a series of nannies and tutors. Seeking to make up somewhat for the time he had not spent with her, he lavished her with gifts.

Devonette became quite entitled. She had never suffered a lack of any kind, always getting every material thing she wanted. She had her way in every possible instance. Needless to say, nannies did not last long around her. She did not develop the ability to have a deep interpersonal relationship as a result.

Winston visited his several sprawling estates periodically to recharge, but his visits always ended after a day or so. Then he was off to work. In point of fact, his favorite location was his rather plain office in one of the software company's office parks.

One of Winston's additional passions was a strange fascination with time-travel. He couldn't say for sure where it had come from, but he felt deeply that it was somehow involved with his mysterious father. As a result, Passway had bought into the government's stalled time-travel research. The research had yielded results, but the method that had been developed gave inconsistent results, sometimes marooning the time-traveler in the past with no way to return and often delivering the traveler to the wrong destination.

He had learned of Kathleen's formula from the government scientists. The fact that she apparently had complete control over time infuriated him. That was something he must have, and no one else should ever be given access to it. The idea that she existed somewhere in time and shared her method with her husband and other allies was intolerable.

He had a group of mathematicians and physicists working on what they supposed was Kathleen's discovery. They had made some theoretical progress, but not enough to give him hope that he could locate and destroy that blasted woman and her caveman husband and all of her friends. Of course, he'd make sure that she would give him her time equation formula prior to her death.

His plans were grandiose and would require time. Time was something that all men have in short supply, so he devoted some billions to health and life-extending technology. That research led him to a small company that was releasing some innovative drug compounds, apparently for minimal profit, if not for free.

He suborned government employees of the FDA as a routine step in that quest. From one of them, he had learned of the strange case of the now missing Professor Wolf, who was apparently much younger than his recorded age. That led to his discovery that Kathleen was behind the company that had a lock on some new health enhancement drugs.

Winston was an intelligent man and, possibly due to his wealth, incredibly arrogant. That Whitby woman having access to two things he wanted was enough to keep him up at night.

Kathleen had formed a shell corporation that invested in a small biotech enterprise and through it, she disseminated parts of her health impacting technology, parceling it out for free, a bit at a time. If he could get his hands on the underlying formula, the only way it would be parceled out would be for vast sums of money. That eventuality would allow him to accelerate his plan for world domination by at least two decades. The elite and heads of states would all bend their knee to him, in exchange for an additional life span. That was a certainty.

He enjoyed thinking about that. Given the ability to extend his lifespan indefinitely, he would have plenty of time to get control of the entire planet. Managing it would be no problem, especially with an AI-based military composed of robots. The plan was good. The major problem was finding Kathleen Whitby. He viewed her as his arch-enemy, although he realized that she probably didn't know he existed. That was something he planned to change.

Chapter Seven

Devonette

Devonette had developed into an incredibly popular girl if you judged her based on the number of followers on two social media platforms. She used five platforms, but her quirky sense of outrage and sarcastic humor worked best with video. Two of the five platforms offered a more seamless video experience, so she used them most. She spent a lot of time thinking of things to post and had come up with a brand that was built on slyly or sometimes angrily disparaging the male sex, her admirers in particular.

It didn't matter much if the boys figured it out. There were plenty of them, and she'd never lacked attention. She was an engaging, sexy thing, and she knew it. Even if she did tell everyone how cute she was, as she usually did in every conversation, there were still plenty of males that vied for her attention. It was kind of boring in a way. The male sex was so predictable. The thing that kept her interest the most was leading a boy on until she figured out precisely how he ticked, where he was most vulnerable, and then using that against him.

When she was sure he thought he was about to win her affections, she would post a video or, preferably, several. These videos culminated in a final denouement in which she made it clear that her target was not good enough for her and hadn't interested her from the beginning. At that point, her followers would heap abuse on the unfortunate young man, and he would inevitably disappear from the sphere of her attention, often angry but always in ignominy.

She had started this process in high school and continued it at University. If pressed, she would speculate that some male, somewhere, would probably be good enough to win her affection, but, in her mind, she didn't believe it. She was far too clever for them, and none had ever impressed her enough for her to consider developing a close relationship. For this reason, her followers knew her as the Ice-Maiden. She was proud of that name. It described her and served as a challenge to an unending stream of young males who sought to get close.

Despite the prevalent attitude condoning casual sex, Devonette took pride in her chastity. No man was good enough, especially when compared with her father, and she had no desire for a relationship with another woman.

Her position was unassailable since her father was worth billions, if not more. She had everything she desired, except total social media dominance, and she was working on that.

There had been a bit of a problem when she found that Daddy was sending her to a public university, albeit a highly rated one.

"I thought I was going to an Ivy League school. That's where all my friends are going. Why are you sending me to someplace out in the middle of the country where no one ever forms valuable connections?" She was angry but knew that displaying too much emotion would only cement her father's decision, so she tried to act reasonably.

"The problem with those Ivy League schools is that the graduates feel they deserve the positions their contacts get for them. In my experience, most of them are barely literate cretins who can't form an original thought. They expect the name of their Alma mater to intimidate the people they meet in the business world. It doesn't work that way. When I meet a competitor, I don't ask for their degree. I investigate their prior performance; their record of successes and failures. That allows me to determine their strengths and weak areas."

"But, Daddy, that's like some kind of meritocracy or something. My social studies teacher and my English teacher taught me that was patriarchal domination. It isn't the way the new world will operate after society is reset."

Winston had sat back, his face going beet red. Devonette knew that this was a sign that she should be quiet and meek. He was usually impassive and unemotional, but now he was exceptionally irritated.

His voice, when he spoke, was calm and carefully controlled. That was another sign that he was angry.

"My dear, you have been thoroughly misinformed. The teachers responsible for filling your mind with that do not deserve their position. I see now that I made a mistake allowing you to go to that institution, despite its good reputation. They erred teaching you that garbage. Rest assured that those two will no longer be teaching there. I'll call the headmaster as soon as we are done here. They're out, and they'll be lucky to find a job flipping hamburgers.

"Now, as to the Ivy League idea. I'm sending you where I know you'll meet some normal individuals. Not that you're on their level, but I want you to be able to get along with them, to know how they think, and to be able to manipulate them. That knowledge alone will be worth far more than the content of the courses you are signed up to take. By the way, I've taken the liberty of selecting your course of study. You will, of course, study hard and earn good grades. You will not deviate from the classes I've picked.

"You expect to succeed me in the business ventures I've started, and I intend that you will. To this end, I've designed a course of study that will prepare you adequately to compete in the lion's game of billion-dollar business that I play. It's vicious and cut-throat, and you will learn how to compete, or you won't be playing, especially with my money."

That was enough for her. She followed his instructions. The money she stood to control when she finished her studies was more than many countries made in a year, and the totality of Daddy's business was incredibly more than that. She knew who ran the show...at present. Besides, it wasn't like she didn't have enough time to have a personal life. She was brilliant, and her studies posed little challenge, especially when she had access to several exceptional tutors.

She averaged two or three video calls a week, speaking to her tutors. They usually knew more than the professors and instructors who taught her courses. That left hours of free time to amuse herself with building her social media following and setting up her little dramas with aspiring boys.

Daddy encouraged her. He approved of her destroying men, not on general principles, but because it was a playing field that allowed her to develop her abilities to manipulate males. This would, Daddy assured her, translate well into the business world. His only restriction was that she keep the family name out of her actions.

When she complained about the poor qualities of her phone videos, he set her up with a professional video studio with staff that provided professional quality to her efforts. As a result, she had a vast number of followers who generally fell under the definition of "mean girls" and were always ready to pile on any target she selected.

To an impartial observer, Devonette had a certain power granted by her cuteness and wit. Still, on closer inspection, her life was a meaningless whirl of unfulfilled conquests, interspersed with rejections of calculated cruelty and seasoned with frantic searches for targets who could keep her fans interested.

The only private time she had was at night. Her private home was secure, and her bodyguards kept watch outside through the night. They were the best the firm of Barton-Massara could provide, and they were hand-selected by her father. Most of them were ex-military, in great physical shape, and able killers. Nothing could happen to her. That gave her an incredible feeling of security, and she didn't mind the loss of privacy. There was always a man following her on-campus or wherever she went, but the men were discrete and almost impossible to detect.

While University was a venue for hunting unsuspecting men, she studied her course material with the tutors and worked to make acceptable grades. Daddy wouldn't like it if she embarrassed him by flunking. After studying, she'd do yoga for an hour, then go to bed with Irwin, content that her house was being watched carefully.

Irwin was probably the only entity that Devonette cared for. He was a stuffed tiger that she'd had forever, now sadly out-of-shape and worn. Still, despite the patchy fur, she couldn't sleep without him by her side.

"Irwin, I think I have another boy that is going to love me. All I have to do is to make the right moves in History. There are about five hundred students in the lecture hall, and I'd all but given up on finding anyone interesting. I saw him just today. He sits in the very back. Not a good place." she sniffed. "He's good-looking and should have the sense to sit where he can be seen."

The lights were out in her apartment, and the tiger was only visible in the faint light of the alarm clock and the green glow thrown off by her charging cell phone. Irwin, as usual, agreed with her, so she snugged him closer to her chest and continued.

She spoke a little louder. There was no reason to whisper. Her apartment was large and quiet. "I, of course, sit in the front middle. That way, everyone can see me. I suspect most of the others spend more time watching my responses to the lecturer than they do watching old Professor Higgins. He's a bore, anyway." She snickered quietly to herself. Her dramatic reactions to Higgins were carefully calculated to catch the eye of the students seated behind her and impress them with how vivacious she was compared to the overweight professor. The strategy always worked to her advantage. Higgins could say nothing since she wasn't overtly offensive, just possibly a little overactive with yawns, hair flipping, and other gestures.

She had recently discovered that she could make the old man lose his train of thought by casually exposing her thighs. He seemed always to notice, and the results were hilarious. He would stutter, then turn away, trying to remember what point he had been making.

She made a game of that. How many times could she interrupt the lecture during one fifty-minute period? Of course, she was careful to make it seem like she was unaware of the commotion. It wouldn't do to have Higgins figure out he was being manipulated.

As for the boys in the class, she'd had twenty-three of them seek her out after class, clumsily attempting to engage her interest. Their efforts were wasted. She had reached the point that not just any male would do. She selected the best-looking, the most athletic, the best specimens for her carefully orchestrated attacks. She felt that her followers were most impressed when she emotionally destroyed attractive men, ones that they could only dream about. It was part of the equation that she was far more desirable than the poor drones that followed her. Her train of thought slipped for a moment. Maybe they were dronettes? Was that a word? She shrugged the question off. It didn't matter anyway.

This semester, she was working on the football team. She had already disrupted the general team spirit by luring several players into a losing competition for her attention. She had decided to destroy the starting quarterback by gradually wedging herself between him and his long-time girlfriend. Then, if she could time it correctly, she would drop him just before the big Homecoming game. That would create a real stir among her followers.

However, the man she'd noticed sitting in the back of the class had caused her to delay her plans for a time. He would be fun to toy with, and she had nearly all semester for the quarterback. Homecoming wasn't until late this year.

The fact that the student who always sat in the back had ignored her as she brushed past him as they exited was an added inducement. Men just didn't do that. Plus, he was about as perfect a specimen of a human male as she'd ever seen.

He wasn't as large as some of the football players, but he moved with an economy of effort and a fantastic gracefulness that betokened extreme fitness. When she'd brushed against him in the crush leaving the lecture hall, she'd momentarily thought she had bumped into one of the columns supporting the foyer of the building. His arm had felt rock hard.

He'd turned his gaze on her for an instant, then dismissed her from his attention as not worthy of consideration. She'd seen it in his blue eyes. There had been a flash of interest, then an invisible barrier had slid between them, and she was left wondering if he had seen her.

The feeling of being ignored had been overwhelming and uncomfortable. It made her wonder if her mascara was smudged or something. She had gone directly to the restroom and checked her appearance in the mirror. She had frowned at herself in anger. She looked, as always, perfect. Black hair, startlingly blue eyes, flawless complexion. Yes. She was perfect. He couldn't have just lost interest after that single glance. That had never happened before. Never in her life had a male been indifferent to her. Such a slight couldn't be allowed to pass without repercussion.

"Irwin, I think I'm going to enjoy making that guy regret his brushing me off. He'll be crawling after me within a week. Oh, and don't you worry about the quarterback. Dewayne's already hooked. If his girlfriend only knew how he'd returned my smile today! He looked like a jackass eating cactus; his lips were pulled back so tight. She'd better be working harder at keeping him satisfied, or he'll be out of her clutches faster than a tiger can strike."

In her imagination, Irwin affirmed her statement but qualified it. "That guy isn't worth much. He's small-change to you."

"Yes, but sometimes I like easy challenges," she muttered in response.

She hugged the hapless stuffed animal and rolled onto her back with a yawn.

Chapter Eight

Thoughts of Home

Cole had walked across campus, entered the small house that his mother had purchased just off campus, and then fixed some food to eat while he read the history assignment. He sat at the kitchen table, a sandwich and chips at his hand as he worked through the Visigoths' first incursion into Rome. It was hard going. The author of the text didn't seem to be able to write in a readable style. The reading was a dry recital of facts, names, and dates with a minimum of analysis.

Cole periodically came up and took a bite of his sandwich, then tried to think of the actual situation on the ground in Rome of that time. It was no use, he concluded. The text had almost zero analysis. It was up to him to try to figure out what the invasion had meant to the hapless citizens that were caught up in the action. Their society had changed as a result, but was it dramatic, or had it been so slow and imperceptible that the average Roman hadn't noticed until after the fact?

He took a drink of water, then laughed out loud. "I guess I could always go back and ask someone. Ha! But then I'd have to learn Latin. It's not worth it. Besides, Mom wouldn't let me. There's a slight chance of changing some minor facet of history that could persist."

Kathleen had expanded her time-equation model to the point that she understood that almost all changes that a time-traveler could introduce would gradually diminish, given enough time. It was possible, but the odds were vanishingly small, that a novel element introduced in the time frame could multiply its effect enough to change the time where she'd originated.

This result had been cross-checked several times until she had ceased to worry about it. Once Serensaa had demonstrated her innate talent for traveling through the space-time stream, Kathleen had come to the conclusion that there probably were, or had been, or would be, a large number of humans that could travel through time.

A human might slip into another time inadvertently and never be able to return, or perhaps, some people had gained mastery over their ability. The Sasquatches certainly had. They'd been traveling through time for...well, there was no way to quantify it, given that they regularly went back to the Jurassic or earlier, and they had not caused a disruption. At least as far as she could determine, the Sasquatch travelers had almost zero impact on the flow of time and events. Of course, that might have something to do with their extreme focus on privacy and stealth. They did not usually appear to humans, and most modern humans were unaware of their existence, except as a semi-mythical creature that only a few kooks tried to find.

Cole shook his head. It was easy to get lost in thought. The history book was so dull that he found it difficult to concentrate. His thought turned to Lola. She'd be waiting for him somewhere around the homestead.

He visualized her and mentally placed her beside a human girl. Lola looked alien and odd in a way that made her seem frightening, but he knew better. Her mind was a bright, active, and pure thing. She wasn't self-absorbed, the way the girls he'd met in his classes were. Despite being a deadly killer, she didn't have a mean streak in her. Based on the posts he'd seen in his forays into social media, humans had a propensity to gang up on victims and abuse them cruelly.

Another thought struck him. The analysis of the life-extending formula his father had gotten from the Sasquatches indicated that it was primarily compatible with humans. Lolita and Fancy had partaken of it, and it seemed as if they had benefited, but their benefit was in terms of vitality only. They would probably die after their normal lifespan. Of course, no one knew how long that was. The existing knowledge of the species was an open book that was being filled out as time went by. The same scientist who analyzed the red paste had speculated that the Deinonychs would live about as long as humans, or maybe a little longer. He had based that supposition on modern birds. Parrots sometimes lived to nearly a hundred years. Deinonychs, as birds' distant relatives, could possibly attain that age.

Studying their species longevity back in the Cretaceous was likely to be useless, though. Based on what he knew from observation in the Pleistocene, not one predator in a thousand lived to more than middle age. Hunting and fighting with prey that outweighed them several times tended to make for a short life generally terminated by injuries. For a relatively small Deinonychus, the numbers were probably even less favorable. Belle had weighed almost 70 kilos. Lolita tipped the scales at 45, although her daughter, Lola, was larger at 50 kilograms. That was most likely due to better nutrition rather than genetics since Lola's father had also been small.

In any event, he would most certainly outlive Lola. That was a sad thought. She would inevitably grow old. He had to encourage her to find a mate of her kind. She would age, and he wouldn't. She needed a mate who would live and die in tandem with her. He, on the other hand, had plenty of time. He could keep Lola company throughout her life and then find a human girl after she was gone. "I can devote myself to Lola and not cause her the anguish she will certainly feel if I show up with a girl. That's the least I can do," he told himself.

He visualized Lola again. She wasn't alien at all. To him, she was his best friend. Knowing her the way he did, he knew she would be waiting for him to show up. With that thought, he turned to his book, read the rest of the assignment, carefully taking notes as he turned the pages. There was no sense in reading it twice. If he could summarize it, that would suffice as a study guide.

He finished, put the book away, and gathered up his plate and glass. His father had taught him a campsite was always supposed to be cleaned and ready for the following user. It made sense. If he came back to camp injured and unable to lay a fire, for instance, the fire he'd laid before leaving could be a lifesaver. He washed his dishes, stored them in the cabinet, then went to the bedroom.

The modern clothes came off, revealing a muscular body for an instant before he slid his buckskins on. There was no sense wearing the fragile modern clothing home. The leather pants and tunic were far more durable, with the added benefit of making stealthy movement easier. He laughed to himself. Lola would probably have a fit if she saw him in modern clothes. She wouldn't understand why he'd wear such non-functional stuff.

Lola, now she posed a problem that he couldn't entirely solve. They were so close mentally that she was like a part of himself. He had no problem admitting that he loved her, but she continually acted as if she needed their relationship to extend to a level that wasn't possible. He was not a deinonychus. They could practically read each other's minds while hunting.

They acted as a bonded pair, but they couldn't be mates. He felt as if he were failing her in some way, but there it was. He was human; she wasn't.

He sighed. He'd have to figure out some way to convince her to find a suitable mate. They'd have to go back to the Cretaceous to do so. She wasn't interested in any of the available males in the group. None of her cousins had met her standards.

He looked in the mirror as he washed his face. It had just struck him. If she needed a mate of her kind, then so did he. He grinned. Eventually, maybe. There were plenty of women on campus, and more than a few had displayed interest in him. There had practically been a fight among the girls in his chem lab to determine who would be his lab partner. He'd chosen a plain and somewhat out-of-shape girl to settle the escalating situation.

Sandy was friendly, but she was not going to get a good grade. He had to help her with the lab work and had gradually given up on tutoring her. Now he let her copy his experimental results, making a few changes so that it didn't look as if she were cribbing.

The other girls continued to appear at the wash station when he cleaned his equipment, but he could flirt a little with them and then brush them off. Not one of them was attractive to him. Some were cute, even beautiful, but he wanted a mind behind the face. Moreover, he needed to have a flexible and open-minded woman to fit into the primitive life he loved.

None of the girls he'd met so far fit that requirement. They were almost exclusively caught up in a semi-virtual life on social media. Their conversation was shallow, and he couldn't see any point in it. It was simply easier to concentrate on his studies, being pleasant to his admirers but not engaging with them other than on a strictly academic basis.

That girl that had bumped into him after history had been outstanding in looks, but one glance had led him to the conclusion that she was another of the same mold—probably devoted to her social media friends.

He allowed himself to fantasize a moment. She would be amazing to have a physical relationship with, but there had to be more than that to keep his interest. If she thought like Lola, who loved hunting and the wild, then maybe she and he could have a meaningful and lasting relationship. But that was just a dream. It couldn't happen for any number of reasons.

He dried his face, then slipped into the spiritual-time world, heading directly to the stone house porch. Lola would be waiting there for him.

Chapter Nine

Hunting for a Mate

Lola wasn't on the porch. Cole glanced around the compound but saw no sign of the Deinonychus flock. He stood for a moment, scanning the distant hillside. Not there, either.

BW came around the corner and climbed the stairs, making a whuffing sound. The wolf took Cole's hand gently in his mouth in greeting. Cole laughed, then grasped the wolf's muzzle in return. The formalities over, BW sat, tail gently wagging, and watched Cole's face for a clue as to what he would do next.

"Where did they go, BW? Where's Lola?" He didn't expect an answer, of course, but the wolf stood and paced over to the front door.

"Well, if you think she's in there, I'd better go check." He followed and went inside. The wolf hesitated but then turned and lay on the stones where he could see the yard.

As soon as he shut the door, he heard the clicking of claws on the floor, and Lola came out of the library.

"Hi. I've been reading a book about animals. Kathleen showed me how."

"You learned to read in a day?" He was nonplussed.

She looked down, then glanced up with her head turned so that he could see only one eye. "Not very well. But I can sound out words, and I think I'm getting better. Want to see?"

"I've got a better idea, Lola. What if we organize a trip to the Cretaceous and see if we can find you a mate?" In his ears, his forced cheerfulness sounded flat.

She didn't answer immediately. Instead, she straightened, raising her head to its full height. That brought her face up to the base of his neck. His perception flipped for a moment. Suddenly, he was staring at the face of a killer dinosaur. It was a view that would frighten any human. Just as quickly, he thought to see the hurt in her. Her face was expressionless, except for her eyes, but he knew her well enough to understand how she felt.

"Okay. Let's go look for a mate for me, but there's no hurry. I can wait. Maybe you need to study for college. If not, would you help me with my reading?" She bobbed her head in a positive gesture.

"You know I'll happily help you with reading. What made you decide to learn?"

She made a kind of coughing sound. "Ugh. I thought if you were learning from books, then I should also. I..." She paused, searching for a way to explain herself. "The knowledge is there. Books are wonderful that way. I should know more than I do. I think you'd like that, and besides, I'm curious about things."

"But, Lola, you already know how to survive, how to get along in the world. You're a great hunter. What more do you need?"

She seemed irritated in her response. "Why do I need more? I need more because it's there. Why do humans need to know things? Maybe if my body had hands instead of claws, I'd be able to write. Maybe there would have been Deinonychus scientists. I want to know how things work. Why they work the way they do. That's all."

He rubbed his forehead unconsciously, then answered. "I didn't mean that you shouldn't learn, and I don't want you to be angry with me. I just never thought you would want to read."

She clicked her teeth together. It was a sign of agitation. "That's the point. You don't expect things from me. You think I'm just an animal, a dinosaur with a bird brain. You lead me to think that you care for me, but you don't hold me to the standards you would expect of a human female."

Cole reached out and touched her face. She jerked back but then stepped forward and wrapped her wing/arms around him.

"I'm sorry, Cole. I don't mean to be angry. I want you to be proud of me." She pressed her jaw against his neck, then said, "I'm ready to go look for a mate if you think this is the right time to go."

He replied softly. "I'll go talk with Mom and Dad. If they have time to take us, we can give it a try."

⸻ ⸙ ⸻

Cadeyrin and Kathleen were in the kitchen, seated at the table discussing something quietly. They stopped when the two walked in.

Kathleen asked, "What are you two doing? You look like you're going to a funeral."

"We've decided that we should try and get a mate for Lola. She doesn't think any of the flock here are suitable, so we're going to have to go back and search for someone in the Cretaceous."

Cadeyrin nodded. "She should realize that she won't be able to speak to any of the Deinonychs back then. We should take Lolita. She has experience in interacting with wild males."

"Yes. Lolita has to come. She can prevent any mishaps. We don't want Lola to get injured due to a misunderstanding," Kathleen added.

Lola pulled herself to her maximum height in an affronted manner. "I can talk to others of my kind. We don't always use English. Most of our communication is based on gestures, you know."

Kathleen smiled gently. "Yes, dear, but you're so used to being around humans that you might miss something that your mother would pick up."

Lola nodded. "Okay. I see that. I was going to ask her to come, anyway. She can point out desirable males to me. I probably can't tell what ones will make a better mate. I am too used to humans, I guess."

⸻ ⸙ ⸻

They assembled on the porch in the morning. Jason Gridley had decided to come, although Annie objected.

"It's dangerous back there, Jason. I think we've been through too much for me to feel at ease with you gone. And, don't offer. I'm afraid to go myself. I'd rather that you stayed here. Besides, we could have some kind of emergency here. Logan and Serensaa are capable, but you're the warrior." She looked embarrassed. "You and Cadeyrin, I mean."

Cadeyrin laughed. Nothing seemed to offend him. "Grid is a modern warrior. I'm just a poor primitive hunter with sharpened sticks."

Gridley grinned. "You certainly give a good account of yourself with a rifle for a caveman. I'd pick you anytime as a companion in a dangerous situation." He turned to Annie. "Look, Baby. I survived back there with the girls and a knife and some sticks, as Cadeyrin calls them. I'll be careful. Besides, Lolita is going. She will warn us if any dangerous creatures show up."

Kathleen added, "Yes. We won't be more than a second, your time."

Annie nodded slowly. I always forget. You can leave, be gone a day or a week in your time, but then snap back here, and I'll have just said, 'Be careful.' I won't even have time to miss you." She sighed. "Alright. Go ahead, but don't you let any monster eat my husband."

Lolita raised her head. "No monsters there. Just fluffy, yellow quacks, and they too stupid to be much trouble. I take good care of Grid. No worry, Annie."

Everyone laughed, and Annie nodded. "You keep him away from those yellow things. Acrocanthosaurus, aren't they? They're like a T-Rex, and those are dangerous."

Jason said, "They are big, but they're also stupid. They're the apex predator back then, but that's because they are big enough to go after the Astrodons, the big sauropods. The girls killed an Acro back when Kathleen came to rescue me."

"Maybe they did, but now you've only got Lolita."

Lola squawked. "And me! I'm good at fighting."

"You've only fought with the animals here. A big dinosaur might be a lot more difficult."

Lolita snapped her jaw with a clopping sound. "Not worry, Annie. I takes care of. Now, we go. Quit talking. We be quiet when we arrive, 'til I see if anything bad nearby." She turned and looked out over the yard, obviously ready to leave.

Kathleen took Cadeyrin's hand, and the others took hold. Everyone had to be touching for Kathleen to transport them. They had decided that she would do the job since she had a specific reference she could plug into her time equation that would bring them back slightly over one hundred million years in the past. There should be plenty of potential mates for Lola then.

Annie started to say, 'Goodbye,' but the group was already fading into a blurry haze. It flickered out, and the porch was empty. BW whined, and Annie said a worried prayer under her breath.

⸺◆⸺

The hill had disappeared. Odd-looking trees covered the area nearby, and there was almost zero visibility in all directions.

Lolita looked around, then said, "We gots to move. No see anything here."

Kathleen checked to make sure everyone was touching, then shoved the group into the inter-temporal space. She moved more slowly this time, checking for a good exit point. After a few moments, the landscape faded into view again. This time, they were on a hillock overlooking a rolling plain that seemed to extend for miles. There was a line of trees in the mid-distance, probably marking the path of a river. Groups of animals could be seen far out over the plain on either side of the river.

Cadeyrin, Grid, and Cole positioned themselves in a rough triangle, each ready to use his heavy rifle. Cole carried a hunting rifle chambered for .300 Winchester Magnum cartridges. This would take down almost any animal of reasonable size. Cadeyrin carried one of their two double-barreled elephant guns, an old .500 nitro express rifle. It kicked like crazy but would knock an Acro flat, providing that the shot was well-placed. Grid carried a dressed-out M-4. It was light, and the cartridges weren't powerful enough for the larger animals, but the weapon made up for that with its integrated grenade launcher and high rate of fire. Besides, he had said someone needed to be able to shoot something small for supper without blowing it all to bits.

Kathleen was armed, of course. She always carried the same rifle, a Ruger Mini-30. It was a short carbine with very manageable recoil. The bullets hit with considerable impact, and it could carry a 30 round magazine. She had a bag full of such magazines slung over her shoulder. If they were attacked, she was prepared to defend herself.

In the mid-distance, a pair of giant beasts pushed through the trees, coming out into a slough filled with water plants – reeds of some sort. Cole thought to recognize the plants as cattails or something similar.

Gridley pointed and said, "Sauropods. Probably Astrodons. They look like a pair. Uh-oh. Look, there comes the rest of the family."

A trio of smaller Astros followed the huge adults. All five waded into the slough, lowered their heads, and proceeded to munch on the reeds. Although they stood in one place, each Astro could reach a wide arc of reeds by sweeping its head back and forth. After each bite, the beasts raised their heads, vegetation hanging from the sides of their mouths. They chewed slowly, gradually drawing the ends of the reeds in and swallowing wads of masticated greenery which made lumps in their throats. As they ate, they surveyed the area, keeping an eye out for intruders.

Lolita watched critically. "They think they too big to be lunch. They wrong." She looked at Lola. "You, me, we could kill one. Climb on sides, kick claw in. They cut open easy, and guts fall out. Then they die, and we eat."

Lola shuddered visibly. "Okay, Mother. But, we don't need that much meat, do we?" She turned her head away as if to deny the image that Lolita had painted.

Lolita cocked her head and studied her daughter. "Oh. You too used to eating deer? Astros good meat, but maybe you right. Too big. Too much meat go waste."

Cadeyrin put his hand on Lolita, getting her attention. "If we kill one of those, there will be lots of scavengers here within a few hours. Wouldn't the smell draw an Acrocanthosaur?"

Lolita bobbed her head. "That true, but what is Acro whatever-asaur?"

Grid explained. "That's what we call the big yellow ones."

"Oh. Forgot. Fluffy yellow Quackers. Yeah. They can be bad. Eat everything, too. We kill them once. You remember, Grid?"

Kathleen had been there too. The three sisters had systematically ripped a single Acro to shreds. If it had caught one of them, a single bite would have killed them, but they were too fast for it. She said, "Lolita, we are here for Lola's sake, not just to hunt."

Lolita lowered her head, her feathers smoothing down. They had become fluffed out as she thought about conflict. "You're right. I was being too selfish. We're here for Lola. Any males will be over by the river somewhere. That's where they're more likely to find food."

Cole noticed with amusement that Lolita had used proper English for once. It wasn't that she couldn't use it correctly; she just didn't bother. Trading brevity for perfection was common sense to her.

The group headed towards the river, keeping watch in all directions. The Astros raised their heads and stared at the oncoming group but didn't move from the slough. Lola thought they felt safe in the deeper water. They were correct. A Deinonychus couldn't reach them in the muck. They would only be vulnerable when they reached the hard ground. Of course, an Acro could wade in and attack them, but there were none in sight.

Lolita stopped at a large pile of dung. She sniffed delicately. "This be Yellow Fluffy shit. One here yesterday, maybe."

A few steps farther and there were several smaller piles of scat. Lola's mouth opened slightly, and she drew air over her tongue. Lolita didn't have to tell her that the piles were Deinonychus dung. Two were from the same male. They were heavy with pheromones. Instinctively, she knew that he was healthy and looking for a mate. The idea excited her and disgusted her simultaneously. Was she some kind of animal to be excited by poop? Her mind denied her interest, but her body still responded, even though she willed it not to.

Lolita looked at her daughter. "This one might be good. We go try to find him and check him out. Okay?"

Lola bobbed her head affirmatively but without enthusiasm. She was familiar with Deinonychus males, of course. There were six males in the flock that lived around the stone house. Two were older and were Belle's surviving spouse and Fancy's mate, while the others were chicks of her age or younger. She was familiar with their ways, and none of them interested her in the slightest.

Belle's mate had even shown some interest in her in the last year. He knew she had reached maturity. The idea of taking up with her Aunt Belle's mate wasn't at all attractive, and he had given up after a few attempts to court her. The younger chicks weren't ready to court as yet, but she didn't care. They seemed to be too close – family. Her genes wanted someone that wasn't related. Kathleen had explained to her that closely related creatures shouldn't mate. The chicks would be likely to be sub-par or even deformed. She wasn't sure what genes were, but she planned to read about them. They sounded interesting.

They approached the river. The trees formed a thin screen at this point. It was easy to see the water and the opposite bank. The trees were thicker over there.

Cadeyrin abruptly turned and led them northward, staying a hundred feet or so away from the trees and brush.

"A group of your kind went along this way," he said to Lola. "They were keeping out of the trees because there was something in there they were avoiding." He paused to point an all but indecipherable scuff in a bare patch between some weeds."

Lola sniffed dubiously at the spot. There was some Deinonychus scent, but it was faint. Obviously, Cadeyrin was a superior tracker. Cole was not nearly that good. She looked at the hunter with a new appreciation.

Grid said, "If they were avoiding it, we should also."

Cadeyrin grunted affirmatively.

They moved quickly, covering several hundred meters, keeping their heads up and eyes open.

Lolita stopped abruptly. She sniffed deeply. Once, then again in deep whuffs. "Something near. Don't like smell. It smell like one of us, but different. I never smell it before." She backed slowly away from the trees, scanning the bushes as she moved.

Cadeyrin motioned the rest of the group back. "Let's get some distance here," he whispered. "I think we're being watched."

There was a stir in the bushes. The tops spread apart in a path leading directly towards the group. Whatever it was, must have realized they had detected it.

The final screen of undergrowth parted with the cracking of breaking branches. A head as big as a man's torso came through first, followed by a long, low body. The beast's shoulders were lowered to the level of its hips, and its back was as high as Cole's face. It walked leaning forward, carrying itself horizontally, counter-balanced by its long, stiff tail.

Lola stared, astounded. It was as if she were seeing one of her own kind but magnified to ten times her size. She watched the creature's eyes as they scanned the group. The monster focused intently on Lolita.

Lolita stepped forward and bobbed her head in greeting, but the big raptor wasn't there for a social visit. It ignored her signal. Instead, it raised its head and screamed a battle cry at them. Its feathered arms lifted, and the finger claws spread in a threatening manner.

Lolita's crest dropped. She kept her eyes on it and said, "It going to attack, but it's not sure of us. There's another one behind. When they get clear of bushes, we have to fight." She stopped talking, lifted her head, screamed in return, and flexed her wing/arms into attack mode.

The giant raptor screamed a second time. The volume of its cry made Lolita's sound like that of a baby. Lola jumped at the sound, then strode up beside her mother and went into attack position. The giant raptor swiveled its head and evaluated the two Deinonychus first from one eye, then the other.

The bushes crashed again, and a second oversized raptor joined the first. The two raised and lowered their heads, alternately screaming.

Cadeyrin had moved slightly forward and to the left of the two Deinonychus. He aimed, then waited until the first raptor started to lunge forward. The Nitro-Express boomed like a cannon, and the attacking raptor staggered and stopped. It looked at the man dubiously, then abruptly collapsed.

The raptor's mate nudged the first but got no response. Its eyes fixed on Cadeyrin, and it screamed, even louder and more ferociously than before. It knew precisely which of its opponents had done the damage.

The express rifle boomed a second time just as the raptor began to move. The beast spun to its right, staggered in a circle, and then stopped facing them. The heavy bullet had shattered the creature's right wing-arm, but the wound wasn't close to being damaging enough to stop the creature.

Kathleen and Gridley opened up at that point. Their bullets were smaller, but there were many of them, and the steel-cored projectiles went deep. The raptor lunged forward, trying to catch Cadeyrin in its jaws. Its lunge was knocked off target as Lola and Lolita crashed into its left side.

Lolita clawed her way to its back, kicking mightily with both of her killing claws. Lola kicked a claw into the creature's thigh, jumped high, and bounced away.

The human weapons had gone silent as the mother and daughter attacked. Kathleen was in the process of inserting a new magazine into her carbine. Grid had already reloaded, and Cadeyrin's double-barreled rifle was just clicking shut with fresh ammunition.

The giant raptor fell to the ground as Lola bounced off, landing on its side. It lifted its head, trying to regain its balance, but the combined attack had been too damaging. It struggled but couldn't right itself with its smashed right arm.

Lolita was standing off to the side, perhaps twenty paces away, watching with her head cocked at an angle. Lola had moved back beside Cole. He was in the rear of the group, his Win-Mag shouldered, but he had not taken a shot as yet.

Keeping his eyes on the struggling creature, he said, "Lola move away. Protect your ears. I'm going to shoot."

She obediently dashed behind him a few steps, then turned to watch after she'd raised her arms to cover her ears. His gun was almost as loud as his father's, and she appreciated the warning. Her hearing was too valuable to risk injury from the muzzle blast.

The Win-Mag jumped as Cole shot, and the bullet cracked as it struck the big raptor's temple. The shot was perfectly placed, and the creature dropped its head, twitched slightly, then was still.

"Well. That was exciting," Cadeyrin said in an understated manner. "What are those things?"

"Some kind of dromaeosaur, I guess. They look like our Deinonychus on steroids," Kathleen answered.

Cole moved forward slowly, his rifle still shouldered. Sometimes big game was deceptive, and these creatures were too large and too well-armed for him to take chances. The killing claw on their toes was at least nine inches long. "I think these are Utahraptors. They're the only ones that would be this large in this place and time."

Gridley nodded. "That's my guess, too. I did some homework before we came. Living back here for months as I did, I was always at a disadvantage in not knowing what creatures I might encounter. Last night I spent some time in the library and looked up everything I could find in our books. If we keep coming back here, we should get a better selection of paleontology books, though. The ones we have don't have a lot of information in them."

Kathleen snickered. "If we come back here much, we'll be the ultimate authorities on the fauna. We can write our own books."

Lola walked close to the two carcasses and scrutinized them. One was male, and the other was female. They were remarkably like her, only much larger.

It made her feel odd, killing something that was probably intelligent. She shook her head in denial. The big raptors had the opportunity to avoid conflict, but they had chosen to attack. It boiled down to them or her and her friends.

Lolita made a warning sound at that moment. A group of seven Deinonychs was approaching from the north. They were moving slowly with their heads raised as they tried to make out the details of what had happened.

Cole said, "They heard the commotion and decided to investigate. The gunfire wouldn't mean anything to them, but the screams told them there was a fight to the death. Now they're coming to see if there's anything left over to eat."

Lolita caught Lola's attention. "The large male in the front is the one we after. He young and other three pairs are mated couples. He got no mate. Maybe you like him? You go introduce yourself. Slowly, slowly, and no making like you fear or want fight. Understand?"

Lola hesitated, then took a few steps forward. She looked back. Cole was looking away, his posture stiff as if he didn't want to watch. Lolita motioned her on. "Go."

She turned and looked at the oncoming group. The male was larger than her, but he seemed unsure of himself. The other six adults sensed that something was happening between the two and stepped to the side to watch.

She walked forward, feeling like she was going to her execution as she did. The male was good-looking, certainly. His feathers were bright and glossy, and he looked strong but perhaps a little ungainly.

She stopped twenty feet in front of him and looked coyly to the side.

He bobbed his head in greeting, and she responded with a single nod. That was apparently enough to encourage him. He strode forward, turned, and pushed his shoulder against hers.

That was too fast. The movement should take place much later in the courtship dance. At this point, it was too intimate. She jumped to the side and snapped at him. He ignored her affronted attitude and tried to nudge her again.

Suddenly, it was all too much for her. The blasted idiot wasn't going to court her properly. She wouldn't cooperate with someone who just wanted to have sex at their first meeting. She spun in a circle and ran back to the group of humans and her mother.

The confused male took several steps in pursuit, then stopped and looked at one of the mated pairs as if to ask, "What did I do wrong?"

He looked at Lola again, but she had moved back and was now standing beside Cole.

"I...I can't do this, Cole. I know I should, but he's a...a beast." The absurdity of what she had said came through to her, and she began to shake. "But, so am I!" she wailed.

Cole didn't speak. Instead, he wrapped his arms around her and pulled her close. She buried her face against his neck and gasped out, "He's a perfect male of my kind, and I can't stand the idea of mating with him. What is w-wrong with me?"

He tightened his arms and said softly, "Perhaps this isn't the right time for you. It's a big step – choosing a mate. Many human females have responded the same way you are in much the same situation. There's nothing wrong with you. You're perfect as you are, but maybe you don't need a mate right now." After a moment, he added, "We're all beasts together in a sense. We all have physical bodies of various sorts, but it's the mind inside that counts in the long run."

Kathleen and Cadeyrin had come over to where Cole was comforting Lola in time to hear that last statement. Kathleen looked at her son with approval, then whispered to Cadeyrin, "That's an amazing insight. You have a brilliant son." He smiled but said nothing.

Lolita had gone forward and introduced herself to the newcomers in a flurry of bobbing heads and carefully hidden hand claws. Somehow she had communicated to the seven members of the Deinonychus group that they were welcome to feed on the dead Utahraptors. They seemed to be hungry because they didn't waste time addressing themselves to the closest carcass, spending only a few glances at the strangely shaped humans. Food came first as far as they were concerned. Besides, Lolita had shown no fear of the humans, so they must be reasonably harmless.

Kathleen came close and said, "Lola, listen to me. It seems this was a mistake on our part. We thought you were ready to meet someone, but we were wrong. However, you absolutely must get over the idea that Cole is the perfect mate for you. That won't work out for either of you. You need someone of your own kind, just as he does. How will you feel when he finds someone and brings her home? Have you thought of that?"

Lola made a distressed sound and pushed closer to Cole. After a few seconds, she said, "I know all that. I think I'm going to learn to read better. If I can concentrate on learning, maybe I can feel better about myself. I have to live my own life, and I don't expect you to keep worrying about me. It's not fair. Besides, I want to learn things." She didn't try to explain her vaguely held belief that she might find acceptance for herself in her own mind if only she knew enough.

Kathleen exchanged a frowning look with Cadeyrin. He nodded slowly, then said, "That's a good approach, Lola. I've known several men who studied to become a shaman, and some of them didn't seem interested in having a family. They were more interested in knowledge." He didn't mention that he had followed his father in the study of shamanic knowledge and still found Kathleen critical to his emotional well-being.

Gridley had been standing by watching with a worried expression. "That's settled. I'd feel better if we left. The racket we made is going to draw some Acros for sure, or maybe more of these monster raptors. If we keep messing with Utahraptors, sooner or later, something bad is going to happen. They have to be a lot smarter than the Acros, and that means they're more dangerous."

Kathleen called Lolita, and the small Deinonychus came trotting over from where she'd been sampling some Utahraptor. She had clamped her muzzle on a chunk of bloody meat. As she arrived, she flipped it up, snapped, gulped twice, and swallowed the piece. "We go now? Lola not got mate yet, but maybe this boy not the right one. That okay, Chicky. We find you one sooner or later." The last was addressed to Lola, who had finally released Cole. She was looking around in a distracted manner as if she hoped to find her composure wandering in the general vicinity.

She bobbed her head, then said, "Okay. I'd like to go home now, I think."

The group linked hands, and Kathleen transported them forward. The last thing Lola saw was the young male looking at her. She thought he looked disappointed, but she didn't care. That was his problem. She had her own.

Chapter Ten

Stalking Cole

Devonette was not a slacker. Her father had ensured that she learned to apply herself. He made it clear that she would only take over his business interests if she proved herself capable. She was diligent and industrious when she had set a goal for herself. It took a little doing, but she got herself transferred into the same recitation section as the boy who sat in the back. That was a start. She figured it would be easier to learn who he was if they were in the same class.

Additionally, she would have more opportunities to interact with him. She planned to be circumspect. There would be no blatant attempt to attract his interest. She was too good and too devious to be that careless.

⎯⎯◆◊◆⎯⎯

The recitation instructor was a first-year grad student, and she was an idiot. That wasn't just Devonette's opinion; everyone in the class recognized it immediately. The instructor's explanations were odd combinations of word-salad that bore little relation to either Professor Higgins' lectures or the textbook.

Devonette fully believed in the power of women – most specifically, the power of one woman – her, but she didn't view the world through the distorted lens that Janice Ellison used. According to Ellison, all history was distorted, being told, as it was, from a strictly white Euro-centric male viewpoint. Ms. Ellison offered alternate interpretations that involved elaborately contrived scenarios designed to show how the principal actors were female. Men, in her explanations, did not have original thoughts and, if left to themselves, would lie around all day, drinking. It was up to women to decide to go to war, migrate, build cities, and so on.

By the end of the first class, all the students had tuned the hapless Janice out. Devonette was a late-comer, transferring during the third week. Ms. Ellison, having realized that she wasn't getting through to her students, spent a significant part of each lecture focusing on Devonette. She seemed to think that Devonette was destined for greatness. On that, at least, they could agree.

The class had only five more minutes to go, and everyone had gathered up their papers and belongings. The instant the bell rang, the entire class jumped up and crowded through the door.

The boy who always sat in the back was named Cole Whitman. Devonette had acquired that information the first day when she stayed a little late to ask a flattered Janice a question about what she'd missed. The class roll had come out when Devonette had suggested that she would feel more at ease if she knew the names of the other students.

At the second recitation session, she had contrived to sit beside Cole. He was courteous, but that was it. He didn't seem aware that the most desirable girl was seated beside him.

He also seemed to be taking notes as Janice spoke. He couldn't seriously think the woman had anything important to say.

It took some restless movement on her part to position herself so that she could read what he was writing. His notes were clear and, she thought, surprisingly insightful. He had seen through Janice's ideological bias, and his notes were oriented towards points that would enable him to pass the two tests that the recitation session would have. Those two tests accounted for ten percent of the total grade for the course.

A slight feeling of respect struck Devonette. Obviously, Mr. Cole, whatever his last name, was intelligent enough to plan on manipulating his way to a good grade. After a bit, she smiled slightly. The expression was intended for herself, but a boy two rows away smiled back and looked at her hopefully. She frowned in irritation. Men.

Her ultimate triumph would be even sweeter if Cole were as smart as his actions indicated. She'd have to move carefully, too. It wouldn't do to arouse his suspicions.

To this end, she formulated a plan that involved asking him questions about the course material, showing interest in his answers, but acting as if she were simply using him as a resource. She'd flirt a little, then act cool. That had worked for numerous men in the past. There was no reason it wouldn't work now.

She followed Cole out of class, but he didn't linger and his long strides outpaced her. It was frustrating. She'd decided to allow him to take her to lunch, but he was already a ways ahead and walking like he was leaving campus. There was a way to handle that, though.

She touched her watch and spoke quietly into it. A moment later, a tough-looking man dressed much like a student strode onto the sidewalk and started following Cole. She smiled. Randy would track him home. That would be another piece of information she could use.

She went to lunch alone, thoughtfully using the time to make notes of possible strategies.

She was concentrating on her laptop when a shadow loomed over it. She looked up. Randy was there with a slight smile on his face. He was always business-like around her. She knew he got paid too well to allow himself to relax. If he made a pass at her, she would tell her father, and Randy would be out of a cushy job. They both knew it and, although she took some liberties with him, Randy always behaved.

"He lives on 43rd street in a ranch-style house. I watched for a bit, and it doesn't look like he has roommates. I told James to take over. He'll watch to verify the living alone thing. Do you want any more information, Ms. Passway?"

"Randy, be a dear and find out who owns the house. I'd like to know who his landlord is." That would be a possible approach. She could arrange for pressure on the landlord to evict Cole. If that happened during finals, the disturbance could affect his grades. She was not interested in how well he did, but anything that could make him vulnerable was important.

"Yes, Ms. Passway. I'll have a report for you by tomorrow."

She sighed. It would be nice if it were sooner, but she knew that Randy would be busy keeping an eye on her until she got home. That wouldn't allow him time to do any research.

"Thank you, Randy. That'll be all."

He didn't say anything, just stepped back politely, then turned and disappeared.

———◆◇◆———

Her watch chimed at 7:00 AM. Carefully placing Irwin between the pillows, she stretched, then got up and padded into the bathroom where her phone was charging. Daddy had taught her always to charge it in another room. He said the EMF waves from the device often interfered with sleep and, worse, he'd pointed out, that the phone could be hacked and set to record any sounds she made at night. She didn't think she made sounds when asleep, but he thought it was potentially hazardous, so she followed his instructions without questioning them.

The chime was a text notification from Randy. He wanted to make sure she knew he had sent an email regarding Cole Whitman. She opened the mail program and read the information.

It appeared that the subject might not be who he passed himself off to be. James had watched the house all night, and there had been no sign of occupancy. It was definite that the target had entered, but somehow he had left without their noticing. James admitted that it was remotely possible that Cole might have left through a rear window and vanished between the neighbor's houses, but that would mean that the subject had noticed the surveillance. He didn't think that was likely.

The other alternative was that the target had stayed in the house with no lights and no activity all night. The two men sometimes used a highly sensitive laser eavesdropping device. When focused on a window, it would pick up the vibrations from any sound inside. Randy had taken it over about 10 PM, and they'd activated it.

It had sensed no sounds from inside. Randy joked that it was almost as if Cole had disappeared into thin air, but he made it clear that he didn't consider that reasonable.

The second part of the message deepened the mystery. The house was owned by a Florida corporation called CADKAT, LLC. That corporation, in turn, was owned by a second one. The tracing took some time, but they'd contacted an outside resource who had better access. The second corporation was called Daoifla Investments, LLC. That one owned several other corporations. The research was still ongoing, but one outstanding fact had surfaced. One of the corporations owned by Daoifla was Piskat, Inc.

That meant nothing to Devonette. However, the report had gone to her father before Randy had forwarded it to her. Dear old Daddy had come through again. He recognized Piskat as a privately held medical research company. He'd become aware of it from a different line of inquiry.

In fact, he had made several efforts to purchase the company that had released a highly successful medication that had some life-extension properties. The holders had refused to sell at any price.

This refusal was so unusual that he had taken steps to find out who they were, and the result of the investigation, while not definitive, implicated Kathleen Whitby. The listed agent for Daoifla was the law firm in Minneapolis that Winston knew represented Kathleen Whitby.

The research had cost tens of thousands of dollars but had come to a dead-end at that point. The employees of the law firm who could be bought knew nothing. Whoever was responsible for Daoifla's legal work wasn't talking.

Winston briefly considered having one of the senior attorneys kidnapped and tortured but put that on the back burner. Given enough time, something would come out, and he had assets in place to glean that information.

This new line of research was precisely the serendipitous result for which he was hoping. They could concentrate on the corporations turned up by Randy's source. The possibility that Cole was related to Kathleen Whitby had set the researchers off on another path.

Cole "Whitman's" school records had given them his social security number. That had led to his birth records in 2001 in Columbia, Missouri. That appeared to be a dead-end until the death records had been checked. There had been a Cole Whitman born in February of 2001, but the infant had unexpectedly died of SIDS in March of that year. They had even found a picture of a tombstone that confirmed that information.

Suddenly, the inference that the name 'Whitman' was most probably 'Whitby' seemed highly likely. The only problem was a record from Brainard Lakes Regional Hospital of a Kathleen Whitby giving birth to a boy named 'Cole' in 2016. There was no way that child could be the young man Devonette had her sights on.

Randy ended with a note of caution. Her father had insisted that she stay away from Cole Whitman. If he was who he might be, Daddy didn't want her arousing his suspicion. She was to leave him strictly alone. Besides, he might be dangerous.

She laughed at that last. There was no man that she knew of who could overcome both Randy and James. The two were deadly. She shivered deliciously at the thought of them ripping through bodies. Anyone who planned to kidnap her or otherwise injure her had better have a pre-paid funeral plan.

"Irwin, my Daddy says I'm to leave Cole Whitman alone. What do you think of that?"

The scruffy stuffed tiger asked a critical question. "Did Daddy say if he means Cole Whitman or Cole Whitby?"

"Why, he said Cole Whitman, of course. So, that means if his real name is Cole Whitby, I can continue with my plans, doesn't it?"

Irwin agreed with that interpretation, but he advised caution.

"You will have to be careful not to let Randy and James know what you're doing. They'll tell your father, and that could be bad."

"Yes. I will have to take care, won't I? If I work carefully, I can make it appear like he is chasing me. That's the point, really. Then if Daddy asks why I didn't leave him alone, I can say it wasn't my fault. After all, what man could resist me?" She smiled at her reflection in the mirror as she said that.

Irwin agreed again. "Now that that's settled, what will you do?"

She thought for a moment. "If I can set up a circumstance where he and Dewayne can meet, and I'm present, I can act like Cole is stalking me. Dewayne and the rest of the football team will probably beat him up. Then I can come back to him later and act sorry about it. That will give me the opportunity to charm him. He's going to regret acting indifferent, that's for sure."

The problem with that idea was Dewayne wasn't entirely under her control. She had continued working on the quarterback during the past two weeks. It wasn't like that was difficult. She'd sometimes had four men on the string at the same time. Dewayne's girlfriend was becoming suspicious, but that just made the game more fun.

There was an obvious place where she could stage the confrontation. Dewayne and several members of the offensive team almost always stopped at a local coffee shop for lattes after practice. They weren't supposed to, but the coach hadn't found out yet. All she had to do was to get Cole there at the same time.

Chapter Eleven

Depression

Lola stood on the porch, looking out at the long stretch of hillside and the trees along the crest. Her mind seemed out of control – whirling from thought to thought and unable to focus on a single topic. This was an unusual feeling for her. She was usually happy and able to concentrate on a single idea until she was satisfied that she'd thoroughly examined it.

Now, she felt sad, and her sense of shame and embarrassment was almost unbearable. Everyone had gone to great lengths to help her, even endangering themselves in the attempt.

Those Utahraptors were frightening, and it didn't require much imagination to see how the whole thing could have resulted in someone getting killed. And, what had she done? She'd been so disgusted at the abbreviated courtship dance of the young male that she had run to Cole and practically denied her own species.

That, she thought, was the sum total of her problem. She was happy with her body and felt at ease in it, but she wanted…she wanted…she drew a deep breath and forced her mind to admit what she did want. She wanted Cole as her mate and not just in spirit.

She recognized that her desire ran smack into the solid barrier of reality. She couldn't have what she wanted in the way she wanted it, but so far, she couldn't see a way around the problem. She had inherited a significant degree of stubbornness from Lolita, and perhaps that was a contributing cause to her inability to give up on the idea.

What was worse, as she had shown everyone her deepest, heartfelt desire. They must be thinking that she had lost her mind.

With that thought, she leaped off the steps and trotted across the yard, heading up the hill. Perhaps there was a chance she could find some peace in the wilderness. She certainly couldn't stay here and face any of the humans, not after this.

⸻◆⸻

She scanned the tree line as she approached the top of the hill, hoping that the old Sasquatch would appear. If he did, she would ask him for his opinion. He was the longest-lived creature she knew. Perhaps his vast experience held an answer.

The Sasquatch didn't appear, so she pushed on through the trees and headed down the far side of the hill. Cole would miss her even if the others were relieved that she was gone. He'd search, but she intended to be far away by the time he got back from school.

She wallowed in self-pity without realizing what she was doing. He'd be sad, but he probably already had some human female he found interesting. She imagined some girl in the far distant future holding his hand.

Her next thought nearly drove her to her knees, if it were possible to feel worse than she already did. Why should I expect him to act differently and against his nature? I'm just a freaky animal and not even in my own time.

If Kathleen hadn't brought her mother and aunts back when she rescued Grid, there wouldn't be the problem known as Lola.

Grief overwhelmed her, and she broke into a sprint, moaning as she ran. She knew it was impossible to run away from the problem, but she simply had to do something.

She stopped, gasping for breath when her thighs were burning so badly that she couldn't take another step. The pain helped her focus, and she felt a little more in control, mentally.

She stood, head down, until her heart had slowed and her thigh muscles recovered. When she started moving this time, it was at a slow jog that she knew she could maintain.

Three hours later, she was drinking from a spring-fed slough. The water was undisturbed and clear. That was nice. She didn't like muddy water, even though it was sometimes all that was available.

Sensing eyes upon her, she raised her head and discovered a dire wolf watching her from the far side of the slough. They weren't common in this area. Kathleen had told her the English name, but Cadeyrin called them Daoifla in his native tongue.

The creature was slightly larger than BW and far less attractive to her eyes. Its body looked too heavy, and proportions were off, making it look bulky with thin legs. Overall it had a dubious and untrustworthy appearance.

There was a slight sound from down the bank. She turned her head slightly, looking out of her right eye in that direction. The tall grass moved a little. Whatever it was, it was heading towards her. When she looked back, the dire wolf had vanished. She took a deep breath. She was being hunted. The stupid creatures didn't know what she was, and they weren't cautious enough to leave her alone.

She trotted back through the reeds to the small knoll from which she'd come. It was a clear hillock with short grass covering most of the top. Once there, she stopped and watched the tall grass and reeds around the slough.

There were four of the Daoifla stalking her. They had spread out and now were trying to come at her from three sides. She thought of Cole's warning that she should be more careful. Even a minor injury could prove serious when one is alone. What would he think if she ended up being killed by some overgrown and ugly beasts?

Still, she knew she couldn't run from them. Their endurance was greater than hers, so she would have to fight. The old Sasquatch came into her mind. He had given her the gift of time and space. There was another choice; she could enter the spirit domain and move away. The idea was strange but reassuring. It was an option that she hadn't considered before.

The Daoifla burst from the weeds simultaneously, snarling as they trotted towards her. In response, she closed her eyes and entered the spirit land. It wasn't as confusing as it had been. She looked around, trying to orient herself.

There was a towering black thunderhead far off in one direction. It flashed with bolts of what appeared to be internal lightning. That was something to avoid. She only wanted to get away from her hunters, and that was simple. She moved in a way she couldn't describe, then re-entered the real world.

The sun was shining, and she was standing on the rolling plain that she'd crossed before she found the slough. The hillock was about a kilometer away to her left, and she trotted quickly, heading on a path that wouldn't bring her near her pursuers. They'd be surprised that she had disappeared and, best of all, there would be no scent trail that they could follow.

The land ahead of her dropped into a valley, and she moved down over the verge to keep out of sight. She didn't want the Daoifla to see her from the top of the hillock. That was easy. She could avoid any predator that might hunt her.

What if she used her new mode of travel to go far away from the humans? She could do that easily but was it a good idea. She remembered overhearing Kathleen saying something about traces left by travelers in the spirit world. If she traveled that way, perhaps she would leave tracks that could be followed. She didn't know if that was possible, but it seemed like a better idea to keep trotting.

Several hundred meters later, she considered going back to the correct time for her species. That was frightening. There were creatures back there that would think nothing of killing and eating her. Of course, there were creatures here that would do the same thing, but she was familiar with the mammals of the here and now. She could handle them. The memory of the Utahraptors was still fresh, and she would not willingly approach one of them again.

So, going back was out. How about going forward? What if she went to the future and found out about Cole's college? Would he be pleased if he found out, or would he lecture her about the dangers?

She'd been there. The old Sasquatch had taken her forward to that time. She knew, somehow, that she could return on her own. It was something to think about, but if she went forward, what would she do?

Along with her stubbornness, Lola had acquired a tendency towards fast decisions. She knew that she sometimes allowed her natural aggression to convince her to act precipitously. She had developed the habit of compensating by analyzing situations more fully.

Her mental state betrayed her at this point. She was depressed, and her mind was tired of thinking that led in apparent circles. She stopped, took a deep breath, then said, "If I don't go, I won't know if I can." With that statement, she shut her eyes and entered the spirit world.

The landscape was different. Frighteningly dark and ominous this time. The distant storm she'd seen before was closer. Near at hand were billowing black clouds. She hadn't seen any of this when the old Sasquatch had taken her forward, but maybe she had been too startled to notice.

Forming an intention to go to the future and find Cole, she scanned the surroundings again. An opening had formed in the billowing black clouds, and without conscious effort, she found herself moving toward it rapidly.

This is better, she thought. It must be the correct path. I'll come out in some bushes at his University place and stay hidden while I look around. The black clouds had surrounded the opening and now were curling over the top, forming a tunnel. It wasn't solid; instead, it flowed, almost closing and then reforming. Should she enter?

There was a sudden sense of threat followed by a wash of fear. She stopped moving and looked closely. Something was moving at the mouth of the tunnel. It formed out of insubstantial wisps of cloud, clumping together into an amorphous mass.

As she watched, horrified, her sense of danger increased as the mass split into two chunks that flowed slowly into almost recognizable shapes. She strained, trying to make sense of what she was seeing. The shapes changed, writhed, then formed into long bodies with glowing eyes.

The eyes were fixed on her. Wonderingly, she moved back a little. That sign of fear and intimidation acted like a catalyst on the shapes facing her. They writhed again, extruded legs and wing-arms, then took a more upright position. They moved forward, and now she saw. They were two of the enormous raptors they'd faced in the Cretaceous. Two of them, and they gave every sign that they were about to attack.

She looked around, but the landscape had changed. Now she was surrounded by roiling black clouds. The two Utahraptors were swaying their heads from side to side, gauging the distance they would have to lunge to grab her. The clouds closed in more tightly, leaving her no possible escape.

She was going to die, and her fear was suddenly a source of embarrassment. If Cole knew that she had been killed without fighting back, he would be ashamed of her. She flexed her wing-arms into her attack position and screamed hopelessly at the two monsters facing her. They screamed back, and she lunged at the one to her right.

It gaped its jaws, exposing needle-sharp teeth. She ducked under its jaw and struck at its neck with her hand claws.

The result was unanticipated. Something happened, but she wasn't sure how or what. She was now flying away from the tunnel and the two raptors, heading directly toward the towering black storm. The clouds spun, and lightning flashed. She tried to stop, but her sense of orientation changed, and she was falling into the darkness.

Lola entered the storm and was buffeted by gale winds like a dry leaf. She closed her eyes in response to a nearby lightning flash. It was so close that she could smell ozone almost before the thunder roared.

Something grabbed her at that moment, and she struggled to turn her head and bite. It could only be one of the raptors. Before she snapped, a calm thought entered her head.

"Little one be still. You should never enter this place. Those who do always come out changed, if they come out at all."

Her eyes opened wide. It was the old Sasquatch. He was holding her in his arms like a human would hold a baby. She tensed, then relaxed. If he had wanted to hurt her, all he had to do was to let the storm take her.

He spoke again, not out loud, but in her mind. "What possible reason could you have to be here?"

She formed her intent to see Cole in the future. Before she could finalize the thought, the old one answered.

"I see, perhaps more than you now understand. You are like a lost child, knowing neither whither nor whence to go in search of your heartfelt desire. I will assist, although I'm not sure that your intent is well-considered."

Time passed, or not, she couldn't be sure, but now they were at the entrance to the tunnel. The two big raptors were still there. She flinched in the old one's arms, but he simply moved forward. As they drew nearer, she could see the Utahraptors shrinking in size. By the time they were at the tunnel mouth, the two monsters had withered to the size of small lizards.

She must have asked because the Sasquatch answered. "There are many guardians in this world. Their job is to test your intent and will. They feed on your fear and grow strong when you face them unless you are completely sure of your intention. As you see, they are tiny things, things that sense the fear in your mind and manifest as your worst nightmare. They have no power over you now that you know their secret."

They flew through the tunnel. At first, it was dark, but she became aware of faintly glowing light. The light rapidly brightened, and they flew out of the tunnel into an open area that glowed with a clear light. The old one set her down and pointed.

"That spot over there will respond to your intent. You will come out in some thick bushes. Be sure not to let the humans see you. You are far from your own time, and they will not respond well to your presence. Now that you know the secret of the guardians, you will have no trouble returning to the past and no trouble coming forward to here and now, should you desire to come again." The Sasquatch moved away, then stopped. "I am troubled. It is not our way to assist other travelers in the spirit world. Especially when their goal is one we don't agree with or fully understand. Take care, little one." With that, he faded and was gone.

Lola turned and exited the spirit world at the spot she had been shown.

❖

There were flowering bushes all around her and a great deal of noise in the near distance. Humming and growls that sounded like some fierce animals were preparing to fight, the sounds of humans talking, music of a sort different from what she had heard her humans play. She crouched near the ground, shivering. Now that she was here, what would she do? What could she do?

A voice spoke nearby, one she recognized. It was Cole. She wormed her way near the edge of the bushes and peeked through a tiny gap in the leaves. He spoke to a human girl who wasn't very attractive if she was any judge. At least the girl didn't meet the standard set by Kathleen, or Serensaa and Annie, and their two daughters. Lola held still and listened.

"No, Sandy, I'm sorry, but I was just looking for a reliable lab partner with no complications. I, uh, I'm already spoken for, if you must know," Cole said.

Lola could see the concern in his eyes. The unattractive girl, Sandy, didn't respond well to his statement. Her face fell and crinkled up into an expression of sadness. She choked out a short sentence. "I'm sorry. I made a mistake. I...I thought there was..." Her voice faded to an embarrassed silence, then she said, "I'm sorry." She turned and walked quickly away.

Cole stood there looking sad, in turn. Lola wondered what was going on precisely. That unattractive female couldn't be one he thought of as a mate. That much was clear to her, but she didn't understand the situation at all.

Cole was talking to himself in a low voice. "Damn women. I don't understand any of them. I didn't mean to hurt Sandy. That black-haired girl in my recitation class is another one that I've got to watch. The only female I understand is Lola. She's like a clear jewel compared to these conniving modern women. I could be happy just hunting with her. I don't even know what I'm doing here." He started to walk away as a couple holding hands approached along the sidewalk.

Lola watched Cole's path. When he went by another patch of lilacs, she had transferred through the spirit world to that location and watched him from close at hand. This was a new form of stalking for her, and it seemed very useful.

He walked between two large buildings and across a wide space, stopping to allow a vehicle with people inside to pass. There were no more bushes she could hide in, but there was a narrow gap between two buildings on the other side of the yard. She transferred there.

When he left the campus, Lola watched from under the front porch of a run-down house. Then she jumped down the street and watched from behind a group of cans overflowing with garbage. The stench was incredible, and she tried to breathe through her mouth to avoid it.

Two more jumps, and she was between a house and a vehicle parked beside the wall. Cole turned up the sidewalk that led to the porch of a smaller house across the street. He stopped, did something with the door, then entered, and the door shut. She felt a sense of relief. Now she knew which house was his. She studied the building until she felt she could return directly through the spirit world.

A loud voice shouted, "What the hell? What is that behind the car?" Then it said, "I think I drank too much beer. I must be seeing things."

A second male said, "Looks like a damn ostrich or maybe an emu. Do we have a zoo here in town?"

She didn't wait for the answer. The spirit world opened, and she fled back down the long tunnel to the Pleistocene.

Chapter Twelve

When a Plan Comes Together

During the next week, Devonette tried twice to get Cole's attention. Both times were spectacular failures. She felt as if she wasn't even there as far as he was concerned. Finally, she decided to resort to direct physical action of a sort that she had never used before. If she couldn't get him by her usual methods, she would have to rely on the fact that he seemed to be an utterly decent guy. She'd followed him to his chem lab and noticed that he ignored all of the women there, also. That made her feel less frustrated.

A horrible thought hit her as she walked away from the chemistry building. What if Cole was just not interested in females or any kind of person, for that matter? She thought about it for an instant but then decided that wasn't the case. Her intuition had told her that he was interested in her the first time they'd met. It was just that he kept himself under firm control. It seemed like he analyzed every possibility of an encounter before he acted, and he always acted in a manner that kept other people at a distance.

She waited until they were leaving the Wednesday lecture section. The crush of students poured through the doors and down the ten steps to the plaza in front of the lecture hall. It was always somewhat of a stampede, and she was careful to avoid the crush as much as possible.

This time, she waited beside the door until Cole came out. He was packing his notes into a small pack he always carried and appeared distracted. That made it easy for her to walk into his path as he reached the top step. She intended to collide with him and drop her book in response. She had carefully loaded it with individual sheets of handwritten notes that would be sure to fall out and go all over. If he were as decent as she thought, he would stop and help her recover the scattered papers. Then she could show gratitude and ask him to go for a cup of coffee or a latte or something. All she needed to do then was to make sure it was at the same time that Dewayne and his cohort were there.

Devonette was firm and reasonably fit, but she was not athletic. She collided with Cole as she had intended. He was rock hard and didn't give much, and she staggered back directly into the path of another girl rushing to get to her class across campus. Devonette bounced off her and went down the steps. She managed to grab the center railing and break her fall, but her grip didn't hold, and she landed hard on the steps, head downward. Stunned and hurt, she started to roll on down, but her fall was stopped by a firm hand that caught her arm. It hurt, and she groaned in pain, then stopped when she realized that Cole was holding her.

"Are you okay?" he asked.

She tried to smile in response, but her face wrinkled as she realized that she really wasn't okay. "My side hurts," she whispered. She wasn't lying; it did. She'd never been hurt that much in her entire life, and it was almost unbearable. She looked frantically around. Surely there was something or someone nearby that could make the pain cease.

Cole knelt and helped her into a seated position. Two other boys were gathering up her scattered papers. One of them brought her the stack and her book, then hovered beside her as if he were going to take credit for saving her. Cole took the book, shoved the papers inside the front cover, and placed it beside her.

"You may have cracked a rib. You hit the edge of the step hard. Is it okay if I check your ribs? I'll be careful, and I know what I'm doing. I've broken a few of mine in the past."

She nodded. This wasn't going as she'd planned, but it was working so far. She doubted that she would have had the courage to try it if she'd known she might get injured in the attempt.

He held her arm and carefully felt along her side, pressing gently. She gasped when his fingers touched the sore spot.

"That's the place. It's a rib, alright. It may be only bruised, but it could be fractured. We'd better have you get an x-ray to find out for certain. Can you walk? I'll help you to the walk-in clinic."

She stood, careful to avoid moving her torso. An incautious move caused her to wince and gasp in pain. He held her arm, steadying her on the steps.

"What's your name?" he asked.

"Devonette Passway. I'm sorry. I must seem like a baby to you."

"No, Devonette, not really. Rib injuries are excruciating. It helps to breathe shallowly. Believe me, I know from past experience." He didn't see fit to mention that his experience with broken ribs had involved a bison kicking when he thought it was dead and safe to approach.

Devonette saw James approaching, striding through the clots of departing students as if they were no more than irritating insects. She motioned to him with her fingers, a prearranged signal to stay back. He slowed, looked puzzled, then came ahead. She made another peremptory motion, but he climbed the steps anyway, his brow knit in either concern or anger. She couldn't tell which.

"Hi, Miss. Is this guy bothering you?" he asked.

She was angry. He needed to go away and let her work. She was hurt, and it would only be worth it if she could get close to Cole. This lummox wasn't helping. "No! I fell, and he's helping me. I'm fine."

Cole interjected, "Not so fine. I think she might have broken a rib or two. I'm going to take her to get an x-ray."

James grabbed her arm and tried to pull her away from Cole, who had his arm around her shoulders. "I'll take over now. You go about your business."

Cole didn't show any sign of emotion. He simply grabbed Jame's wrist with his left hand and squeezed. James gasped and let go of her arm, then grasped his wrist with his other hand to support it.

Cole said in a calm tone, "I can manage. Thanks." He belatedly thought to ask Devonette, "You are okay with me taking you to the clinic, aren't you?"

"I'm perfectly fine with it." She addressed James, "Thanks for the offer, but this is a friend of mine. We're in the same class, and I think he's all the help I need." She followed up with the same flick of her fingers. This time James got the point. Still frowning and supporting his wrist, he turned and strode away across the plaza.

She contrived to snuggle a little closer to Cole. He still had his arm around her shoulders. The movement hurt, and she gasped. His arm tightened protectively.

"Don't move like that. You'll only hurt yourself. Let's see about getting you off the steps and to the clinic. Can you walk okay?"

She leaned on him as they descended. At the bottom, she paused, breathing hard but trying to limit her rib movement at the same time. She leaned on him, surprised at the intensely masculine feel of his body. Her heart rate accelerated despite her wanting to feel nothing toward him.

"I can walk by myself now," she said, thinking to distance herself from him. No man had ever made her feel precisely the way he did, and she was sure that it wasn't a good thing considering her plan to destroy him socially. She moved away, then reconsidered. How would she get him to fall for her if she didn't give him a taste of how appealing she could be? She pretended to stagger slightly, and he immediately put his arm around her again.

The trouble was, she wasn't getting any sexual signals from him. He seemed totally fraternal, helpful but not influenced by her in the way she desired. It was frustrating. At least things were moving in the way she wanted, even if the personal cost to her was higher than she'd planned.

◆◇◆

As it turned out, Devonette had cracked two ribs on the step. Cole waited until she was finished with the emergency treatment. They left the clinic with the clinician's admonition that she should consult with her personal doctor and possibly see a specialist. She walked through the door on her own, slightly ahead of Cole.

James and Randy were waiting across the street. They started forward, but she flicked her fingers again, and they halted, pretending to examine the side of a parked car. She looked out the corner of her eyes to check Cole's position. He was directly behind her. She took the opportunity to make a little private smile to herself, secure that he couldn't see her expression. This was working out. Her ribs felt better with the support, and it didn't hurt so much to breathe. She had the undivided attention of, she hesitated, then admitted to herself, the most attractive male she'd met in her life.

If she could contrive to engage his affection, even a little, things would work out. Without conscious recognition, her plans had modified themselves. She now wanted to experience more of a relationship with him than she'd initially thought. There would always be time to dump him publicly when she got tired of him. It would be more fun this way, she told herself. Still, deep inside, there was a little voice that cautioned her that she risked getting her own emotions too involved.

Cole suddenly asked, "Who are those two guys across the street. The one that wanted to help you and his friend? They've been following us like they know you."

She drew in her breath sharply. He was more perceptive than she'd thought. No one ever noticed James and Randy since the two specialized in being unobtrusive. He had identified them almost immediately.

Cole added, "And, what's this little finger signal you've been giving them?"

She flushed, turned around, grabbed his arms, stood on her tiptoes, and kissed him. It was the only thing she could think of at the moment. He responded slightly, then drew back and said, "I still want to know who they are."

She was blushing now. "I...uh, my father's rich. I don't like to tell anyone. No, I'm not even supposed to hint to anyone in case they get ideas about kidnapping me. Those two are my bodyguards. They'll stay back, though. I signaled them to leave us alone."

He smiled. "So, you had help at your call, but you let me help you instead? You strike me as someone who doesn't trust other people easily."

Devonette had never been so flustered. The damned boy could see right through her, and that made him even more desirable. She would enjoy destroying him. She'd make it a spectacle that he'd never forget. The next instant, she felt compelled to lean forward almost against her will. She moved closer to him.

"I did, but you were so helpful and so nice about it that I decided you were safe. I don't have many friends, you know. I guess I just wanted to feel like I could have someone care who wasn't being paid to care, if you know what I mean."

Cole didn't answer directly. He glanced across the street at James, who happened to be rubbing his wrist at the moment. "They're too obvious. Your father could do better with his money."

She bristled up. Her father never made mistakes. "Those two are the best of the best. They're highly experienced – Navy Seals or something like that." Internally, she flinched. He had the ability to elicit a reaction from her before she could even think of what she was doing. It must be that she was distracted, maybe with the pain or something.

She tried to soften her attitude. "No. I'm sorry. It's just that they are supposed to be good at surveillance. I don't know, though. You picked them up easily. How did you do it?"

He laughed. "Some of the best hunters have trained me. Those two don't fit in well. They cover it up, but their motions are a little delayed. That's caused by analyzing other peoples' responses to what they do."

Hunters? That was intriguing but cryptic. She filed it away for later. She needed to get back to her plan. Maybe it would be a good time to remind him that she was injured. She gasped, intending to fake pain, but the gasp hurt, and she groaned, holding her hand to her side.

He said, "Breathe carefully. You won't be able to draw sudden or deep breaths for a week or more without pain. Rib injuries are bothersome because they take a long time to heal, but you're okay."

She essayed a tremulous smile. "You make me feel like an idiot. Would you walk me home? It's not too far, and it would make me feel better. I do trust you, despite you thinking I don't trust easily. I know you'll get me there safely."

He laughed softly, then said, "I can do that, but how about the two over there. Isn't it their job to take care of you? I don't want to intrude."

"They just watch me. If I pretend they're not there, it's almost as if I'm a normal person. They don't care as long as they get paid." She pulled her lips down in a pouting and semi-sad expression. "I meant what I said about wanting to feel like someone cares who doesn't have to."

He nodded. "I can see how you might feel overprotected. I'll walk you to your door. I've already missed my lit class, but it's not a problem. I've already read the book and the teacher never says anything valuable in class. She just rambles about diversity and equity, then says the test will cover chapters x, y, and z. It's sad, we're paying for experts in subject fields to impart their expertise to us, but all we get are mediocre scholars at best who want to teach us their biases."

She couldn't help herself. His expression was so doleful that she laughed, then grabbed at her side.

"Devonette, you'll have to stop that. It will hurt every time you forget." He paused, looking at her. She felt transparent before his intense gaze. "But, that's reality. It does things we don't like when we try to pretend that it isn't really there."

"What?" He was puzzling. Most boys and men, in her experience, would be talking about things they thought would give them status in her eyes. Cole was talking about ideas. That was something new for her, and she decided that she liked it.

"What I mean is that reality has a way of sneaking around and biting you on the rear end when you ignore it or think you can control it by simply imagining things working out the way you want."

"I guess I see what you mean. It does seem that way. I mean, I never worry much about things hurting me. This is the first accident I've ever had, uh, I mean major accident."

"Two fractured ribs aren't major in the grand scheme of things." He smiled as he said it, negating any implied criticism.

She took his hand and pulled. I live over three blocks and down a few. I'd like to go home and rest now, I think."

He allowed her to hold his hand as they walked. He held hers loosely, not gripping too tight. His grasp was firm and dry. She could tell from the feel of his fingers and palm that he could easily crush her hand if he wanted. She remembered how easily he'd made James let go. The thought made her feel deliciously vulnerable, particularly as she was positive he would do no such thing.

She thought about talking as they walked, but, somehow, it seemed better to walk in silence. She could think of nothing but trivia to talk about, and he definitely wasn't the sort who filled his mind with trivial thoughts. Maybe he'd appreciate a girl who was quiet. She didn't know.

She felt insecure in her ability to charm him. That was a novel feeling, too. Men were usually so predictable it was boring. They wanted to impress her, get her alone, and make physical advances. Sometimes she let them have a little bit of success, but only a little bit. The object of her game was to keep them trying until they were so invested in her that they would be devastated when she dumped them. This man beside her was of a different type, and she wasn't sure how to toy with him or even if she wanted to play with him. The small voice inside her cautioned her again. She could find the tables turned if she wasn't careful. He was amazingly attractive, both physically and, now that she knew him a bit, mentally.

They stopped at the front of her house. Daddy had purchased a home for her to live in while at college. He wasn't going to have her in some dorm or student housing. He'd told her that she was not to join a sorority either. She was an elite, and she was being groomed to run a multi-billion dollar empire. Developing long-term relationships with ordinary people wasn't something he wanted her to do.

Her house was older, but it had been extensively remodeled. She walked to the door and turned as Cole stopped.

He let go of her hand and said, "Here you are. Take care of yourself, and remember to take it easy on those ribs." Before she could say anything, he started to turn away.

She blurted, "Stop! Not yet." It sounded stupid, but he did stop and turned back to face her, a smile on his face.

She grabbed him and kissed him. He responded slightly, she thought, but maybe she was deceiving herself. She blushed and stepped back.

"That was for helping me. It was sweet. I owe you for this."

He shook his head. "No, you don't. I would have helped anyone."

She frowned. His statement hurt her pride. She wasn't just anyone, and he should have been able to see that. She stuttered, "I...I, uh, I didn't mean it like that. Will you let me buy you a coffee or latte or espresso or something, at least?"

He shrugged. "I drink coffee sometimes. Maybe we could meet for that, but I don't need you to buy it for me. I have money adequate for my needs."

Aha, a little bit of temper, then. She gloated inwardly. He did have emotions and could be tempted to respond. That was hopeful. Maybe she could figure out how to manipulate him with some practice. It was a refreshing challenge.

"I'm sorry. I didn't mean it like that. It's just that I want to do something for you in return. Could we wait until Friday? I'll probably be recovered enough by then to meet you at the coffee shop near the stadium. Are you good to meet me at four?"

That was when Dewayne and friends usually showed up unless they were heading to an away game. They got out of practice earlier on Fridays.

Cole shrugged again. "No offense taken. I can meet you then. My last class is at one, so I'll be available."

She leaned forward slightly, but he didn't take the hint. He turned away, then looked back and said, "See you then."

She stood on the step and watched him walk away. Gods! He was graceful. It would be a real shame to have the team beat him up. She couldn't wait to see it, but, as she thought that, she had to suppress a novel qualm of guilt.

Chapter Thirteen

Learning

Lola faded back into the world near the steps of the porch. She hadn't precisely planned where she would come back, but this was as good a location as any. Her attitude was not so depressed now that she'd taken affirmative action. The sense of helplessness that she'd had before had faded, as had the thought of fleeing to avoid the situation.

Besides, Cole would be back soon, and she wanted to see him. Perhaps they could hunt a little before it got too dark. She fluffed her feathers against the cool from the stone foundation and settled down on her legs to wait. It wouldn't be wasted time. She found she had a lot to consider.

◆◇◆

Cole stood inside his front door, thinking. Devonette was charming and, despite his intention to remain aloof, he was breathing faster than usual. He'd tried to act like her kisses hadn't been anything special, but it had been difficult to suppress his natural reaction.

He was wary of her. Every instinct he had screamed that she wasn't trustworthy. Something about her was just too studied, too planned, too manipulative, but he couldn't think of precisely the right word to describe it. Maybe too artificial was a better way to put it. In any case, he felt that she was dangerous in some fashion.

He tried to think of it as if he were a man of the present instead of who he was. Well, he had been born in the present, more or less, but years of hunting with his father and wolves, and, most especially, Lola, had given him a different perspective.

That was it. Compared to Lola, Devonette was opaque in her motives. He could see just enough to recognize that she was both untrue to her nature and, probably, unfaithful to others.

In contrast, Lola was crystalline. She was a dinosaur, true, but she had a transparent, loyal nature. She had never told him a falsehood. He didn't even know if telling a lie was possible for her. She viewed the world in a straightforward manner and approached problems with the same enthusiastic attack she used when hunting game. He felt at ease with her. He didn't with Devonette. He felt like he had to be on his guard at all times.

Still, there was a physical issue. Devonette's kiss had pushed all of his buttons. He shook his head ruefully. If she had an inkling of how close he had been to losing control. He shook his head again. He wasn't quite sure what he would have done. She might have been receptive, it certainly seemed that way, but there was still a hidden reserve about her that he distrusted.

Besides, there were her two bodyguards. He'd said nothing to her, but the two had watched the scene in front of her door. When he left, one had trailed him, trying to stay out of view, but neither of them seemed to know how to do that effectively. He grinned mirthlessly. Neither bodyguard would be much of a success hunting. They were civilized and used to people who were ninety percent oblivious to their environment. The two men had an edge against unsuspecting modern city-dwellers, but not against him.

Even he had difficulty with the plethora of stimuli in the city environment. It was easy to see how people just turned off their attention. So much was happening at once that it was easy to get overloaded. He usually was operating at less than half his normal attention band-width.

He sighed, then walked inside. There was no reason to stay in the house. He was caught up on his assignments, except for maybe something in the Lit class he had missed. That wasn't going to be a problem, though. He'd read through the book in the first week. The assignments were usually only a chapter or less, so he simply refreshed his memory by scanning them in a few minutes.

His buckskins were waiting in the bedroom closet. He changed, then looked around. The house was secure, all locked up, and everything turned off except for the light on a timer scheduled to come on at random times during the evening.

He closed his eyes, faded into the in-between dimension that led between time and space, then headed directly for his parent's house.

A short or long time later, there was no accurate measurement, he appeared in his bedroom in the stone house. Heading for the kitchen, he encountered Serensaa. She greeted him, then moved in front of him to stop him.

Serensaa was a Clovis culture woman who spoke a variant of Cadeyrin's native language. She wasn't the linguist he was, though, and her English wasn't as good as Lolita's. She compensated by being direct and not wasting time with niceties.

"Cole, you got problem with Lola. She hurting inside bad. I know. I see this. She girl just like me. I fall in love with Logan when I first see him in Florida swamp. I no hide it. I act on it. I know what I want. Lola got no way to act on you. She different body, but." She paused and held up her finger in an admonitory way. "But, she still love you. She not ready to be Deinonychus. She think she be human. Who can say? Maybe she be human in mind. You got to fix problem. She can not do it by herself."

He nodded slowly. That was the crux of the matter. His trouble was much the same. He would be the first to admit that he loved Lola, but what kind of love was it? She filled a need he had for a faithful and loyal companion. She often seemed to read his mind, notably when they hunted together. She was intensely female, despite her ferocious appearance and killing claws. The image of Devonette crossed his mind. That girl was made for him, or, he paused, someone like him, anyway. Her body was perfect for physical love. He smirked. She would have a difficult time ripping the throat of a deer with her teeth.

Serensaa mistook his smirk. "You no grin at me. This serious. You hurt Lola. Maybe she not recover. Maybe die of broken heart."

"No. Serensaa. I don't want to hurt Lola. She's precious to me, but I can't figure out our relationship. I know she wants a family, and that's something I can't do. I'm hoping that everything will come clear to both of us, but..." He looked down, conscious that his eyes were moist. "I'm maybe as unhappy as she is. I don't know."

He pushed past the small, beautiful woman and rushed into the kitchen, but it wasn't much better there. His mother and Annie were working on some kind of stew. They both looked at his face, then turned quickly back to their work, ignoring his distress and allowing him time to recover.

He tried to put a brave front on the situation. "Hi! I'm back. Is that what we're having for supper? Stew?"

Kathleen nodded, then said, "Lola is outside by the steps. She's been huddled by the stones for over an hour. You'd best go get her before she gets a chill." The weather wasn't precisely cold, but the evenings grew cool as night approached.

He nodded and turned to the hall. Lolita was standing in the doorway, but she backed up and allowed him to exit.

"You go outs? Lola out there. Sad, I thinks. Not good she not want mate we try to find."

"Yes, Lolita, I agree. I'll go get her and try to cheer her up a bit."

The little raptor made a non-committal sound in her throat, then went into the kitchen. He could hear Annie as he headed for the front door.

"Lolita! You let that meat be. It's for the stew."

Lolita, her mouth sounding full, answered, "But, I no likes it cooked."

Kathleen's voice followed him out on the porch. "There's plenty, Annie. Lolita, leave some for the rest of us, please."

⸺◆⸺

Lola looked up to find Cole looking at her from the steps. A glad rush went through her heart. "You're back! I've been waiting. I learned – " She stopped abruptly. Maybe she shouldn't tell him that she could travel to the future. He might disapprove of her spying on him. She improvised. "I learned that I can't walk away from my feelings. I was going to go for a long hunt, but it didn't help, so I came back and waited for you. I've been thinking while I waited."

He came down the steps, and she met him at the bottom. He sat on the bottom step, and she moved close. He ran his fingers along her neck in the same way he'd done many times before. It generated a thrilling feeling that flooded her mind. "I like it when you do that."

"I know, you're making your 'happy' sound. That deep hum you do when you're pleased."

She hadn't realized that she was doing it. She'd been so engaged in the sensation of his clever fingers scratching her neck. "I guess I was." She changed the topic. "Is there time for us to hunt a little before your mother has supper ready?"

He thought about it. "Not really. She and Annie are making stew, and it's nearly ready if your mother doesn't eat all the meat before they get it cooked."

She was amused. "For as little as she is, Mother eats a lot. She burns a lot of energy."

Cole stood. "Let's go up the hill to the trees. We can walk along the edge up there for a little while. We've got that much time at least."

⸺⬦⬤⬦⸺

There was a large boulder at the verge of the hill, some meters from the tree line. Below the boulder, the ground sloped gently down under a carpet of short grass. The two found themselves near the glacial-carried rock, and the grass looked inviting. Cole sat with his back pressed against a smooth spot on the boulder while Lola settled down beside him. Her anatomy wasn't designed for pure sitting. She either had to rest in an upright position, balanced on her projecting pubic bone and propped by her legs and tail, or lie on her side, her legs extended. She chose the latter position with her head resting against Cole's thigh.

She liked that position best since it gave him no excuse not to rub along her neck with his fingers. It wasn't long before she was humming in satisfaction.

They were silent for a time, and then Cole paused in his ministrations.

"Lola?"

"Yes, Cole."

"If you were human, you know that we'd be mates."

"I know it. Same, if you were a deinonychus."

He laughed. "I hadn't thought of that. Turn about is fair." He looked away for a moment. "It's a sign of how arrogant we humans are. We like to think of ourselves as the apex of creation or evolution. It's part of our mindset that we're different from animals. We are the only ones who speak, do mathematics, and do--oh, all sorts of things that animals don't. It's been said that the difference between a cat and a man is that both know they're in a room, but only the man knows that he knows he is in the room."

She interrupted, "What kind of cat? A saber tooth?"

He grinned. "See? It's my arrogance. I assume you know everything I do. But, in a way, that's good. In light of you and your kind's mental abilities, humans aren't alone at the apex of all animals. It's just that humans and deinonychs were never meant to co-exist. Our scientists estimated your kind were barely more intelligent than, oh, say, a vulture."

She snorted. "Vultures stink. I can eat meat that's been around for a while, but not what they eat. Ecchh!"

He ignored her comment and continued. "I guess what I'm saying is that I've learned something from you. There is no limit on caring, on love, I guess. If the world were the way we think, you and I would not care for each other. You'd have a deinonychus mate, and you'd be happy. You're not. I know you're sad, and I am too. I don't want to hurt you, but...oh, you know!" He flung his hands up, lacking the right words.

She raised her head and pressed her muzzle against his neck. He cradled her jaw and held her face close to his in return.

She whispered, "You know and trust me. I would never hurt you either. I'm unhappy, it's true, but as much as you don't want to hurt me, I don't want to hurt you. I tried to make myself see that young male as a mate, but I couldn't bring myself to do it. It just seemed wrong. Wrong for me, at least. If you find a human woman that you like, up in the future, I want you to take her as a mate and be happy. I'll be happy if you are. I've decided to try to learn things. I think that I'd be happy if I could learn until I reach my capacity. I wonder if I can learn as much as a human."

He sighed. Her aspiration told him more about her mindset than she had spoken. She wanted to be human so that she could have him. Since she couldn't physically be a human female, she hoped, maybe subconsciously, to show that she was the equal of humans mentally. In that light, her aspiration was pathetic. Viewed another way, it was laudable. She should be allowed to learn as much as she wished.

It seemed to him, on reflection, that all intelligence, regardless of the physical form in which it was housed, should be treated with the same respect. There was a requirement for fairness that he felt within himself. It told him that Lola had natural rights conferred on her by her intelligence, and they were the same that he had. Perhaps some humans might not see it that way, but he and Lola were the same in terms of self-awareness. They both deserved proper treatment.

Maybe the same thing could be said for computerized Artificial Intelligence if it ever reached the point of sentience. He didn't know. That was something he'd heard discussed in a physics class. But, to him, Lola was as deserving as any human girl. It was a pity that she wasn't a human, or..." He smiled. She'd turned it around in a manner he had not previously considered. "If he were one of her kind."

The thought of Devonette intruded into his attempt to analyze their relationship.

"There is a girl at college that I've just met. She's attractive physically. Very attractive, but I somehow don't trust her. She seems too contrived and too calculating. Oh, Lola! What are we going to do? I'm so comfortable with you. You know our minds complement each other. I understand what you felt when you looked at that young male deinonychus. He didn't seem quite right to you. That girl I was speaking of—she doesn't seem quite right to me. Neither one of us is normal for our species. Maybe I'll study along with you. Do you think we could be happy studying together?"

She was taking deep breaths, a sign of emotion. "I'd be happy if I were able to be near you, regardless of where it was, but I can't ask that of you. You should see if this girl will be a good mate. Maybe if you took the time to know her better?"

He laughed. "That's almost exactly what Lolita told you about the male we tried to fix you up with."

There was a distant clanging. Annie was whacking the bottom of a skillet with a spoon or something far off down in the valley. Dinner must be ready.

They got to their feet, and she started down. He moved quickly and caught her neck. She turned, and they wrapped their arms around each other for a long time, content in their closeness. Annie clanked again off in the distance. Lola turned her head to look, then they reluctantly released each other and started for the house.

Chapter Fourteen

Best Laid Plans

The weather was rainy on Friday morning. The old stone of the campus buildings looked shiny in the damp, and the odor of damp mildew permeated the breeze. Cole went to his history lecture. Devonette greeted him at the door.

"Do you suppose they'll notice if we sit together?" she asked.

"The grad assistant takes roll by checking for the total number of empty seats. I don't think she'd actually notice if someone had changed places. We can ask the guy who usually sits beside you if he'd mind changing with me," he said.

Devonette winced inwardly. The guy who sat beside her most likely wouldn't give up his seat willingly. He had made it clear that he considered her a prize that he was trying to attain. She'd have to give him some sort of consideration if he gave up his seat to Cole.

Outwardly, she smiled and said, "I'll ask him. You wait back until I give you the signal to come down. What's your seat number?"

"Row W, seat 21."

"Okay. Wait for me to wave to you."

She descended the steps and took her seat. Raymond was already there. He smiled at her and started saying something about the upcoming test, but she didn't listen to the words.

He was startled when she turned a brilliant smile on him. That hadn't happened before, and the unexpected attention almost dazed him.

"Ray, would you do me a huge favor? I'd be very grateful if you did." She carefully didn't associate any action with her promise of gratitude. Fortunately, Ray was so overcome, he almost broke his neck, nodding.

"Yes. Anything for you, Devonette."

She smiled her most seductive smile, and the remaining will drained away from him visibly.

"Ray, I have a bet with someone, and to win, I need you to change seats with someone for this class."

He looked dubious, and she hastened to say, "Just this once. I'll be grateful if you'll help me."

He nodded again, although not so enthusiastically.

"Go up and take seat 21 in row W. That way, I'll win my bet. They won't count you absent because your seat here will be occupied. Don't worry, I've got it all figured out. I don't know who will sit here, and that's part of the game." She pushed gently on his arm, nudging him to move.

He stood, turned, and looked, but there was no help for it. If he wanted to be on her good side, he'd have to oblige. She'd made that clear without actually saying it. He gathered his things and climbed the steps.

Devonette watched until he sat in Cole's seat, then moved her head to summon Cole. He waited for half a minute before he headed down. She started to feel irritated, but then it became plain that he meant to convince Ray that he hadn't been watching from above. That was devious enough to appeal to her sense of intrigue.

She had seen that Cole was someone who thought things through before acting. That characteristic meant more difficulty for her. He wouldn't be subject to acting without thought. She would have to be careful.

He sat down, and she acted surprised, then leaned toward him and said, "Poor Ray. He didn't want to give up his seat. I can't imagine why."

He glanced at her from the corner of his eye. Her expression was similar to a cat who had just caught a mouse. He nodded slightly, then relaxed.

The lecture was boring, as usual. The only thing that livened it slightly was Professor Higgins was more inebriated than usual. The man actually had difficulty speaking, slurring some of his words, much to the hilarity of the class.

Midway through the lecture, the grad assistant dimmed the lights and started a video. Devonette slipped her hand onto Cole's forearm in the darkness. He glanced at her, then moved to take her hand in his. She smiled, her teeth visible in the dim light.

"Are you going to be able to meet me at the coffee shop at four?" she asked.

"I'm planning on it. I'll be there unless something unexpected comes up."

"What could happen that would delay you?" Her sense of competitiveness was aroused by the idea that anything could keep a man from meeting her.

He shrugged. "Oh, I don't know. Maybe if I got hit by a car or something."

She laughed. That attitude implied that she had definitely hooked him.

⸺◆⸺

Ray was waiting at the door after class. They had split up, Cole exiting from the other aisle at her request. She had told him that she didn't want Ray to be too disappointed. Inwardly, she appended the word 'yet' after disappointed. She didn't have any plans for Ray. He wasn't attractive enough to fit her profile, but it was nice to know that she had him hanging on and ready to be disappointed.

Raymond tried to walk with her, but the two were going opposite directions, which didn't work out for him. He left after reminding her that he hoped she was suitably grateful. He hadn't been able to hear from the back.

She shrugged. He was whining – a complainer. He didn't realize that she would never have any interest in him. He slouched away, and she turned, expecting to see Cole waiting for her. He wasn't there. She scanned the area and saw him heading for the Chemistry building. He was too far ahead to catch, and she fumed to herself. The idiot! She wanted him to accompany her to her psych class, but he didn't have the sense to wait. She was going to enjoy seeing him humiliated by DeWayne.

She didn't calm down until halfway through psychology.

Cole opened the door to the coffee shop for Devonette. It was crowded inside. Six men who looked like athletes were crowded around the counter, boisterously placing their orders. Devonette didn't stop. She walked to the counter, got in line, and waited. One of the athletes smiled and said, "Hi, Devonette."

She nodded at him but otherwise ignored him until she had placed her order. Cole crowded behind her and waited his turn.

Devonette contrived to back into him and gasped, pretending to be affronted.

She glanced over her shoulder at Cole and made a predatory smile at him, knowing DeWayne couldn't see her expression. The fool smiled back as if that would save him.

She turned toward DeWayne, who had started to frown when she had gasped. It wouldn't take much to set him off. He was a real hot-head. She mouthed the word 'Help.' He straightened, then stepped threateningly toward Cole.

Cole was placing his order when a hand grabbed his shoulder and jerked him around.

DeWayne was sure of himself and putting on a show for Devonette. Besides, his friends were nearby, ready to assist.

"What the hell you doing, feeling up my girl?" he spat.

Cole didn't answer but looked at Devonette. She didn't meet his eyes but looked down. That was enough to cue him that this was some kind of set-up. He turned and strode toward the door, intent on taking it outside.

Surprised and offended that he had received no answer, DeWayne screamed, "You don't dis me, asshole!" Then he grabbed Cole's shoulder and jerked him back.

When he felt the hand on his shoulder, Cole raised his right hand, spun, and wrapped it around DeWayne's arm, then caught the quarterback's neck with his left hand and jerked. DeWayne was pulled off-balance, and he stepped forward trying to catch himself but tripped over Cole's outstretched leg. He fell forward and caught himself on his hands.

He jumped to his feet, but Cole was out the door before he recovered.

"Get 'im, boys!" He waved his hand at the door.

The largest part of the offensive line slammed into the opening, struggling to get through two at once.

Cole was trotting away by now, but the halfback had made it through the door and sprinted to throw a block into Cole's back.

Cole heard him coming and spun in time to sidestep neatly. The halfback went on by, tripping over an extended leg. He rolled and came back to his feet. By that time, the larger men had caught up with the action.

Cole found himself surrounded by men who all outweighed him. The situation had moved beyond simple evading tactics. He straight-armed the throat of the first man that threw a punch, then put a fist directly on the nose of the one beside him. Those two went down, holding the injured parts of their anatomies.

The other three men looked at each other, then moved forward cautiously. The closest received a devastating kick to the side of his knee. It was his weak point, having been injured repeatedly in prior weeks. He yelled in agony and dropped.

By now, DeWayne had arrived. He ran through the group and threw himself on Cole, who simply used DeWayne's momentum to throw him with a judo-like move. DeWayne slammed on the sidewalk, his forehead making a clonk as he struck.

Cole stepped clear and stared the two remaining men down. "Do you want to try?" he asked.

They glanced at each other, then bent to help their comrades.

He looked around. No one was threatening him, so he strode off, heading for his house. He inspected his hand pessimistically. He might have broken a finger on that one's hard head, but otherwise, he was okay.

Inside the coffee shop, Devonette was practically in tears. This hadn't worked out the way she had planned. Cole was supposed to be down and humiliated. Instead, he'd beaten the best part of the football team.

The barista was calling the police, and she had to figure out how to make Cole think she hadn't planned this absolute mess. That was going to be difficult. She had belatedly realized, when he looked at her, that he understood it was indeed a set-up.

James came in, bursting through the door. He looked angry. "Come on. The cops are coming, and you don't want to be here. Your father will be very unhappy if you are involved."

He grabbed her arm brusquely in a way he'd never done before. She started to say something, but he jerked her toward the door.

"Ouch! That hurts." She tried to pull away, but he held on and hustled her out onto the sidewalk, then across the street. He dragged her down an alley and forced her to practically run. He didn't stop until they were nearly three blocks away. Then he turned to her with his eyes squinted up in anger. "You are an idiot. You can't risk being involved in some stupid fight. I might have had to step in, and that wouldn't be good for anyone involved."

She could see his pistol, showing through a gap in his jacket. He might have used it if he'd thought she had been in danger. That would be a mess. Maybe enough of a mess to force her father to move her to another school. She started to shake. Things had gotten out of her control, and she hated that. Control was what she lusted for the most. Loss of control was a personal failure, and she wasn't used to failure. She wouldn't accept it.

She followed James quietly as he led her to a dark sedan. They got in, and he drove her to her front door.

"Now go in, study or whatever you do, and stop planning fights. I'm going to report to your father. You'll have to explain yourself to him." He held up his hand, palm toward her. "No. I don't want to hear it. I'm just the paid help. I got you out of what might have been an embarrassing situation. I hope that no one there knows your name and gives it to the police."

So what, she thought. I was an innocent bystander. I don't know what happened to make those men attack that guy. Sure, I kind of know him. He's in a couple of my classes. And, yeah, I know the men. They're football team members, but I had nothing to do with the fight.

They'd never hold her responsible, even if DeWayne or one of the boys gave her name. Cole wouldn't involve her. She was absolutely sure of that. It wasn't in him to take revenge that way.

She thought about it. DeWayne would probably not blame her either, but he could if he ever realized she'd incited the altercation. Of the two, she trusted Cole more. She grimaced. What was she doing? Trying to get the most desirable man she'd ever met hurt seemed stupid in retrospect.

And, he had handled himself amazingly well. No one had managed to hit him. He'd laid out four out of six men then jogged away casually. She cringed to herself. He might have come back for her. No, he certainly would have come back for her, except he knew. He knew that she'd arranged for the fight. He might not know why, but she was sure that he wouldn't forget it easily.

Now, what was she going to do? She felt torn inside. The video of the fight she'd recorded on her phone couldn't be used against Cole. DeWayne and the others were the fools here. She'd save it, of course, but it was worthless for her immediate purpose.

She went to the bathroom and stared at herself in the mirror. She looked distraught. She was angry with James for mishandling her. Angry with Cole – why did he have to be such a good fighter? Angry with the football team. Those idiots. They were tough. They should have made mincemeat of him.

Finally, she concluded that she was angry with herself. Underneath her anger, there was a sense of regret and guilt. That was something that never bothered her. Guilt wasn't something she was used to feeling. One part of her mind wanted Cole to think well of her, to pursue her until he caught her. The thought gave her a warm feeling in the pit of her stomach.

The next second, the warmth turned cold. He'd never think well of her after this. What could she do?

Chapter Fifteen

Repercussions

Saturday was horrible. Daddy wasn't happy with her. Randy picked her up and hustled her to the airport to meet her father, who had taken the unprecedented step of flying out in the Gulfstream. He'd never visited her at college. As far as she knew, he'd never visited the middle of the country at all.

When she climbed up the steps, the steward had instructed her. "Take a seat. Mr. Passway is busy at the moment. He'll see you when he has time."

She sat and waited, looking down the short hall towards the private cabin where her father presumably was conducting some business. After thirty minutes, she was startled by a presence at her shoulder.

"Give me one good reason I shouldn't jerk you out of this school and send you to a convent in Europe."

Her father had been out of the plane, and she hadn't been aware of him entering.

"I'm sorry, Daddy. It wasn't my fault," she started.

He was the only man that she couldn't charm. He sometimes allowed her to feel as if she were manipulating him, but when he was angry, nothing, absolutely nothing, caused him to deviate from his planned course.

He didn't say anything in response. Instead, he took a seat opposite her, took a bottle of water, and took a swallow. Then he scrutinized her face.

"Tell me what happened."

She started to explain the fight, but he held up a hand. "Start with what you thought you were doing, disobeying my instructions. I told you to stay away from this Cole Whitman kid. You went right ahead with your childish plans. Randy and James have told me that you continued seeing him. Now explain yourself, Missy."

This was very bad. She'd never seen him so angry. She took a deep breath and started. "I didn't think you meant that I was to leave him alone totally. Oh, I understood that from the guys, but they sometimes put their own spin on things. I thought I could have Cole wound around my finger if I had a little time to work on him. He's a bigger challenge than anyone I've ever encountered. But," she paused dramatically. "But, I was making progress. I even got him to kiss me, and I know for sure that he wasn't planning on doing it. He's amazing, really. Stronger than your bodyguards and very calm in his ways."

He interrupted, "So, you seem to be the one who's getting hooked here. How is that possible? I thought you were the ice maiden. No boy has ever survived once you set your sights on him. Continue, please."

His very politeness frightened her. She'd feel better if he screamed at her and punished her somehow. This was spooky.

"Uh, I slipped and fell on the stairs, and he helped me."

"Yes, I know all about that. Broken ribs and all. It seems that you had to give up acting for a real injury to get his attention."

"Well, I didn't mean to hurt myself. It was some fat girl who collided with me. I was only going to drop my books. Anyway, I survived. It hurt, but I found out I can deal with that." She sounded pleased with herself. She knew that but handling that pain had been something new for her, and she was proud that she had gotten through it without breaking down.

"Cole helped me get to the clinic and then waited for me to get treated."

"Yes. I know. James was upset that you didn't let him take you to the hospital."

"I didn't need him. He was interfering with my plan. If I had to suffer, I wanted to make it worth something. So, when Cole walked me home, I got him to promise to meet me for coffee. I thought I could get the football team to humiliate him. It didn't work out. He can really fight well, and He beat them all. Four of them, anyway. He stared the other two down, and they were afraid to fight him."

"So, why isn't he wound around your finger now, as you put it?"

She couldn't help herself; she flushed, then felt moisture on her cheeks. She'd never cried in front of her father since she was very young.

She drew a shaky breath, hiccuped once, and said, "I screwed up. I can't believe it, but I did. I arranged it so they'd go after him, but he saw right through me. He knows it was my fault. He took off, and I don't know where he is now."

"So," he drawled it out slowly, "you don't know how he saw through you. Maybe it was because your great plans are childish. I hoped that you'd learn to deal with people so that they would willingly do what you wanted. I hoped that you'd develop the sophistication to help with my business. The family business. I thought you were the right person to take over when I was ready to retire. I'm starting to think that I was wrong."

She shook her head in denial. "I... I'm always successful. It's just a minor mistake. I can recover from it. You'll see."

He sneered. "I'd better see. I've had my team research him completely. He's the son of Kathleen Whitby. That's almost certain. I want Ms. Whitby badly. She's responsible for my father, your grandfather's death. I intend to get this Cole you seem sweet on and hold him hostage. Once his mother shows up to rescue him, I'm going to take revenge on her by setting Kang on him, and then I'll give her to Kang. She has some very valuable secrets, and he'll persuade her to talk. Whitby may not be in one piece by the time she decides to yield the information I want, but she'll give it to me before she dies."

Kang was the one person in her father's employ that Devonette truly feared. The man was a Korean who was an expert in both martial arts and torture. She suspected that he acted as an assassin for her father, but she had no actual evidence. The man was immovable. He never showed any emotion whatsoever. Cole was not going to survive his attention, which meant she'd have no chance to prove that she could succeed with him.

"It's not necessary. Give me a chance, and I'll get Cole to tell you what you want," she blurted. She wasn't sure what it was, but if Cole's mother knew something, then Cole probably knew at least some of it. She was hopeful that she could get it out of him. He'd been responding to her, that was certain.

"I see." Her father frowned. "I'll give you a chance to make up for your actions. You'll have until next Saturday to get him to disclose his mother's time-travel method. After that, I'll give you another two days to find out about the longevity drug she has."

Time-travel? Where had that come from? "He knows how to travel in time?" she asked incredulously.

"To all accounts, he can jump across centuries. That's an ability that I want badly. Can you imagine the uses to which I could put that? It would be worth a fortune. The fact that he doesn't use it to gain power tells me that he's one of the idealistic common people. Stupid, actually."

"How do you know he travels in time?" she asked.

"James, come here for a minute, please."

James came up.

"Tell this young fool what you've found out about Cole Whitby."

James grinned. "It's like this. We checked his house. Used the laser eavesdropping equipment. Once he goes in, he does a few things, and then the house gets still as a tomb. He's not there. At first, we thought he sneaked out somehow, but we broke in when he was at class and planted some cameras. He came home, changed to some crazy leather Indian clothes, and then disappeared."

She shook her head. "Disappeared? You mean he walked off-camera?"

"No. He blurred out. He faded away right in front of the camera. The next morning, he was back in the house. We didn't see him fade back in, but one moment the place was vacant, and the next, he was there, changing his clothes to the stuff he wore to class. We know his mother travels in time. The government had several run-ins with her over it."

Her father interrupted. "Unsuccessful run-ins. They were working on a method of traveling in time, but they gave up. It was too unpredictable. Whitby has some kind of formula that allows her to control time somehow. She's always been at least three or four steps ahead of the government and ahead of our competitors, too. In addition to the time formula, she has a mystery drug that they're using to create some of the products that Farlife has released. We, of course, have extensively analyzed those products. They're innovative. Almost unprecedented in concept and quite complex. We need the original drug to analyze. I want you to get me that time formula and a sample of the drug. I don't care what you do to achieve that. If it takes away your celebrated and famous virginity, that's fine. Just get it. If you do, I might forget that you disobeyed me. Do you understand?"

She understood alright. Daddy was unforgiving. She'd seen him and knew what he was capable of doing to people who disappointed him, who failed him. She had no intention of being dumped on her own. Her comfort depended on his money, and the idea that she might have to work to earn a pittance was repugnant. She didn't even want to imagine anything worse than that, although he was capable of doing worse. Working for her living was quite bad enough.

As she was descending the steps from the plane, he came to the door with a final instruction. "I took a look at your social media presence. It surprised me. What you're doing is not the image I want to be associated with my business. You will stop it immediately. I'll have one of my people check in two days. Your social media presence better be gone. It's a security risk, besides creating a negative image that I don't want to have to deal with."

The social media ban was horrible, but maybe she could make something of it. She thought she could set up a blog and get some of her closest followers to promote it. She'd do it under a pseudonym with no pictures of herself, but everyone would know it was her. Maybe she could even migrate most of the videos over there. Daddy didn't know much about social media, and she doubted if his people would work on finding her if she kept her head down, but that was for later. Cole was first.

Daddy had flown off, and James had returned her to her house. She had asked where Cole lived, but he would not disclose that fact. Her first chance at getting back into Cole's good graces was going to be Monday at the history lecture. She sat down to figure out all possible combinations of what she could say and how Cole might respond. She concentrated as if her very life depended on it, as it might.

Chapter Sixteen

Knowledge

Cole arrived on the front porch. That Devonette! He shook his head ruefully. He'd been a fool to get involved, even the slight bit he had, when his instinct had warned him. He shook his hand irritably. His knuckles were still sore where he'd slugged the one guy on the head.

The question was, would any of them press charges, or would they try to seek him out and get revenge on a personal basis? He'd never seen any of them on campus, but it was possible that he might encounter them. Then again, he didn't usually hang out where the student-athletes did. He was studying STEM classes, and he doubted that they were taking many of those.

They'd be more likely to see him as he walked home, even though his house was far enough away from the coffee shop that he'd never been there before. Maybe it would be better to drop his classes and come back a semester later. Or, earlier. He chuckled. With all of time at his call, he could avoid problems with an ease that average humans couldn't imagine.

Lola was sitting on the floor in front of a low table, a tablet computer propped up in front of her. She had difficulty with books. They weren't easy for a hand with long claws. She could swipe the tablet with the back of a knuckle, and she preferred it. The limitation was that books had to be downloaded, and there was no Internet in the Pleistocene. He had to carry the thing forward to load it with the books she wanted.

He looked over her shoulder. She was so engaged that she barely acknowledged his presence. He was startled to see that she was two hundred pages into a text on human anatomy. He'd brought that back to her only three days ago. As he watched, she swiped to the next page. She was reading about the human reproductive system at the moment.

He thought about that. Had she gone directly there, or was she reading the entire book? The first option might indicate that she was still obsessing over him. The second meant that she just happened to be on this chapter.

She turned another page. At that rate, she was going to be through with the book in another day.

"Are you reading every page in that thing?" he asked.

She turned her head and nuzzled against his arm.

"Yes. It's fascinating. What I'm wondering, though, is are there any similar books based on my anatomy?"

"I don't think so. Remember, those humans up there have never even found a complete fossilized skeleton of a deinonychus. They've been restricted to making educated guesses about your structure. Probably the closest I can come to such a book would be one that deals with modern birds. They're your indirect descendants, although you studying bird physiology would be equivalent to me studying monkey anatomy and trying to generalize to humans from that."

She nodded, her attitude serious. "Cole, I enjoy this topic. I don't know why. I like the physical structure of animals." She paused, then made an amused noise, "Akkk. Even human structure. Studying it shows me that we're similar inside."

He wondered if part of her interest was due to her having killed and eaten so many animals. Would a predator be interested in prey anatomy? Probably.

The other part of her problem was longing to be human, but it seemed like this might be a reasonable way to cope with it. "Maybe you'd like to read books about healing. About dealing with injuries. Medicine. What do you think?"

She didn't respond immediately. When she did, it was with a positive tone. "I think I'd like that. It would be a good thing to know. Maybe I could tend to the other deinonychs or the wolves when they get hurt. Would that be possible?"

"Sure it would. You would have difficulty with human medical tools, but we could fix something up for you. Besides, there are many aspects of medicine that don't require instruments. I'm not an expert, but let me find someone on campus who can help. There is an associated medical school. I'll ask around and see if there's a professor there who could help."

"You're not going to go and ask them if they can recommend a course of study for a talking dinosaur, are you? They'd be more likely to insist that you were having some kind of mental problem." She made her laugh sound again.

He ruffled the small feathers around her ear. "You're pretty funny. You know that?"

She hmmmed, deep in her throat. "Yesss. Now go and get something to eat or whatever. Maybe you've got studies to do, yourself? I want to finish this chapter before I quit."

He walked out of the library, heading across the great room toward the kitchen. He'd created a monster of sorts. She was devouring books with all the gusto she applied to hunting. He wondered exactly how much capacity she had for learning. It would be interesting if she were at a greater-than-human level. What if she was a genius? Would all deinonychus be at that level, or was his Lola special?

The others didn't seem nearly as perceptive as Lolita and her daughter. Maybe it was due to Lolita. Her mother was impressively astute. He hadn't known her father. The poor creature had died from some lung disease about the time Lola was hatched. He'd have to ask Lolita if Lola's father was especially intelligent. She'd tell him, he was sure.

The two girls were in the kitchen. Both Rowena and Ashlyn, Grid and Annie's daughter and Logan and Serensaa's, studied at California colleges in the sixties. They hadn't wanted to go as far forward as he did, and they maintained that they enjoyed the relaxed party-like atmosphere that prevailed in that milieu.

"Hi, Cole!" Rowena said. "How's life treating you?"

"Not so good, Sis." They weren't related, but having grown up together, they treated each other as siblings.

"What's that mean?" she asked.

He explained the entire mess.

"Wow! That was dumb of you to get involved." Ashlyn was not the least bit reluctant to point out his mistake. She always held a strong opinion and was usually quick to let others know what it was, even if that wasn't the most tactful approach to interpersonal relations. He was used to that, and it was welcome at this point since it reinforced his judgment.

"Yeah. I really stepped in it. The thing is, Devonette is extremely attractive. I guess maybe I'm not immune to cute girls. That's why I put up with you two.

Rowena laughed. "Cole, you're an ass, sometimes. But, listen, I can see your position. You're what the girls in the sorority would call a hunk. There isn't any female I know who wouldn't want to get close to you. On the other hand, the only two women of your age you are really familiar with are me and Ash. It's not like you had a lot of opportunities to go on dates. You're still learning. I'll bet she's kicking herself all over the place, wishing that she hadn't set up the date at the coffee place. She probably didn't know those guys would be there."

He was dubious. When he remembered it, it seemed to him that Devonette had looked guilty, but maybe his memory was faulty. It had been a tense moment, and he had been more focused on possible aggressive moves by the guy who had been yelling at him. He shrugged it off.

"Well, I learned not to do that again, anyway. Besides, I'm a lot happier back here. There's something incredibly peaceful about knowing you're the only human in thousands of miles."

Rowena said, "Don't forget your folks and ours. They're here, too, at least most of the time."

"Yeah. I'm better in the woods with Lola, for sure."

The two girls looked at each other meaningfully.

"Don't you think that maybe you and Lola are too close? Sometimes, I mean," Ashlyn asked.

That irritated him. "She's my best friend."

Ashlyn persisted in her critique. "You mean your best animal friend, right?"

"Not at all." This was too much. Lola was not an animal. "She's my best friend regardless of species. She understands me, and I understand her. When we hunt, we don't have to signal each other. It's like our minds are linked. We work as a perfect team."

One thing about Ash, she wouldn't let go. "Yeah. But she isn't human. There's no way a dinosaur could understand what it means to be a higher thinking being. She isn't –"

He interrupted her loudly. "She is so a higher thinking being. Just now, she told me that she would like to become a doctor."

"What? Haha. The very idea. Lola a doctor?"

He started to speak again but stopped, his mouth partly open. Lola was standing at the door. Her face didn't show much emotion, but as he watched, she visibly drooped.

Ashlyn turned, saw her, and shut her mouth with a snap.

Rowena tried to smooth it all over. "We were talking about your desire to be a doctor, Lola. What do you think?"

Lola's eyes flashed. She had recovered quickly. "If I'm interested in the subject, and, if I have the ability, I see no reason why I couldn't learn to treat Deinonychus illnesses and wounds." She paused, then said slowly, "Humans, too. I'm studying physiology right now, and I find it quite interesting."

Ashlyn said, "How are you studying it? By looking at people?"

Lola answered softly. "No, I'm reading the texts Cole brought me. I've read almost all of Gray's Anatomy at this point. I'm also reading through some other biological texts."

Cole never thought he'd see it. Ashlyn was at a loss for words.

Rowena asked, diffidently, "You mean you're reading human textbooks?"

Kathleen entered behind Lola. "Yes, she is. Annie and I taught her to read last month, and she learned faster than any human. She's been studying for hours every day while Cole has been at college. I think you've done her an injustice. What do you think?"

Ashlyn looked down. "Sometimes, I jump to judgment too quickly. I seem to have been wrong. I'm sorry, Lola."

Lola made a slight noise in her throat. "That's the way you've always been. I thought maybe in college, you'd learn to slow down and look things over before you decided."

Ashlyn flushed. "I must have missed that topic, but I think I've just been tutored on it."

Cole said, "Come on, Lola. Let's go outside." He pushed past his mother and went into the great room.

The two walked down to the barn, neither speaking. Finally, Lola said, "They think I'm an animal. I thought they were my friends."

"Oh, Lola. I don't know what to say. Humans are egotistical. I think we are unwilling to admit that we may have equals." He looked at her, then put his hand on the back of her neck near her shoulders. "I know that you're my equal. You and I, we're the..." His voice trailed off. They weren't the same.

She finished the sentence. "We're similar mentally. As you said, we often know what each other is thinking. I think that's the same. What they said, Cole. They don't think I can learn to heal, either my kind or yours. I think I can. I'm going to prove it to them."

He smiled. She was always ready for a challenge, and she was stubborn. If Lola said she would do it, she'd try until she succeeded.

He pointed down the valley. There was a small group of mammoths moving far down the way. A herd of camels followed them, staying unusually close to the mammoths. They both knew what that meant.

The camels were afraid of something and were using the mammoths for security.

The distant camel herd suddenly bolted for the near side of the mammoths, which had bunched together. Whatever was frightening them was near enough to be an immediate threat.

Cole didn't worry if a predator got a camel or any other animal. It was the way nature worked. However, having a predator large enough to kill a camel living near their house and barn was undesirable.

"Lola, wait while I get a rifle, then we'll go down there and see what the problem is. Okay?"

She was looking carefully. Her eyes were closer to those of an eagle than his, and her vision was acute. After a few seconds of observation, she said, "It looks like a cat of some kind. I saw its back in the tall weeds."

"Okay. Wait. I'll be right back."

He collected a medium rifle from the gun room and met Cadeyrin as he was coming out.

"Hi, Dad."

The big man smiled fondly. "Going hunting, Cole?" When Cole was young, he had worried about his son, but not so much now. The beasts were dangerous, but Lola and Cole hunted together, and they were more than a match for any predator in the inter-glacial period.

"There's some kind of cat down the valley. It's harassing some camels. Lola and I thought we'd go down and see it off. Can't have it deciding to raid the chicken coop or something."

Cadeyrin nodded. "Supper will be ready in an hour or so. Don't go too far."

"Okay."

The two caught up to the camels after following them for a while. The mammoths were upset, and it was best not to go too close.

"Whatever is out here has gotten the mammoths stirred up. We need to watch closely," Lola said.

He nodded in agreement.

Lola suddenly grabbed his arm with her fingers, holding her claws away from his skin. "It's over there," she whispered, pointing with her muzzle.

He looked where she was looking and saw a brief glimpse of tawny hide slink into a patch of tall grass.

"I'll get it to run out, and you shoot it," she said.

They'd done that before. Lola was good at teasing a predator into a charge while staying far enough away to give him time to shoot.

"Okay, but be careful."

"I know that, Cole. You make sure you're ready."

He checked his weapon, ensuring it was loaded and that he had not lost the extra cartridges he'd put in his belt pouch.

She trotted close to the camels. They eyed her warily but didn't recognize her as dangerous. There were no large bird-like predators in North America in this time period, although there were some in South America. The camels had never seen anything like Lola, and they looked curiously at her, their fear momentarily forgotten.

She trotted in a direction that quartered toward the tall grass where the cat was lurking. Cole raised his rifle and waited.

When she was near, but not too near, she paused, then began to slowly move away, dragging one of her feet as if injured. The cat would be surprised that she suddenly showed a disability, but it wouldn't want to miss the apparent chance for easy prey.

The grass stirred as if a strong wind were blowing over part of it, then a lion came trotting out. Once clear of the grass, it accelerated to full charge and headed directly toward Lola.

Cole took his shot, and the big cat fell, rolling over and over. It thrashed its way to its feet and looked around. The noise that had hit it hadn't come from the direction of its prey. It fixed its gaze on the distant human, standing in the open.

It was still able to run, and run it did, directly at Cole. He worked the bolt, ejected the spent cartridge, and slid home another. The cat was nearly on him when he shot a second time. The bullet broke the lion's shoulder, and it slid forward on its side, then staggered to a three-legged stance and came forward again.

By now, Lola had caught up, and she leaped high over the wounded feline's back, kicking directly downward with all her weight. The killing claw on her right foot caught the lion's neck and opened its carotid and jugular. It snapped at her, but she was already away.

The cat seemed confused. It staggered, blood shooting from the ripped artery, then sat down, breathing heavily. Finally, it groaned, fell on its side, and ceased moving.

It was an old beast with both canine fangs broken and scraggly patches of nearly bare hide. It would have inevitably discovered the poultry they kept at the homestead and hung around looking for an opportunity to raid them. Cole told himself it was better to put it down now, but he still didn't feel pleased.

Lola came over to Cole. "You aren't shooting as well as normally. You should have killed it with the first shot."

"I know. I guess I'm still upset. I don't like my life much right now, and I don't like that the girls were rude to you."

Moving close, she put her face against his neck and wrapped her wing-arms around his waist. "It's okay. No one knows what I am. I don't know what I am. I'm too close to you to be my own species, but I'm not a human either. I have to find out who I am, Cole. You have to help me, please. I need help with this. It's too confusing."

He pulled her close, her neck feathers tickling his face. "I don't want you to be confused. It upsets me, too, but don't worry. We'll figure it out together." He silently appended the words, "I hope so, anyway."

Chapter Seventeen

Another Attempt

Devonette waited outside the lecture hall, hoping to catch Cole as he made his way inside. He didn't show, so she slipped in the doors at the last moment and descended the steps to her seat. Once there, she turned and scanned the upper rows. There he was. She'd missed him somehow. As if feeling her gaze on him, he looked at her, then turned away. She wiggled uncomfortably.

Raymond looked at her curiously but didn't say anything. He'd cooled down a lot. He had figured out that she had something going with the guy he'd exchanged seats with, and now he was sulking.

Well, too bad for that. She wasn't concerned with his moodiness, especially when she knew a single smile or a slight touch on his arm could snap him back. He was transparent. All he could think about was her. She smiled a cruel little smile to herself. And, he would never get any closer than he was today, sitting in the seat next to her.

She looked back at Cole, not recognizing that she was, in her way, acting much like Raymond. Why didn't he look at her? She stretched, hoping that he'd think her lifted arms were a signal, but he gave no indication of seeing them.

❖

Cole sat through the lecture, ignoring the droning of Professor Higgins. At least, the old man wasn't drunk today, but he was boring the life out of everyone in the hall. The more Cole thought about it, the more he felt he approved of Lola's self-guided studies. He wasn't getting much from his courses. Probably the best aspect of them was the physics and chem labs. The rest of it was stuff he could get by simply reading. He didn't need anyone to guide him in that.

At the moment, Higgins was trying to put the obligatory social spin on the Roman settlements in England. Cole shifted uneasily. The liberal arts courses were worse than the science ones. They were getting more and more like ideological indoctrination. Many instructors and students were intolerant of anyone who didn't simply recite the dogma unquestioningly. There could be no value in that. The only way men made advances involved asking probing questions of established beliefs.

What would he do with such a theory? Tell a mastodon he was oppressing the other herbivores? What would the average student do when they graduated and hit the workplace? They'd find they were massively unprepared to work at most careers. All they could do would be to teach. He winced, thinking of a whole generation of children being taught that they were members of an evil society.

Viewed from a neutral position, the students were not getting their money's worth from the school. It was basically just daycare for young adults with some drinking and a little sex thrown in. That set him off on another topic. It didn't take too much imagination to picture Devonette claiming he'd sexually assaulted her. He didn't intend to give her an opportunity for that type of revenge.

Exactly what had he done to her? It couldn't be any personal slight. He'd been as considerate as possible while remaining mostly uninvolved. Maybe that was it? She was offended because he hadn't come on to her. She was gorgeous and probably expected men to drool over her the way the guy that sat beside her did.

He glanced at her. The guy beside her was staring at the side of her face. It was almost embarrassing, even from back where he sat. Devonette, however, did not appear to notice.

He came to a decision. He'd talk it over with his mother first, but he thought he'd quit school and lay out a course of study for himself. He and Lola could study together. That was a fun thought. Lola made him feel happy and relaxed. Kind of crazy for a man to be attached to a killer raptor dinosaur, but she couldn't help what she was any more than he could help being human.

The Professor finished up, gave a reading assignment, and the class practically sprinted for the hall doors. He moved quickly, as well. He wanted to get outside before Devonette caught up to him.

She was left behind somewhere, and he didn't think about her as he walked to his Chem lab class. At least, the chemistry instructor hadn't yet figured out a way to blame western culture for chemistry. Still, it might happen.

He snorted in derision. Probably better to cut free from this stuff. The whole culture was non-survival in some ways. He doubted if many of them could find their way out of the deep woods, let alone find food while they were attempting to get out. They were divorced from the real world and had substituted an obsession with digital devices – virtual reality, they called it. It wasn't real at all.

Maybe he'd made a mistake with Devonette. He hadn't researched her online. He'd take a look and see if he could find her once he got back to his house. He didn't want to waste much time on it, though. He was anxious to go back to the past and talk to his mother about his idea.

— ◆ —

Devonette didn't see Cole when she finally got out of the auditorium. She stood at the top of the stairs and searched, but he had disappeared. It was irritating. She stamped her foot in anger. Why hadn't he waited? Any other man would have. That Raymond was lingering around. She pointedly ignored him and set off for her Psych class.

There was a way to find out where Cole lived. One of her followers worked as a student assistant in the admin office. She could look in the school records easily. Cole's address would be there.

She would have to arrange for that quickly since Daddy had given her such a short time to work. She changed direction. Psych would wait. She had to see Monica in the admin office.

— ◆ —

Cole helped Sandy with the lab exercise. She was willing but not very able when it came to precise measuring. The plain girl kept up a stream of cheerful chatter throughout the period. It was distracting since he kept changing focus, trying to remember what she was asking enough to make a sensible answer, and then returning his focus to the exercise.

At the end of the period, she asked him if he could go to a party the following weekend. He walked outside with her and explained that his family lived a long distance away, and he always visited them on weekends. Much to his chagrin, she changed direction and asked if he would come over to her apartment and help her with the lab write-up.

Sandy pushed the idea and was trying hard to close the sale when she looked over his shoulder and froze mid-sentence. Her face practically collapsed.

He turned quickly to see what had elicited such a dramatic change. Devonette was standing right behind him, her face set in a frown and her eyes practically boring holes in Sandy.

Sandy stuttered a bit, then said, "Uh. Never mind. I think I can get through the lab by myself. See you next time." She turned, her face flushing in embarrassment as she walked quickly away.

He turned slowly to Devonette. She had a strained expression that he'd never seen before.

"Cole, I..." She paused as he held up his hand.

"I don't want to hear it," he said.

"Please listen! I didn't know those guys were going to be there. I know the quarterback, DeWayne, but I'm not his girl, the way he said. He's been chasing me, and I have been avoiding him. It was just bad luck he was there Friday."

He searched her face. "You looked guilty as hell when I looked at you." He brushed past her and headed down the walk.

Hurrying to catch him, she said, "I was startled. I didn't know what to do. Oh, please believe me. I wanted to have some quiet time with you, so we could get to know each other better. I..." She paused again, then continued, her face tinged with pink. "I think I've fallen for you. That's never happened to me before. I've always been the one that men chase. Now I'm chasing you."

She was flushing bright red now. Searching his face, she saw no encouragement. "I... what's the use? You'll never believe me." She started to sob, looked startled, as if she hadn't intended to cry, then said, "It's true! I really, really want you. Won't you give me another chance? My heart is breaking."

She looked pathetic, and Cole's internal sense told him that she was, for the first time since he'd met her, not acting, but entirely in earnest.

"I've got to study for a Lit test tomorrow," he said tonelessly. "I'm going home now, but I should have an hour or so free later if you want to go for pizza. We can discuss this then."

Her expression lightened. "Yes. That's wonderful. Where do you want to meet?"

"I can stop by your house, and we can walk to the pizza place south of campus. Would that work?"

Her mind whirled, thinking of what she'd have to do. First, she had to get home and brief her bodyguards. They needed to be entirely out of sight. "I live at 545 S. 43rd. It's a house that my father bought for me. I'll be ready at six if that's a good time."

"Okay. Six it is." He turned and strode away.

She hugged herself, wondering as she did, exactly why she had felt so desperate. Was it true? Did she care if he was interested? Was she actually attracted? She wiped at her cheeks. If the tears were any sign, she did care, and it wasn't solely because of Daddy's ultimatum.

She headed for her house, walking slowly, marveling at her newly discovered range of emotion. So this was what it was like to care about a man. Was it possible that she could fall in love with him? She wasn't sure what love was, but she thought it should be more than just attraction.

She whispered, "Devonette, you're off in the head. These feelings are for your victims." It was funny how she didn't quite believe that now.

Chapter Eighteen

Pizza With a Side of Desire

Devonette found herself pacing back and forth nervously, just inside of her front door. She had given James and Randy specific instructions to keep away from Cole and her and out of sight. She wasn't confident that they'd follow her instructions. They worked for Daddy, not her. They'd probably try to be a little less conspicuous, particularly since Cole had noticed them so quickly.

She paused and looked in the mirror by the door. Her makeup was flawless. She hadn't used much, but then, her skin was flawless, so it didn't take much. She had a suspicion that Cole would be more attracted to a natural look rather than a heavily made-up one.

I hope that he hasn't changed his mind. I want the chance to show him that I didn't mean it. It was truly a mistake. I wasn't sure those football animals would be there.

By now, she'd almost convinced herself that she hadn't planned the incident. She certainly had not expected Cole to wipe out the best part of the offensive line. DeWayne might be out for the rest of the season. He'd slammed his head on the sidewalk hard enough to get a severe concussion. She'd always assumed that the type of men who played football were tough brutes, but maybe they really did need their protective equipment.

With an effort, she stopped her mental wandering. She was so distracted that her mind had been flipping through topics randomly. God! I hope he hasn't changed his mind. I really, really want him to like me.

No! Was that true? Did she want that? She looked at herself again and silently mouthed the words, "I think I'm in love."

Her eyes widened, then she laughed somewhat hysterically. That couldn't be possible. She was the Ice Maiden. She destroyed men, but now she felt she'd be destroyed if she couldn't get his affection.

The doorbell rang. She jumped, then rechecked her makeup before opening the door.

"Cole! I'm so glad you didn't change your mind." She was aware that she was trying to act nonchalant but was failing miserably.

He smiled in greeting and looked curiously at her foyer and living room.

Maybe he wants to come in. That would be even better. Devonette stepped back and moved her arm in invitation. "Won't you come in? We can get pizza later. Maybe we can order in?" She was hopeful. If he'd come in, they could talk without interruption. Every other man she had ever met would jump at the chance.

Cole shook his head negatively. "I think we should eat at the pizza place. It's better if we do. You wouldn't want your father to hear about you having a man over on the first date." He laughed in an apparent attempt to show he was joking.

She said, "He'll never know. He..."

Cole said, "Your two bodyguards are just down the street. They're in a black SUV and are pretending to read a newspaper." He paused, looked comical, then said, "Does anyone read newspapers these days? They'd be better if they were focused on their phones. More natural, you know."

She sighed. Those two goons hadn't paid any attention to her instructions.

"I'm sorry. They have a job to do, and they don't have much imagination. It's okay, though. Daddy doesn't care what I do as long as I get good grades."

He smiled and said, "Still, I'd feel more comfortable if we went out. I don't want them thinking they need to defend you from me."

If he only knew. She'd been trying to keep from throwing herself on him from the second he appeared. The memory of the two kisses they'd shared burned in her mind.

She nodded soberly. "I understand. You don't trust me, do you?"

To her dismay, he nodded affirmatively.

"Not too much. I'm still thinking you arranged that attack the other day. Why would you do something like that?"

She could feel her face heating up. She must be bright red. Something suddenly told her that she should be honest – at least to a limited extent.

"This isn't flattering for me or easy to say. I was angry that you didn't act like I was attractive. I knew they often go there after Friday practice, and I thought that maybe they'd hit on me. DeWayne has the idea I'm attracted to him. If he flirted with me, I thought you'd be jealous, and..." She shrugged. It wasn't entirely honest, but telling the total truth was pointless. It wouldn't help her with her case. "And, I was just stupid. When he went after you, I was horrified. I didn't know how to act. I don't do violence. I have bodyguards that make sure I'm protected. I...I hoped you'd be able to protect yourself, and you were more than a match for all of them. Do you, uh, I mean, are you an experienced fighter, martial arts, or something?"

He didn't answer directly. "Let's go get some pizza." He held the door open for her.

She took his hand as they went down the front walk. He didn't disengage their hands in disgust. Instead, he closed his fingers over hers. His grip felt strong but gentle. She smiled up at him in response, admiring his profile.

⸺◆⸺

The pizza had been good, and Cole acted as if he were starting to believe her. She'd made every effort to be charming and not manipulative – which she realized was manipulative in itself. That was a step up from her previous game. She now realized that genuine behavior was even better than her usual studied affectations. The best part was that she wanted to win this contest, but not for her usual reason. She did like him. She could see herself with the man for an extended time.

He stopped on her front porch and waited as she opened the door.

"Won't you come in for a bit?" she asked.

He paused, as if thinking it over, then said, "I've got to get back to study, but I can spend a few minutes more talking to you."

A feeling of triumph flashed through her mind, and her breathing accelerated.

Inside, she showed him the central part of the house. Living room, dining, kitchen. It was all so middle-class, not like the luxury estates she was accustomed to when she was with her father. Still, she figured it was better than just about all student housing in the area.

She would show him her bedroom next, but he turned back toward the foyer.

"I've got to get some studying in. Got a test coming up, and I need to be prepared."

She allowed her face to show disappointment. "You don't have to go so soon. I'd like it if you stayed a little longer."

He smiled but shook his head. "No, I've got to get going. It was nice, Devonette. I was concerned that you would try to pull something else, but you've been nice to be with. Maybe we can do it again."

She felt panicked. She'd forgotten Daddy's stricture. She needed to find out about Cole's secrets and time was very short. He had to stay longer.

She moved into his arms and wrapped hers around him, placing her head against his chest. The muscles under his shirt felt rock hard, and she could hear his heart beating strongly. Hers was suddenly beating faster. She took a deep breath and let it out shakily as she turned her face up.

"Kiss me, please," she said.

He lowered his face to hers, and their lips met. She'd been fantasizing about their previous kisses, but this was on a whole different level. His lips were amazing. They touched hers with an intimacy that she had never experienced before.

It wasn't that other men hadn't kissed her, but their kisses were hurried and sloppy as if they were in a rush to get on with their physical desires. He took his time, and she understood that he was concentrating on her, on kissing her, and there was no other agenda on his mind. It was heady. She was sharing a physical connection that led to her feeling of an intimate mental connection. She wanted more of that.

He pulled back and looked at her in some surprise. "That was very nice, Devonette. You kissed me like you meant it."

She looked down, feeling his arms around her. When she looked back up, her eyes were shining with tears. "I did mean it. I didn't know what it is like to share something like that."

She raised her lips again, and again they kissed. Her face was hot, and it felt as if her lips were swollen and intensely sensitive. To her surprise, she was breathing hard, and there was a sensation of warmth in the pit of her stomach.

"Don't stop," she whispered.

They kissed again, and she felt it would last forever, but he finally pulled away.

"I...I've got to go now," he said, his voice not entirely steady. "Maybe we can meet on Monday on campus."

Daddy's deadline! "I'd like to see you tomorrow," she said, understanding that he was going to leave, whether or not she wanted him to.

Surprisingly, he nodded. "Okay. I can arrange that. What would you like to do?"

Do? She looked around at a loss. What she wanted to do was to have him kiss her and not stop.

"Uh, maybe we could go walk around campus and then have some food. Is that okay?"

He nodded. "Okay. Walk me to the door?"

She grabbed him at the threshold and pulled him back for another kiss. It broke too soon for her, but after he'd left, she stood facing the closed door breathing heavily, her mind whirling.

If they were going to have food tomorrow, she wanted it to be here, at her house, where they could have some privacy. She looked in the nearby mirror. Her lips were swollen, and her hair was mussed a bit as she addressed her reflection, "Devonette, you're going to have to be faster if you're going to get him to disclose anything about his mother or drugs and time-travel."

She turned and went into her bedroom to pick up her tatty old stuffed tiger. "Irwin, I'm going to put you on the dresser. I think I might have someone else share my bed." She hesitated, then added, "I don't care what Daddy wants. I want Cole, and I'm ready to do whatever it takes to get him."

⸺◆⸺

Cole was still shaking when he arrived home. Devonette was highly desirable. He had used every bit of his self-control to resist the urge to take her in the bedroom and rip her clothes off. He hadn't thought that a woman could affect him that way.

The worst thing was he felt guilty about it as if he was cheating on Lola. But it wasn't even possible to cheat on her. They weren't the same. He pictured himself kissing Devonette, but Lola was watching, her head cocked in her charming manner, and he knew she would disapprove. She'd be hurt, even though he knew she would want him to be happy.

He shut his door, crossed to the bedroom, and changed into his buckskins, then slipped away into time. He'd go talk it over with Lola. Maybe things would become clear to him then.

Chapter Nineteen

Saturday

He'd cheated on Lola in two ways. Cole thought about it, trying to resolve the guilt he felt. First, he intended to meet Devonette again. Her kisses had been too arousing to resist. He was looking forward to another round of them, although he had suppressed his imagination at that point.

The second way he'd cheated was by doing something he'd promised Lola he would never do. He had taken all weekend with her, but he was planning on jumping back to Saturday rather than the following Monday as he would typically do.

Lola wouldn't know, he told himself. She'll think I went to Monday, but I'll meet Devonette on Saturday, then jump to Monday. That will catch things up, and I'll only age an extra day compared to Lola's time frame. She won't know that I did it.

Somehow that rationalization did not make him feel better.

Neither did his lack of courage. When it had come down to it, he'd been afraid to tell Lola about his growing infatuation with Devonette. He'd given her his usual account of boring classes and nothing more.

His mother had happened to be listening as he and Lola talked in the great room. She must have sensed something was wrong. She gave him a strange look.

Later, when Lola was outside tending to her business, he spoke to his mother. The deinonychs could not use human plumbing, so they restricted themselves to an area behind the barn unless marking territory. There was nothing like a heap of predator dung to warn off wild predators. The wolves maintained a barrier of scent in addition to the deinonychs. Usually, other predators did not intrude into the marked area.

She asked him some pointed questions about Devonette. She looked startled when he told her that Devonette's last name was Passway.

"That's impossible! Passway shouldn't have had a child. Maybe there's another Passway lineage." She seemed upset about the issue.

"I don't know, Mom. I'll ask Devonette about it. I think her father is named Winston."

She nodded. "I'll have to ask some of my future contacts to check on him. There's been someone sniffing around our health initiative, trying to buy the company out from under us. Perhaps he's involved. It sounds like he has the cash to do just about whatever he wants. Now, here's my request to you: Don't get too involved with this girl. She may be on the level, or she may be working for her father. There is any number of people up there who wouldn't hesitate to kill to get the time equation."

He nodded and added, "And, the longevity drug."

"Right. The red paste is worth a crazy amount of money. The person who controls it could control the world. They could have anything they desired. The stakes are high." She frowned at him, then added, "I need you to be extra careful."

"That's just the thing," he said. "I've been thinking about what I'm learning at school, and I'm not."

"What do you mean?" She looked puzzled.

"I'm not being taught what I thought I was supposed to learn. The classes are filled with political ideology. That stuff gets in the way of actually learning how to do things. My chem lab instructor has assigned us to groups and grades by groups. The group shares the highest grade. I'm now doing all the work, and the others are coasting. I'm learning, but they aren't. That's not fair. Another thing is, the history prof is a drunk. He's mildly interesting if he's not too inebriated during his lecture, but the recitation session is crazy. The grad assistant tries to imply that the Romans were successful because they discriminated against everyone not of Roman origin. I know that's not true, but I can't say it in class. She'd have a complete fit."

Kathleen shook her head. "That type of stuff was present when I was working on my degrees. I was in physics, and it wasn't much of a problem in that discipline, but the liberal arts people were bad about it. I think you'll have to ignore it the best you can."

He frowned. "I've been thinking. I'm already doing my physics and chem studies on my own. I've read the lit book, and I see little value in deconstructing the stories based on the author's ethnicity. I can't figure out how that would enable anyone to earn a living." He paused, then added, "Unless they were teaching literature, maybe. I don't have that problem. It's not like we'll ever lack for anything."

She laughed but didn't speak.

"Here's what I'd like to do. I think I could arrange for private sessions with some of the science professors, use the Internet for my reading and some classes, and spend more time here, studying with Lola." It sounded idealistically naive when he said it, but his mother nodded slowly.

"You could set up a course of independent study and probably do as well or better than you would if you attended classes. Except for one thing. That's the social experience of interacting with all of the other students."

He objected. "Mom, you told me yourself that you never interacted with anyone socially before you met Dad. You said you were too shy."

"That was me. I had a problem, but your father solved it," she said with a tender smile. "Why don't you try and stick out this semester, and then we'll decide if you should go on your own. I think you're capable of it. You don't need the discipline, thanks to your father's teaching. You're intelligent enough to know what you want to learn. But, maybe you'll have an ulterior motive to attend – I'm referring to this girl, of course."

It was somewhat embarrassing to tell his mother about Devonette, but he appreciated her judgment. Despite her protestations about being shy and socially backward, she was astute and often saw through people, even when they were trying to be opaque and hide their motivations.

"Okay. But, don't tell Lola about her, please."

"That's not exactly fair, Cole. Lola loves you, and I think she deserves to know what you're doing."

"That's the problem. She does, and I love her, too. It's not quite the same kind of love. It can't be because Lola isn't human. I'm happy with her, but she can never give you a grandchild."

"True. Promise me that you'll tell her soon. Don't make her wait and find out you're so involved you want to stay in the future or something like that."

It was his turn to laugh. "Stay in the future? Ha! It's all I can do to slip forward. It's unpleasant up there. People focus on their phones or other electronics, and they don't notice things. It's like their whole lives are virtual. I'll bet they wouldn't be able to deal with the natural world that we live in here."

She shrugged. "That's not your problem. You make sure you can deal with it. I don't want you getting hurt on a hunt because you're looking at a cell phone when an animal is charging you."

Lola came back in at that point.

"What animal is charging? I'll keep him safe. No animals are going to hurt Cole while I'm around."

———◆◇◆———

They'd gone hunting on both Saturday and Sunday. It had been fun and relaxing. The isolation in the wilderness made it easier for him to widen his focus to take in all possible stimuli. That was important since the slightest movement of a leaf might indicate the presence of danger. It was a welcome respite for the self-imposed tight focus that people in the future habitually used. He felt they were suffering from it without knowing there was another way to interact with the world.

He had noticed that the students on campus generally walked around with their attention closed down. They were either concentrating on their phones, listening to music, or, at best, talking to one other person. He wondered how they managed to cross the street without being run down.

He rarely spoke to Lola when they were off together. That was because each knew what was needed and what the other was doing at all times. They were a perfect team in that respect.

By the end of Sunday, he was wondering if Devonette's kisses were worth interfering with the rapport he shared with Lola. Still, Monday morning, under the guise of going to his classes, he transferred to Saturday in the future.

He stood in his bedroom off-campus, shaking his head. "What am I doing? I've got the perfect female, even if she isn't my species. I don't want to hurt her, but..." He looked ruefully at his reflection as he dressed. "But, those kisses. Hmmm."

He was planning on walking over to her house to meet her, but he'd cut the time too close. He would be late if he walked.

"Well, I could jump back a bit, but if I'm going to do that, why not just transfer to her house?" he said to himself.

The hidden camera that monitored his bedroom recorded his presence at one instant, but then he was gone.

Cole popped in at the side of Devonette's house in the shadow of a bushy white cedar. It pressed against the wall and shielded the area immediately behind it from the street. The neighbor's house was oriented so that there was little chance of being seen.

He straightened his jacket. He'd felt the need to wear it since the weather had turned cooler. Then he walked around to the front door.

He rang the bell, and Devonette's voice came from the monitoring camera, "Just a sec, Cole. I haven't gotten ready yet."

He had time to scan the area. Devonette's bodyguards were probably watching, but he didn't see any sign of the two men. Just as well, he thought. The idea that they watched her at all times was a little off-putting to him.

They'd probably report his presence to her father. What would his mother think of that? She said Passway was an enemy and not trustworthy, and he knew that she was almost always correct. He'd have to be careful.

He briefly wondered why he was there. Why walk into a potentially dangerous situation?

Then Devonette opened the door, and thoughts of caution fled from his mind. She definitely wasn't ready to go for a walk.

She looked beautiful and wore just a hint of an irresistible scent. Cole moved to screen her from the street with his body. She was wearing a thin nightgown

that, to him, exposed too much of her to risk answering the door.

She smiled and lifted her arms for an embrace. "It's good to see you, Cole. I thought about walking, but it seemed too cold. Won't you come in? We can talk inside better than while walking, anyway."

He found himself inside with the door shut without quite knowing how he got there.

Devonette came into his arms immediately and lifted her face for a kiss. Cole tried to analyze his feelings, but she was in his arms and her body pressed against his in all the right places. He dropped his head, and their lips met.

An eternity later, they broke slightly. Both were breathing heavily. She looked at him, her pupils wide and dark.

"I've never done this before, Cole. I'm not sure how to go about it, even though I've probably watched more romantic movies than you ever knew were produced. I've had a bunch of men who thought they were my boyfriend, but I never let any of them get close. Not as close as you are right now." She reinforced that by pulling him close, moving as she did to achieve the tightest fit between them.

He was conscious of her breasts pushing against his body through the thin fabric of her nightgown. It felt good, as if it were meant to be. He kissed her again then slid his hand down between them. She moved closer with a moan.

He looked at her. Her eyes were shining, and her face was flushed.

"Don't stop. It feels better than I ever thought it would," she said.

What did that mean? His mind was intent on the dynamic they were creating, but her statement jump-started his thinking.

He pulled back slightly, loosening his arms. "I haven't had much experience along these lines," he said, smiling. "Not that some women haven't made it clear that they liked me. I've never found anyone that seemed to make sense to me."

She smiled, "Do I make sense to you?"

He pulled her close again. "Too much sense. My mind isn't working very well right now. You're too beautiful."

She pressed tightly against him, then said, "Let's sit on the couch. We can talk there."

She sat beside him, then turned into his arms. "I didn't think I'd want you to kiss me and never stop, but I do."

He kissed her again, then slid his lips across her cheek to her neck, just below her ear. She made a throaty sound in response.

"You're giving me goosebumps. Ahhh."

She responded to his nibble by sliding her hand inside his shirt between the buttons.

From the moment her fingers found his nipple, clothes became a barrier for which he had no time. His shirt came off, and then her nightgown. She wasn't wearing anything underneath. He took a moment to appreciate her physical perfection, then pulled her close. This time, their kiss held fire.

He couldn't get enough of her.

After a time, she pulled back and looked deeply into his eyes.

"I'm a virgin, Cole. I've never done this before. I used to enjoy mistreating men. You see, they all wanted me, and I didn't care for any of them. There were always more that tried to come on to me. You're different. I want you. Let's go to the bedroom, please. It will be more comfortable."

He stood, cradling her in his arms. He was breathing rapidly, but it wasn't from the exertion of picking her up. It was from a rising tide of heat that flowed upward from his hips across his body until his vision was tinged with red.

He carried her into the bedroom and lowered her to the bed. His pants came off then, and she reached out a trembling hand to hold him.

"It feels different than I thought it would," she said, wonderingly.

He moved over her, and their lips met again.

A jolting pain struck him with a buzzing sound, and his muscles tightened into infinitely painful cramps. He collapsed on Devonette, and she screamed in pain.

The buzzing stopped, and a voice said, "Get him off her. She got hit by the Taser, too. I'll have to zap him again in a bit."

Another voice said, "Nah. Get out of the way and let me get to his shoulder."

His muscles were relaxing, but then a sharp stabbing feeling hit his shoulder. They'd injected something.

Devonette was cursing. "What the hell? I don't want you two in here. What are you doing? That hurt! I'll get Daddy to fire you as soon as I can call him."

Cole was somehow on his back, staring at the ceiling.

Devonette's face loomed over him. "Cole! They injected you with something. Are you alright? I'm sorry, I want you. I didn't plan this. You've got to believe me. I...I think I love you." She began to sob, her face pretty even squeezed up in grief.

Randy threw some clothes at Devonette. "Here, Miss Passway. Get dressed. Your father will be here momentarily, and I doubt that you want him to see you like this."

She blindly groped for the clothes, then slid out of Cole's sight.

Randy leaned over him. "You're okay. I shot you with some fentanyl mixed with a little prophy. You'll go to sleep in a bit, but you'll be okay. We're not going to kill you; just hold you here until your mother agrees to talk."

Cole felt like he was floating in a warm sea of darkness. He tried to gather his mind enough to slip into the in-between world and travel away, but it kept eluding him. He closed his eyes and floated.

He could hear Devonette's voice. It came from far away in the darkness and sounded hysterical.

"You set me up? My father told you to break in here and tase me? I never want to see either of you again. Get out! Get out!"

He vaguely wondered if the men had gone. Devonette was sobbing now, but it grew fainter, and he slipped away into the darkness.

⎯⎯⎯⎯◆⎯⎯⎯⎯

Lola had enjoyed the weekend since it took her mind off her self-imposed course of study. She found that she needed the respite. Lola had been so intent on learning that she hadn't let up all week. When she and Cole were in the wilderness, she could concentrate on their prey and on what she viewed as a kind of complicated hunting dance with Cole.

He would move along a hillside, below the ridge-line, keeping his silhouette away from the skyline. She would make a counter move through the bushes and trees on the other side of the valley below the hill. They were stalking a small herd of deer, but she was enjoying the sense of being in perfect tune with Cole as they moved from point to point after their prey.

Something bothered her, though. Cole had seemed a little preoccupied. Maybe not quite himself. She couldn't get her claws into the feeling properly, but it bothered her enough to put a shade of worry into their hunting dance.

⎯⎯⎯⎯◆⎯⎯⎯⎯

Monday, when Cole slipped in between to go to his classes, she walked out to the porch and stared at the hillside beside the house. After a time, she trotted down the steps and across the yard, then climbed the hill. The other humans were inside, eating, she supposed.

Her mother, Lolita, was away. She'd had Cadeyrin transport her to where her mate was. He wasn't receptive to humans, so Lolita had taken him off to be with Aunt Fancy and her group. They were presently hunting a range about five hundred kilometers away.

Cadeyrin would check on Lolita periodically and bring her back when she was ready. Right now, she was acting like she was in a mating mood and wanted to see her mate.

Lola sighed. If only she and Cole could be that way. Still, it was almost enough to hunt with him. They made a good team. That was important to her. She held an instinct that told her hunting with her mate was an essential part of the necessary bonding that went into molding two Deinonychus into a committed mating pair.

At the top of the hill, she turned, surveyed the homestead below, then went into the trees. Once inside, she stopped, closed her eyes, and transited into the spirit world. The storm cloud was off in the distance. Now that she'd almost been caught in it, she was always aware of its location.

She slipped through the paths of time, following her mental image of Cole's location. Time passage had no meaning in this dimension, and she could not tell how long her journey took. Eventually, she materialized in a sheltered juniper hedge near his house.

She watched for a while, but he didn't come out. Perhaps she'd arrived after he had left for class. Closing her eyes, she jumped through the spirit world and came out into his living room.

She stood silently, her senses searching. There was no life in the house. He wasn't there at the moment, although she could smell him.

That wasn't right, she thought. His scent seemed old and stale, so he hadn't been in the house for at least a day. She trotted through the rooms, investigating.

In his bedroom, she found his buckskins. They still held his scent, the scent of deer blood, and her own scent from when they had sat on a hill and cuddled just yesterday, but it was fainter than it should be. Where was he?

He had jumped here and was supposed to be going to class, but his scent said he hadn't arrived. He had to have jumped somewhere else.

She looked around, puzzled. Then it struck her. The buckskins smelled the way they should. Their scent held the record of what the two of them had done, but they had been here longer than a day. It was confusing, but she knew that something was wrong.

If his clothes had been here for a longer time, that meant that he had arrived at least a couple of days in the past. Lola felt hurt. He had lied to her. They had agreed that Cole would always ensure that they aged in synchrony. Now, he would be two days older in physiological time unless she made it up somehow.

She made an unhappy sound deep in her throat. That wasn't the real problem, though. She should be concentrating on finding him. Where was he? And, why had he been gone for two days when he should have just arrived?

She could check on whether he would come back, she thought. She instantly jumped forward twelve hours. The house was dark, and it was still unoccupied. The scent record showed that he hadn't returned because his odor was growing fainter.

Something had happened to him.

She would need help, and the only person she knew who could figure out this puzzle was Kathleen.

Chapter Twenty

Prisoner

Cole was aware that he was strapped to a bed somewhere. The room appeared to be an ordinary bedroom, aside from the twelve-inch crown molding. That was overkill as far as he was concerned. It betrayed the fact that the homeowner was wealthy and accustomed to luxury.

It took him a long time to figure that out. His mind was fuzzy and seemed to be working at half-speed or slower. He didn't hurt anywhere. That, at least, was a blessing. If his memory hadn't been affected, the bodyguard had said something about fentanyl and maybe propofol. Whatever it was, he was under the influence of some drug or drugs that made him unable to concentrate sharply enough to translate into the in-between world. The realization slid into his mind that whoever was holding him captive knew that he could easily escape.

It was...he strained to think...Devonette, or rather her father. She had been more than ready to make love to him. What a fool he had been. She probably had hundreds of lovers. She admitted that men threw themselves at her constantly. It was a bit too much to believe that she had rejected them all. Especially considering what he'd observed of his peers on campus.

Her physical presence had so entranced him that he hadn't bothered to check his surroundings. A tinge of humor slipped into his slow thoughts. It was hard to be aware of his surroundings when he had fixed all his focus on the next step in mating with her. He supposed that he could forgive himself. Any other man would have responded the same way. The next moment he was angry. He wasn't other men. He expected a lot from himself, and he should have checked to see if she was alone in the house.

A woman he didn't recognize came in and checked his IV. He had an IV? He hadn't noticed before. She adjusted the flow a little, then felt his forehead.

"That's alright," she said. "You relax, and everything will be fine. I'll be back at noon to check on you again. Mr. Passway will be dropping by this afternoon. He wants to ask you some questions."

She left, seemingly moving in slow motion. He closed his eyes, suddenly dizzy, and considered his situation. It was Passway. Devonette had set him up, or maybe, her father had used her, calculating that she would seduce him. He seemed to remember her screaming and crying. There was no need for an act to impress him at that point. He was already captive. Maybe she had been in earnest with her seduction. She might have been an unwitting victim of a plot to catch him.

Passway. His mother had warned him about that guy. He, of course, figured he could protect himself and instead got trapped like a March rabbit.

Something the woman had done made him sleepy. Maybe she'd upped the dosage of the drug. His awareness faded to a dull gray.

⸺◆⸺

Kathleen and Cadeyrin were sitting on the porch, drinking coffee, and enjoying the sun cutting through the thin haze of morning fog out over the rolling land to the west.

"I'd better check on Lolita today," he said. "She may be ready to come back. I don't think she cares much for that male."

Kathleen smirked. "If they're like humans, it should only take a few minutes for her to get what she wants. Judging from personal experience, I mean."

He laughed. "Woman, you have a wanton streak in you under all that pretend shyness. I seem to remember that you demand more than just a few minutes from me."

They laughed again, and he leaned over to kiss her.

The kiss was interrupted by Lola suddenly materializing beside them.

Cadeyrin jumped to his feet, then recognized there was no threat. Kathleen and Lola began talking simultaneously.

"You can time-travel!" Kathleen exclaimed. "When did you learn to do that?"

Lola squawked excitedly and yelled, "Cole is gone! I don't know where. We have to find him."

Cadeyrin put his hand on Lola's neck. "He's gone? How do you know?"

She explained, speaking in quick bursts, trying to express herself logically when every fiber in her being urged her toward action.

"I followed him to school. To his house, but he didn't come out. I went inside, and his scent was cold. His clothes smelled like they did when he left this morning, but the scent on them was old."

Kathleen looked at Cadeyrin and asked, "What does that mean?"

He was frowning. "It means that his clothes were there for over a day. He didn't go to Monday morning when he left here; he went to Sunday or maybe Saturday. Why would he do that?"

Kathleen's face fell. "I think I know why." She turned to Lola and reached out. "Lola, dear, I'm not sure this is my business to tell you, and I don't want to hurt you, but the only explanation is..."

Lola made a soft, anguished moan. "I knew it. He has a mate there."

Her head drooped, and she pulled away from Cadeyrin, heading for the steps.

"No! Wait, dear," Kathleen said.

Lola paused near the top step and looked over her shoulder.

"He doesn't have a mate yet. He's found a girl that he thinks is somewhat interesting, but her father is possibly my enemy. He could be in danger. I don't know who the father is, precisely, but I've been aware of him. He's been trying to interfere with our health business."

Cadeyrin added, "It goes without saying that he also wants the time equation. Everyone does. Where did he come from? I thought you got rid of Passway before he was born."

Kathleen paused, trying to calculate the possibilities. "I did. I made sure his ancestors never met. He disappeared. I might have made a mistake, though. Time can heal itself. The string of reality isn't easily changed, and that's something that my formula doesn't cover. The math only implies that there might be a more complicated explanation. Based on his age, he could be William Passway's son. That shouldn't be possible. If, as I thought, Passway was never born. Something must be wrong with my understanding of how the time-flow works. I'll have to think about it."

Lola interrupted. "He doesn't have a mate? Maybe we should find him and warn him."

"It's possible he went forward to the weekend to spend time with her," Kathleen mused.

Cadeyrin shook his head. "He might have, but if he did, I'm going to be disappointed in him. He lied to Lola. That's not good."

Lola made a groaning noise. "Mmm. Maybe he did, but where is he now? He wasn't at his house, and his scent was cold. He didn't come back that evening. I checked," she told them belatedly.

Cadeyrin walked to the porch rail, then spoke. "He may have gone off with her, but it is unlike him to not let us know or to return. My sense is that something is wrong, but I'm not sure what."

Kathleen nodded in agreement. "We'd better check on him, just in case. Lola, you should stay here. It's too dangerous for a Deinonychus to be in the future world. You will create a panic, and people may be killed as a result."

Lola spoke plaintively, "Yes, but I need to know if he's okay. I learned how to stay out of sight. I've been hunting by myself, jumping from hiding place to hiding place. Prey never notices me. I'm just as careful in the human future, too. I've been there before."

The two humans looked at each other. Cadeyrin was the first to speak. "She will go there with or without us, you know. She cares too much about him to just let this alone."

"Okay," Kathleen sighed. "Lola, you can come too, but let me do the jumping. I'll select places for us where they won't see you."

Lola nodded, human style. "I want to go now!"

Kathleen walked over to the agitated raptor and stroked her head. Lola looked confused for a moment, then sighed and put her head under Kathleen's arm and began to make sounds that were distressingly similar to human sobs.

"I...muhh...huhh...I couldn't stand it if something happened to him. I know he needs a human mate, but I...huh...I love him!" Her words failed, and her body shook with grief as she sobbed.

Cadeyrin and Kathleen met each other's eyes, and he shook his head negatively. It was a confusing mess. Lola had lived with them for nineteen years, and they had grown accustomed to treating her as a human. She was so much a part of the family that they treated her as a daughter. She acted human, at least, as much as possible for a being encased in a body genetically designed to be a highly efficient killing machine.

Kathleen looked at her husband, and her lips soundlessly formed the words, "What do we do?"

In response, he said, "I'll get some weapons, and we'll go. I have to tell Serensaa and Annie first. Grid and Logan went fishing, so their wives will have to tell them. We don't need a large group for this first search. You and I and Lola are quite enough to check things out."

Lola slowly pulled her head out, made a loud sniffing sound, then moved to put her wing-arms around him.

"Thank you," she said. "I'll be careful and follow your instructions. I promise."

———— ◆◇◆ ————

It took less than ten minutes to collect their gear and tell the women where they were going and why.

Chapter Twenty-One

Face-off

Cole's house seemed cold and dark. The usual energy given off by an occupied house was missing. It was a subtle feeling, but Cadeyrin and, to a lesser extent Kathleen, sensed it.

"He's not here," Cadeyrin said after they materialized in the living room. "He hasn't been here for some time. Lola's right."

Kathleen pulled a slip of paper from the front door. It had been inserted between the frame and the door and stuck out of the crack.

"What's this?" She opened the folded paper and read:

> *You have some information I want. I now have something to trade that I think you want back. Don't leave the house. I'll know, and your son will suffer for your actions. There will be someone there shortly who will take you to a place where we can speak.*
> *If you divulge your information, you'll go free. If not, things won't be so pleasant.*
> *W. P.*

Lola made an angry sound. "They have Cole. We must rescue him."

Cadeyrin had listened to the message, then turned and was now scrutinizing the room.

Kathleen joined him, the two working as a team with their goal unspoken but known by both. Lola dithered a moment, then asked, "What is it?"

"There has to be a camera in here, maybe more than one," Kathleen explained. "Look for a tiny glint of light reflected from its lens."

Lola sniffed reflexively, then said, "There's a faint scent of someone else. It's stronger over here."

She walked to a small bookshelf, inspected it, then asked, "Is this what you're trying to find.? It shines kind of blue."

The two looked. She had found a camera hidden in a book. There was a small hole in the spine where the lens poked through. The book had an opening cut out of the pages, and there was an electronic device there.

Kathleen bent over it for a moment. "There's an antenna. It's hooked to the wireless. They probably are watching right now. They'll know we found a camera."

Lola hadn't been interested in the camera mechanism. Finding it was enough to encourage her to search more. She called from Cole's bedroom, "Come here. I found another one, I think."

A shiny bit of lens showed in the wall plate that surrounded the light switch. Lola pointed it out to the humans, and Kathleen asked, "How did you find it? It's almost invisible."

"It's not to me. I can see the glow easily, now that I know what to look for. There's another one in the wood by the window."

Lola pried at the window molding with her claw, and a large splinter popped off.

There was an embedded camera there also.

Kathleen said, "Lola, you can see a wider range of colors than humans. I knew your vision is sharper than ours, but not that much better."

Lola clawed at the camera, and it came free of the nook that had been carved in the wood. She looked at it carefully, then dropped it and stomped her foot hard.

"I hate those things. They spied on Cole. What do we do next? How do we find Cole?"

Kathleen pulled the two close and whispered, "Are there any more in the bedroom?"

Lola scanned, then said, "No. I don't see any."

Kathleen continued. "Okay. We'll go back to the living room. I'll put the book back and suggest we wait for the people he's sending. Lola, you act angry and say "no." Say you're going back to the past and then jump out of the living room to the bedroom. We'll pretend you aren't in the house. Cadeyrin and I will go with them when they get here. It will be up to you to follow without them knowing. Can you do that?"

Lola nodded earnestly. "Yes. It will be like hunting. I can do it. Then what?"

Cadeyrin said, "You watch from somewhere without being seen. When they take us into a building, jump into a vacant room, then see if you can find us. If we can get Cole out, we'll leave, but I suspect they will want to hold us captive, too. In that case, you attack and distract them. This will be dangerous, and you'll have to be very careful. They will have guns, so don't give them a target. Move quickly."

Lola looked unsure but nodded. "I will try. The part that may be hard is in the building. There might be no place to hide."

"True. If someone sees you, attack them. We'll make the best of the distraction," Cadeyrin answered.

In the living room, Kathleen seated herself where she could be easily viewed from the book camera that she'd placed back on the shelf. She looked at the lens and said, "Alright. Here we are. We'll wait for your men." She glanced at Lola, who had been watching her intently.

Lola made a hoarse scream, flapped her wing arms, then said, "No! I'm not going to be captured. I'm going back to the past."

She disappeared almost instantly, leaving behind a faint ghostly simulacrum of herself that faded more slowly.

Cadeyrin looked directly at the lens and said, "We'll wait. She's too wild. Besides, she doesn't know how to communicate well enough to give you any useful information."

⸻◆⸻

After a time, there was a knock at the front door. Cadeyrin rose and opened it.

Randy and James were on the porch, looking nervous. Randy flinched back and drew a pistol.

Cadeyrin simply smiled and said, "Come in, please. You shouldn't wave that thing around in public. I believe there are laws against it."

He moved aside and motioned the two inside.

Randy shoved the pistol back under his coat but kept his hand on it.

"Uh-uh, big guy. You back up and sit down. I'm not coming in and having you jump me."

Cadeyrin shook his head. "You're nervous. That's bad. It makes you more likely to make a poor decision. We're not going to jump you. We want our son back. You do have him, and he's safe, right?"

James seemed a little more in control. He nodded briefly. "Yeah. We've got him drugged so he can't escape." He looked at the two curiously. "You can travel in time – really? Is that true?"

Kathleen laughed softly. "My husband is proof. He was born over ten thousand years ago. We can jump out of here any time we want. Your guns aren't going to stop us, so you might as well be nice and take us where your boss wants."

Randy started to pull his pistol again, but Cadeyrin said, "Not necessary. We're cooperating, as she said."

Randy shrugged and drew his pistol, then turned toward the kitchen, holding the weapon ready for action.

James nodded again. "That may be, but where is that dinosaur thing? I saw the video. It looks dangerous."

Cadeyrin answered, "We sent it back to the past. It is dangerous. It's a predator, and it's a deadly hunter. It's gone now, and it isn't coming back. We can't reach out and grab something across time. We have to have it right beside us where we can touch it to move it."

He was playing a game with the two. What he hadn't said was that he could grab them at any time, jump them back to the Cretaceous and leave them there. It would be so quick that they wouldn't recover their wits until after he'd marooned them. For that matter, it would be possible to disarm them, but one of them might get off a shot, and he wasn't going to risk that with Kathleen there.

James looked as if he didn't believe that the creature was gone. He backed toward the front door. "We've wasted enough time here. The car is outside. Both of you come on, get in the car nicely, and don't try any tricks. Someone might get hurt if you do."

Kathleen and Cadeyrin exchanged glances. Someone would get hurt, but they didn't intend it to be them.

"Okay," she said.

They exited the house and got in the second row of the SUV. Randy had climbed in and was sitting behind them in the third row, covering them with his pistol. James started the engine, looked both ways, and pulled out.

Neither of the men observed a pair of bright eyes peering at them through the thick screen of the white cedars across the street.

———— ◇ ————

The bodyguards had delivered them to a sprawling estate with lush grounds along a river. They'd been ushered through some mammoth rooms and into a small office. Now they were waiting.

Kathleen said, "This is typical. He'll make us wait to show how important he is and how little we matter to him."

Cadeyrin nodded and said, "Headmen of tribes often did the same thing when I was young." She looked at him with a quizzical face, and he laughed, then amended his statement. "Younger, I should say."

She smiled. "You're just the right age for me, though." Then, changing the topic, "They had better not have hurt Cole. I think they've got some surprises in store for us, but that works both ways."

Cadeyrin held his finger to his lips. "They're surely listening or watching us."

She shifted uneasily. "You're right." She raised her voice, "Mr. Passway, you can quit the games now. Your house is impressive, and we're happy to acknowledge that you have other important things to do. However, we are here now, and we're somewhat impatient to assure the safety of our son. Maybe we can cut a deal."

She looked at her husband. He shrugged. "That ought to work."

James opened the door and said, "Mr. Passway is in the Morning room having breakfast. Would you care to join him?"

He led them to a light and sunny room with expansive glass windows overlooking a manicured lawn that sloped gently down to a gazebo by the water. Passway was sitting, looking at the view and sipping coffee. The remains of a light breakfast were on a small table beside his chair.

He nodded at them. "Have a seat. I believe we have some business to discuss. Would you like some coffee?"

Kathleen nodded, but Cadeyrin, more suspicious, held up his hand in refusal. She looked at him, then said, "I've changed my mind. Our discussion won't take long."

Passway smiled, a shark-like expression on his face as he bared his teeth. "That's good to hear. I presume you've come to try and rescue your son."

She snorted in disgust. "What do you want?"

"Ah. That's the real question. What do I want? I want a large number of things, and you have two of them, I believe. With a complete understanding of time-travel and, what I believe is a secret formula for longevity, I can acquire

the rest of my desires on my own without involving you."

Cadeyrin quietly said, "That's what we thought you'd say, but you didn't add the rest."

"What rest? That's all I want. It's just two little pieces of information." Passway was apparently enjoying himself playing cat and mouse.

"The rest is that you intend to eliminate us when you get what you want. You have the sort of personality that cannot tolerate competition. If we were around, you'd figure we would interfere in your plans."

Having said that, Cadeyrin stood and moved over by Kathleen's chair, then put his hand casually on her shoulder. She glanced up at him, her expression opaque.

Passway abruptly grew tired of the game. "Give me the time-equation now. There's paper and a pen on the sideboard. As for the longevity drug, I'll pay a fair price for the company you have distributing it. You only have to agree to sell. Once I get those things, I'll release your son."

Devonette burst into the room at that point. Her face was red and streaked with tears.

"Daddy, you've got to let Cole go. How could you do this to me? I feel like a fool for not suspecting you'd use me to get at him. He's just a student to you, but he means a lot to me."

She stopped her chest heaving and looked at Cadeyrin and Kathleen, whom she'd suddenly realized were in the room.

Kathleen said, "You must be Devonette. We are Cole's parents, and we are why your father kidnapped Cole. He wants something from us."

Devonette snapped, "He always wants something from somebody. He –"

Passway said, "That's enough, Devonette. Now, leave us. If all goes well, Cole will be released, and you can resume your little game with him, although I hope it won't take too long. I've got other plans for you."

She opened her mouth, but he lifted his finger, peremptorily, and she shut it again. Then she obediently turned and left, giving Cadeyrin a side-long glance from the corners of her eyes as she left.

Passway watched her exit, then returned his attention to the two. "Please excuse my daughter. She tends to become overwrought. I believe she has some designs on your son. Don't think that will affect our business dealings. She's in for a disappointment. He's not a suitable match."

Kathleen said, "She's beautiful. That's one good thing you've created, Passway. Give us a valid reason to assist you."

He looked surprised. "Hello? I have your son captive."

She shook her head negatively. "That's not good enough. We can rescue him at any time. And, don't think your men can stop us."

Passway touched his watch and said, "James, come in here and be ready."

Cadeyrin turned to the door as James opened it, his pistol in one hand and a taser in the other.

There was a sudden shriek accompanied by the sound of breaking glass. Randy came running through the door, shouldering James against the door jamb. He turned and fired three shots that narrowly missed James.

James cursed, "What the hell are you doing? That nearly hit me."

Randy looked through the doorway. "That thing was out there. It nearly got me." He scanned the room outside. "It's not there now. Maybe I got it."

Passway frowned. "What thing? That dinosaur? I thought it had gone back to where it belongs."

Kathleen said, "I don't think you hit her. She could have ripped Randy apart if she'd wanted to. Right now, she's waiting to see if you allow us to go peacefully. If we, all three of us, don't come out within a few minutes, she'll attack again, and she will be serious this time. I'd hurry if I were you. She is somewhat of an impatient one."

Passway nodded. "I see. James, you know what to do."

James lifted the taser, but Cadeyrin moved like a tiger and struck him on the side of the neck. The muscular bodyguard collapsed.

Randy spun, his pistol extended. He got off a random shot, his wrist deflected by Cadeyrin, who followed up with a solid punch to the forehead. Randy's eyes crossed, and he staggered back, then sat down heavily.

Cadeyrin collected the dropped weapons.

Kathleen had been watching Passway. The man's eyes narrowed, but he made no move. He was still confident, she thought.

"Passway, here's what we're going to do. We're getting our son and leaving. You can research time-travel all you want. You've got the money to hire the best mathematicians to do the work for you. I wish you luck with it. As for the other, well, you can purchase the products we see fit to release, just like any other consumer. They will help with your health. I recommend them. As for purchasing the company, maybe I'll let you do that, but you'll find that it owns nothing. Not a patent, not a formula, nothing. I hold that information, and I'm not releasing it."

There was a scratching sound, and Lola appeared at the door. She glanced at Randy, and he lifted his arm to shield his face but didn't move, otherwise.

Cadeyrin turned his attention to Passway. "Give orders for Cole to be brought here. Lola isn't going to wait too long. Look at the killing claws on her feet. Her toes are flexing in preparation to attack."

Lola stared hard at Passway, then flexed her wing-arms into attack position and hissed. Passway flinched slightly.

"I'll have him brought here. He's drugged, so he will be in a wheelchair. Tell her to calm down." He pointed at Lola.

She hissed a second time and took a menacing half-step forward.

Cadeyrin said, "Wait, Lola. Cole's coming."

She lowered her flexed fingers slightly.

Passway looked relieved and spoke into his watch again. "Brittany, get the boy into a wheelchair and bring him to the Morning Room."

There was a muffled answer, distorted by the tiny speaker in the watch.

James moaned and rolled over to his side. Randy, his eyes on Lola, didn't move.

Cadeyrin held one of the pistols, covering the two.

Kathleen now had the second weapon and kept it pointed at the floor, where a slight move could raise it to align with Passway. "We're going to wait until he gets here. You will give no orders or take action to stop us. In the meantime, you're free to ask me questions, but I can't guarantee I'll answer the way you want."

Passway shrugged. "It was worth a try. Next time, I'll not underestimate you."

She smiled grimly. "With any luck, there won't be a next time."

He shrugged again. "If you're answering questions, can you go anywhere in time?"

"No. Not anywhere. One of the restrictions is that travel to more than a few seconds in the future is impossible. It has to do with the conservation of information more than anything else. I can go back as far as I want, and I can come to now, but I can't go into the distant future. The structure of time prohibits it. I could wreck my own present by acquiring knowledge that has yet to develop in the future."

He looked puzzled. "That makes no sense to me."

"It doesn't make any to me either. The math seems to break down when I try to apply it. I know it's true, though, because I can't jump forward. I only suspect the part about information."

He asked, "How about the drug? Does it extend life, or just help with health?"

"What's the difference? If you're healthy, you are quite likely to live longer. How much longer, I can't say. You might wonder if you can live infinitely, but no one can say they'll live forever until they reach the end of time. Frankly, the drugs we are releasing now affect mitochondria in a positive way. I suspect we'll see a large reduction in all causes of mortality as a result."

Passway made a face. "That's just going to pollute the world with more useless eaters. We're over-populated now. We need far fewer people, rather than more. It would be better if your drug eliminated all those who are of low intelligence, for example."

She asked, her tone slightly harsh, "Is that what you intend to do?"

"Why not? The Earth will thank me. It can only carry so many humans. It will be better for everyone if our population is limited."

A woman dressed in a nurse's garb knocked on the door jamb. She started in but stopped dead when she saw Lola and the guns.

"Mr. Passway, he's gone. I got him into the wheelchair, and Devonette told me she'd bring him down here. I waited but then saw her taking him down the hall toward the garage wing. I followed and got there in time to see them leaving in the Bentley."

Passway snarled, "You're a fool. Consider yourself terminated. Leave and don't let me see you again."

The woman practically ran from the room.

Kathleen thoughtfully said, "That wasn't very nice of you. She thought that Devonette was doing your bidding."

"She's a fool. When I give an order to someone, I expect them to obey it, not pass off the task to someone else."

Cadeyrin moved to a position between Kathleen and Lola. He placed a hand on each of them, then said, "It hasn't been nice to meet you, Passway. I'll say the same thing you said to that woman. Don't let me see you again."

Passway blinked. His eyes seemed slightly out of focus, but maybe it was just the misty area where the three had been standing.

He rose, walked forward, and waved his hand through the area, but the mist had dissipated by then.

"I'll be. They really can time jump," he said. "I've got to get control of that."

Chapter Twenty-Two

Escape

Cole felt relaxed. He was cocooned in a warm, fuzzy place. Nothing bothered him except he vaguely realized that he couldn't concentrate well. That didn't bother him. There was nothing on which to concentrate. There had been some pushing and shoving, and then they let him sit, then more pushing. He'd heard Devonette trying to get him to hurry, but it hadn't seemed urgent.

His head rolled from side to side. He hadn't done that. Where was he, anyway? He made an effort to open his eyes. The light was bright, making them water, but he saw enough to tell he was in an automobile. It was going somewhere fast.

He thought about it for a bit. The dash had looked close, so he must be in the front seat. He moved his hand and encountered what could only be the seat belt. The vehicle swerved violently, and there was a series of loud honks.

He opened his eyes in time to see the front of the car swerve back into the right-hand lane, just missing an oncoming truck. His mouth was dry, making it hard to speak. He tried to talk with no result. On the third attempt, he said, "What's the rush? Are we going to a hospital? I'm okay, I think."

Devonette's voice sounded strained. "Try to wake up, Cole. I'm getting you out of there."

The car slowed, then accelerated again. She sounded distraught. "Daddy is going to write me out of his will for this, but I couldn't let you be hurt. I think he was going to have you killed."

He found his face and wiped his hand over his eyes. When he opened them, things were a bit clearer.

"Watch out for that red light!" It was too late. She'd blasted right through the intersection, threading between two semi-trailer trucks. The second truck's driver honked as he braked hard.

She looked in the rear-view mirror. "I think we're safe for a bit. No one is following us."

She patted his leg. "Daddy was talking to a man and a woman. I think they were your parents. He wanted them to tell him how to time-travel."

She flashed a glance at him. "Is that true? Can you move through time somehow?"

The secret had somehow gotten out. He started to deny it but then changed his mind. "Yes. I can go through time. My mother discovered a formula that let her jump in time. Then we learned that there's a more intuitive way to do it. That was from Serensaa. She's a Clovis culture woman. She's married to Logan."

He belatedly realized that his explanation was a little disjointed. He thought about trying again, but Devonette was fumbling with the navigation controls on the dash.

"Damn it! This thing won't let me set it when we're moving. I've never driven this car before. We always had a driver."

The navigation system. There was something about that. Oh, the car probably could be tracked through the GPS. He wasn't sure how that worked, but he thought it was pretty likely that her father would know precisely where they were.

"We've got to get away from this car. They can track us," he mumbled.

Her eyes flashed in alarm as she glanced at him. "What? I...oh, you're right. What am I going to do?" she wailed.

He was feeling less fuzzy now, so he looked at his wrist. The IV needle was gone. In its place, there was a small bandage which he rubbed gently.

"You've got to find a place to park this thing. I can't do it while we're moving. It messes me up. Is there a park or something around here?"

"No. I don't know where we are exactly. How about that grocery store parking lot?"

"Stop there. I'll get us out of here."

The vehicle came to a halt, the tires screeching a little as she locked the brakes. He reached for her hand, but she pulled away.

"What are you thinking? We need to get out of here. This isn't the time to hold hands."

"Give me your hand. I need to be touching you to take you with me."

She grabbed his hand in response.

He closed his eyes and tried to concentrate on the in-between of the spirit world. It was elusive, not coming clear quickly. The drugs were still in his system. He made an effort but couldn't focus well enough to transition.

Her hand tightened. "Cole? The police are coming. I can hear sirens. There's one turning into the parking lot. His lights are on. They're after us."

He made a wrenching effort.

The police cruiser stopped beside the limo. It was idling, but there was no one inside.

⸻ ◆ ⸻

It was suddenly quiet. Peaceful. He hadn't realized how much noise was always present in the modern world. He kept his eyes shut and enjoyed the slight breeze on his face. Devonette's hand gripped his tightly, and he could hear her breathing rapidly.

Her grip suddenly grew tighter, then she screamed. His eyes popped open. She had started shaking, and the blood had drained from her face. He turned to look in the direction she was staring.

There was a group of rhinoceros-sized pigs lumbering directly toward them. The things were huge and looked fierce. Their eyes seemed fixed on the two humans, and Cole realized that he and Devonette were their intended next meal.

He'd never seen anything like these animals. As far as he knew, they were not members of the Pleistocene fauna. It suddenly clicked in his drug-fogged brain. He'd taken them much farther back in time than he had intended. He remembered now that there had been giant pigs in the Miocene, so maybe he'd jumped them back forty or fifty million years rather than the thirteen thousand he'd foggily intended.

Devonette was in an extremity of fear. She was gasping for breath, although she had stopped screaming. She made an effort to regain control and whispered, "Cole, help." She glanced at him, but her vision went immediately back to the pigs.

He had released her hand when he had turned. He gripped her shoulder and took them back to the in-between. This time, he had a clear destination in mind. They emerged in the house his mother maintained by a lake in northern Minnesota.

Cole had been there before a few times. Kathleen had purchased it and used it as a sanctuary when he had been born. There had been a raid and a gun battle with operatives sent by a group that wanted her time equation. The Feds had covered up the battle and taken steps to ensure that it didn't make the news.

Kathleen had thought that she would have to get rid of the place, but there was no follow-up from anyone, so she kept it. It hadn't been used much. A local woman kept an eye on it and cleaned it periodically, but that was the only person who regularly came by.

Devonette had shut her eyes before they had jumped, and now she opened them. She looked around wildly, then burst into tears and threw herself in his arms.

"Those pigs were horrible. They had huge fangs. I...I think they were going to eat us."

He pulled her closer. "Maybe they thought they had an easy meal, but we're safe now. This house belongs to my mother. We don't come here often, but I've been here before. It's quiet and peaceful. We're back in modern time, so there are no large animals."

She looked at his face. "Why did you take me back there and into danger? Was it because I let you get captured? That wasn't what I wanted at all."

"No. I think I was too fuzzy from the drugs. I made a mistake when I jumped us out of the car. I just wanted to get away. I think I took us back to the Miocene. That's about fifty million years or so, and there was a variety of huge pigs then. Pigs are omnivores. Those we saw weren't strictly predators, but they still might have attacked us. Certainly, they were big enough to kill a human."

She started shaking again. "That's what I mean. Can I trust you? You could take me somewhere I could be killed or eaten. You can travel in time. Only there's nowhere I want to go. I'm not interested in primitive times. I need my things, my house, social media."

She was babbling. Cole stroked her hair and cheek.

She stopped, hiccuped, then wiped at her eyes. "I must look awful."

"No, you look beautiful. I'm sorry I took you back there, but you were in no danger. I can always jump us out of harm's way."

She moved close to him, looking at his eyes. "So, you weren't getting revenge on me for what my father did to you?"

He smiled. "No. I don't blame you for that. You were as surprised as me, and I was conscious enough to hear you yelling at them to let me go. I'm just glad you took the opportunity to rescue me."

"Yeah. Well, Daddy is going to be very angry with me, but I can talk him out of it, I hope."

She looked around. "This is a quaint little place. Where's the bathroom?'

"Through that door. That's the guest suite back there, but you'll have to wait for a minute. The water's turned off. The electric well pump is always shut down when the place is vacant. Why don't you have a seat over here, and I'll go turn it on."

He headed for the basement, where the pump switch was located. He flipped it, listened for the sound of the pump, and watched until the pressure gauge started to show it was working. On the way back upstairs, he turned on the water heater.

She wasn't in the room where he had left her, but a quick search located her. She was lying on the guest bed, in the semi-darkness. It seemed to be evening outside.

"Cole?" Her eyes were dark and wide in the dimly lit room.

"Yes?" His heart was suddenly beating rapidly.

"Remember what we were doing when you were captured?" she said softly.

"How could I forget?" He sat on the edge of the bed and bent to kiss her.

Her arms opened and pulled him down. The kiss was slow and passionate. He felt as if no time had passed since he'd been kissing her in her house.

"This time, there won't be any interruptions? Will there?" she asked.

He answered by unbuttoning her blouse. She smiled and pulled him down for another kiss.

———◆○◆———

The night fell, and the two lay together under the sheets. He had dozed, but now he was awake and thinking about what they'd done. It was as if she had given him a precious gift. It had become apparent that this had been her first time. There was some blood on the sheets.

He briefly wondered how he'd explain

that to his mother. They'd made love, then kissed and talked. After some time had passed, they had a second time. Then they had slept. When they awoke, he would have tried a third time, but she had been too sore."

She was asleep again. He considered the future. Was Devonette the woman he had been unconsciously seeking? She was pretty, beautiful, in fact. However, he didn't know her well. She had set him up with the football players. She didn't seem to take well to being ignored, but maybe that was understandable. She had said that she was used to men chasing her.

In her favor, she had never let any man catch her. He smiled, at least until he came along. She was intelligent, but was her personality one which he could love?

That thought struck him like a bucket of cold water. Was her personality as lovable as Lola's? What would Lola think of his actions? He pictured her head drooping in her expression of sadness and depression. Was there some way he could keep his relationship with her and simultaneously be with Devonette?

It would be easy to do if he didn't bring Lola forward or take Devonette back. Neither would know that they were sharing him if he timed his jumps back and forth carefully. A sense of shame came with that thought. He couldn't cheat on them at the same time, even though it was possible.

He'd have to introduce them, and maybe Lola would understand. Perhaps if she saw that he had a mate, she would decide to take one of her kind. He knew that she viewed him as her mate, but he could never give her the family she desired. She was smart. Smart enough to recognize that she couldn't fight reality. It would have to work, but would it? He didn't know.

━━◆O◆━━

The problem arose in the morning. Devonette had decided that she wasn't as sore as she had thought in the middle of the night, and they had slept late after that.

When they woke, the sun was well up. He'd decided that he needed to get the introduction over. It might be premature. Devonette hadn't precisely promised to marry him, but he felt confident that she would.

However, she balked when he told her that he wanted to take her back to meet his parents.

"I've already seen your parents. My father was talking to them. Your Dad is a good-looking man. Then that horrible bird-thing attacked Randy and James. That's when I took the chance to steal you out of the house. The thing is, I don't want to go back in time ever again. There are monsters back there, and I'm not going to put myself where they can get me."

He explained, "Look, Devonette. That was a mistake. I'm sorry I took you back then. In the time where my parents live, there are no giant pigs."

"But, what animals are there?" she asked.

He stopped to consider. He had to be honest. Lying wasn't something that he could do easily. "Well, there are predators, just like today. You know, lions, bears, wolves, and...uh...things." He'd just remembered the saber-toothed cats.

"What kind of things?" she asked suspiciously.

"Uh...other kinds of cats. Mammoths, herds of bison, lots of smaller animals, and camels. There are lots of camels."

She wasn't to be distracted. "What other kind of cats?"

He sighed. "Saber-tooth cats. Some are pretty large, but there are some smaller ones, too."

She shook her head in denial. "No! I'm not going back there, and that's final."

"But, they aren't a problem for us. I can always tell when they're around, and I carry a gun, too."

Her eyes narrowed. "You use a gun?"

"Of course. It's the easiest way to protect myself. My father sometimes uses his bow and arrows, but he's used to that. I can use them also, but a heavy rifle is best when you're up against a large bear."

He was making things worse. Now she was drawing away from him.

He tried to pull her close, but she pushed at him.

"Cole, I don't like guns. I don't like cats. There's nothing about that time I like, and I'm not going back there with you. If you want to be with me, it has to be on my terms, understand? I'm a modern woman, and I live in the modern world. You can live with me. I'll get Daddy to give you a position in one of his companies, and we can have a nice, safe life."

Well, at least she was thinking about a future together, even if it was one that he didn't relish. The idea of being locked into the present time and having to spend the rest of his life fitting into the constraints of modern society wasn't something that appealed to him.

She quit pushing him away and moved close again. "You know you want me. We can have a long life together, and it will be safe."

She didn't know how long it might be. If he married her, he would want to give her the red paste. It would be no good if she aged and he didn't. They could potentially be together for hundreds of years. Would they grow tired of each other? His parents showed no signs of that. They were still in love, and they were old. They'd been together longer than he'd been alive.

That was a stupid thing to say, he belatedly realized. He was almost twenty, so maybe they'd been together for more than twenty years. That wasn't long for some married couples. The problem was none of their research had indicated how long human life could be with regular doses of the red compound. The old Sasquatch was possibly thousands of years old.

He tried to imagine living with Devonette that long. It was difficult. In some ways, her personality grated on his nerves, but maybe that would fade, or he'd become used to her. He certainly wanted her strongly right now. She was so beautiful.

"I've decided what I have to do, Cole. I'm going to get cleaned up, and you're going to take me to see my father. They won't taser you, and you can always jump out if you are in danger. I'll convince Daddy that having us together is for the best. It would be good, though, if you gave me some information to show that having you around would help his business."

"What do you have in mind? What could I tell you that he would want to know?" He was puzzled.

She shrugged airily. "Oh, maybe how to travel in time, for instance. I'm sure he'd be able to use that in his business. He's a billionaire, you know. He has lots of different businesses, but I'm sure they could find a use for jumping in time." She paused, then added, "As long as it doesn't involve me, of course."

"Devonette, I can't let the time formula out. My mother wants to keep it secret, and it's her discovery, so it's her right. She says, if modern humans had it, they would misuse it. It wouldn't be long before they messed up the time-stream and caused paradoxes that would screw up the world. I just can't tell that. The other thing is, none of us use the time-travel formula now. We take a shortcut that we learned from Serensaa. She's a contemporary of my father who can jump through time instinctively. I don't think most modern humans can do it, though. It takes a certain spiritual mindset that is mostly incompatible with the way moderns view the world. I can do it because I was raised away from society. I'm a product of the natural world, just as you're the product of society. I don't know if I could teach you to time-travel on your own."

She frowned prettily, then said, "Okay. I'll provisionally accept that, but we'll have to discuss it more at a later time. How about the drugs your parents are distributing. Daddy said they have a company making some amazing discoveries in life extension or health improvement, or something along those lines. Can you tell me anything about that?"

His instinctive warning sense started to prod at him. It was starting to seem like she was grilling him. Was it possible that she'd been told to seduce him just to get the secrets he knew? That was a nasty thought, but her actions kind of seemed that way. He decided to address the suspicion head-on.

"Did you just have sex with me to get me to spill my secrets for your Dad?"

She looked hurt. "That's not nice. I wouldn't have had sex with you if I hadn't wanted you. You've got a way about you that makes me want you. I've never felt this way about any man before. I'm not some cheap woman who has to screw for a living. I've got plenty of money. I didn't have to spread my legs for you."

She had worked her way up from hurt into anger. His approach had been a mistake.

"I didn't mean it like that, Devonette. I wanted you. I still want you. You're the nicest thing that's ever happened to me. Don't be angry, please."

Her anger faded. "I didn't do what we did just to get you to talk, you foolish boy. I did it because I wanted you so much I couldn't help myself." She smiled. "I still want you that much. It's just that I know my father. He's going to be difficult about this, and it would help if I had some way to make him see it was all for the best."

He temporized. "I understand. I'll do what I can, but I can't give him the secrets I've promised to protect. Maybe I can help him with time-travel research, though. Does he have people looking into that?"

She looked disappointed. "Yes. He has a group that is studying it, but they haven't made much progress beyond what the government already had done."

That sounded suspicious. The government had sent people back in time and had sent men to raid them. The men had no way to return, however. It was a government-sponsored one-way trip. It hadn't turned out well for the men who were sent back. The government hadn't even told them they wouldn't be coming back.

"What does your father have to do with the government?"

"I think he bought the time-travel information from them, maybe. He doesn't tell me all of his business dealings. Is that a problem, Cole?"

"Hmm. I don't know. My mother doesn't like the government, but you see, they've been chasing her for years trying to get her formula. They've been a problem with the drugs, too."

"Ah-ha! I knew you knew something about the life-enhancing drugs."

"Well, I do, but the components aren't easily available. You have to travel through time to get all of them, so, you see, it comes back to the time secret again."

She looked thoughtful. "That might be enough to keep Daddy happy for the time being." She looked at him coyly. "I think I've recovered now. I mean, if you want to make love to a woman who might be selling herself to get secrets."

He laughed. "You're too beautiful for me to worry about it. Come here!" He pulled her close and made a growling sound as he thrust his face against her neck. She squealed, then giggled. He kissed her, a long, slow, passionate kiss. Things became very serious after that.

———◦———

They showered together, then dressed.

"Can you take me back to my house, Cole? Maybe you shouldn't be with me when I talk to Daddy. At least, not the first time. If I can get him to see that this is for the best, then will be plenty of time for him to meet you."

He nodded. "We've already met, but I was so drugged that I don't think I made a good impression."

She laughed. "Okay. Take me home. Then you can talk to your parents. Maybe they'll come to the future again so that I can meet them formally."

Chapter Twenty-Three

A Mess

Lola was watching as the car stopped in the parking lot. A landscaped berm lay at the north edge of the lot with a line of blue spruce along its top. They were large trees with thick foliage, and it was no problem for her to find a hiding space inside the screen of branches.

She saw a slight blue flash come from the car. It was always that way. The humans couldn't see it, but she knew her vision covered a wider range than theirs. Every time someone jumped through time, it released a bluish flash when they entered the in-between world.

She started to jump after them but stopped. She didn't know when or where Cole was going. Probably he'd make for home. She closed her eyes and slipped in-between to check the Pleistocene compound.

He wasn't there. Logan was sitting on a chair on the porch while Serensaa trimmed his hair. She was good at it and enjoyed using the steel scissors. She'd told Lola once that she'd never imagined such an excellent cutting tool. Although they weren't as sharp, they worked ever so much better than a flake of chert.

Logan had told her that Cole wasn't there. She hadn't wasted time chatting after that. She jumped back to the future, going to Cole's house. That could be the place he went. Besides, it was the only place she knew where he would be likely to be in the future.

When she materialized, there was a jolt of crackling energy. She fell to the floor, her body wracked by cramps. She wanted to kill the men who came forward, but she couldn't move because of the intense pain from the wired darts in her breast.

One of the men loomed over her, and then she felt a pricking sensation in her back. The lights faded as her eyesight grew dim. The last thing she heard was one of her attackers saying, "I hope that wasn't an overdose. This thing might not respond to fentanyl the same way a human would."

The other man answered, "Don't make no difference to me. Boss says catch it. We did. If it dies cause of the drug, well, that's his problem, way I figure."

⸺⬥⸺

Cole and Devonette transferred to her father's riverfront mansion. He brought them out of the in-between dimension at the gazebo by the river.

Since his arm was already around her slim shoulders, he kissed her. When they broke, she said, "This place is just one of Daddy's houses. He only bought this one because I was going to school here. I couldn't understand why he wouldn't let me live here, but he insisted that I had to act like one of the common students."

She laughed, "That's stupid. He bought me a house. It's small, but still a house, and it's all for me. I don't know any other students that have their own house."

"Well, I do, but there may not be many others," he answered.

She looked at him inquisitively. "I guess your folks probably have plenty of money themselves. I'm not very creative, but I can think of many ways to get rich if you can jump back and forth in time."

"Yeah. That's one of the reasons they don't want it to get out. It would attract the worst people and complicate law enforcement. It would be easy to commit crimes, and you could arrange it so you'd never get caught." He hadn't quite admitted his parents were wealthy. In fact, he'd never thought of it much. They always seemed to have enough money to do whatever they wanted, although they didn't seem to want much. He'd always thought of them as being content with life in the past. Money was useless there. What counted was the ability to hunt, garden, and do things for yourself. That was real. Money was only an artifact of civilization, useful for complicating and ruining lives the way he saw it.

She kissed him again. "You can go hang out somewhere for a while. I'll probably sleep here tonight, so I'll call you tomorrow."

He reminded himself to make sure he charged his phone. He didn't use it that much and had taken to leaving it off the charger overnight.

She turned and headed up the winding path to the house. He watched from the gazebo for a few moments, then faded into the spirit world. When he came out into reality, he was in the living room of his house off-campus.

A chair was lying on its side, and a few colorful feathers were on the floor. Lola had been here! But, she couldn't travel in time by herself. She hated the sensation. Maybe his mother had brought her, but why? And, what did the chair and feathers signify?

He searched the house, moving quickly through the rooms. Nothing else was disturbed. Then he saw it. There was a brown smudge on the floor near the front door. Closer inspection revealed that it was a partial footprint. The only place there was any damp dirt was outside to the side of the house. The planting bed there was in the shade and retained moisture for days. It hadn't rained recently, but perhaps he should look.

There was a full print in the damp earth of the bed. Someone had been in the house, and somehow Lola had been involved. Cole was suddenly sick with worry. It was one thing if she had come to his house by herself or with his mother. If someone else was there, it was likely to be one of the men hired by Passway. There wasn't any blood splashed around, which meant that Lola had not been able to defend herself.

She could be like a buzz saw when she got angry. Deadly claws on both hands and feet and a mouth full of razor-sharp teeth made that an easy response. She also didn't shed feathers easily. They had to be pulled out, and she wouldn't allow that if she could fight.

Cole stood on the porch with his head down, thinking. He rubbed his forehead, then looked over his shoulder. There were no apparent witnesses, so he initiated a jump there in plain sight, something he wouldn't normally do.

Serensaa and Logan were on the wide porch when he arrived at the compound. They were sweeping some hair clippings up. From the looks of Logan's hair, she had just trimmed it.

"Hey, Cole. What are you doing here? Don't you have a class or something?" Logan asked.

Serensaa smiled at him but continued sweeping up her husband's locks.

"Have you seen Lola? She was at my house. How did she get there? Is Mom or Dad around?"

Logan, hearing the stress in Cole's voice, straightened to answer. "Lola was just here looking for you. She jumped out but didn't tell us where she was going. Did you teach her to travel through the spirit world? I didn't think she knew how. None of the other Deinonychs can."

"I didn't teach her. I thought maybe Mom had brought her forward or something," Cole said.

Serensaa quit sweeping and fixed her sea-gray eyes on him. "Maybe Lola didn't know she could go through time, but she loves you. She is drawn to where you are. You need to find her."

He asked again. "Mom or Dad? Are they here?"

Logan shook his head negatively. "I don't think so. They went off to check on you with Lola. She came here looking for you earlier and told them she couldn't find you. She thought something had happened to you. They left, then she came back just a short time ago, but she left immediately."

"Damn! For the record, I did something I promised her I wouldn't do. I jumped to Saturday rather than Monday. There's this girl up there, and..." He wasn't sure how to go on.

Serensaa and Logan exchanged glances. Logan said, "We sort of understand how that works. You don't have to tell us all the details. Just give us the overview, so we'll know how to help."

"Uh, I...Devonette and I were in her house, and her father's men tasered and drugged me. They were holding me captive. I think that Passway wanted

Mom to come to my rescue. The next thing I knew, Devonette had me in a wheelchair and hustled me into a car. She got me out." He paused, gathering his thoughts. There was no need to describe what happened in the lake house. "Then I jumped us back too far, then we went back to her Dad's house, and she went in. I went home and saw Lola had been there. She lost some feathers, and it looked like there was a struggle. I'm afraid they tasered her, too. I thought she might be here, but she isn't, so she must be in the future at Passway's place."

He looked out over the hillside for a moment, regretting the mess he'd created. When he turned back to the two, he had made up his mind. "I'm going to get a rifle and go back. If she is in Passway's power, she will need help fast."

Logan frowned. "Look, Cole, a rifle isn't easy to hide when you're in a city. If you need to be armed, take a pistol and wear a coat so it can't be seen. We'll go with you if you give us some time to get changed."

He addressed the last part to Cole's back. Cole was already inside the door and opening the gun-room door. He selected a 9 mm Glock and then jumped through the in-between to his room, even though it was up the stairs and just a few steps away. There he grabbed a jacket. Logan was right about carrying a rifle. The firepower would be welcome, but it was too difficult to conceal. Someone would see it, and the police would get involved. That was something he didn't want.

Things were bad enough as it was. He had a Deinonychus running around a university town, men who were searching for him, his parents might be involved and might even be in danger, and Devonette was probably getting hell from her father.

He slipped the jacket on and made a wry face in the mirror. It was going to be challenging to go back to school. Maybe he'd inadvertently made the decision he'd been trying to raise the courage to make. He might be stuck studying independently along with Lola. Then his composure broke. He had no guarantee he could find her. If she'd gotten hurt trying to locate him because he'd lied to her, there was no way he could ever live with himself.

There was a clatter on the stairs, and he heard Logan calling, "Cole? Wait for us. We'll be ready in a few minutes."

They needed to change to modern clothes, but he wasn't going to wait. He didn't want anyone else involved. It would only make it worse.

"You stay here. I don't want help," he yelled out the door.

Before the two could answer, he initiated the transition and was in the spirit world. He headed directly to Passway's gazebo a couple of seconds after he'd previously left.

Devonette passed through the patio doors, having just turned away from looking at him before he had jumped back in time. He followed her, trying to plan as he went.

He reached for the doorknob, but the door swung open. Devonette stepped through with a frown.

"Cole! Don't come in here. I told you to go hang out somewhere for a few hours. I thought you disappeared a few seconds ago, but now you are here again. I know Daddy, and he won't want to see you until I get this straightened out. He'll have you drugged again. What do you think you're doing? I expect you to follow instructions."

"I'm looking for Lola. I think he's got her captive now."

Judging from the look on Devonette's face, that probably hadn't been the right thing to say.

"Who the hell is this Lola? She'd better not be some girlfriend."

"No. She's my, uh, my adopted sister. She's a deinonychus, and she's smart. She talks." How do you explain something like that to anyone? Devonette's face went through a series of expressions. Angry, then puzzled, then angry again.

"You expect me to believe that?" She stopped, then a look of understanding appeared on her face. "Oh. So that was what that thing was. It attacked the boys. I mean James and Randy. That was when I grabbed you, and we got to the car. I didn't see it clearly. I saw something that looked like an ostrich or a big chicken. It was only there for a moment."

"She's not a chicken. She's a raptor, and she's around here somewhere, I'm sure of it." He was still trying to figure out a plan that would allow him to search the house.

Devonette put her hand on his face and stroked his cheek. "Cole, Cole, let me take care of it. You do what I said. Go back to your house or something. I'll deal with Daddy and, if your dinonike, or whatever, is here, I'll find out. I'll call you this evening when I have some privacy."

He started to object, but she shoved at him. "Go, now, before someone sees you." She noticed his jacket for the first time. "And, where did you get that ugly coat? You didn't have it a minute ago. Oh, never mind. Just go!"

He was confused. Maybe the best thing to do was to go home. "Alright. I'm going, but you call me as soon as you have a chance and know something."

"Okay," she said. "Now, go!"

Her eyes widened as he faded into a misty outline, then disappeared.

She whispered, "So, that's how it looks. Daddy will have to have that. That's a given." She smiled a tight smile. "So will I. I can use it as long as I don't have to go back where those monsters live."

Chapter Twenty-Four

Lola

Time seemed to stand still. The room had a light on the ceiling, and it glared in her eyes, but she was too tired to do anything about it other than to keep them closed. Things came to her in bits and pieces. She was lying on her side, which was not her most comfortable position. It made breathing more difficult and always made her wing/arm go numb.

The men that had brought her in checked her bonds once more then left. She paid no attention to them. They weren't essential to her current thoughts. Cole was. So was she. She could see the two of them side-by-side, standing in a clearing. The sun was rising, and a thin layer of ground fog made the light sparkle and shine on the nearest trees. It was so beautiful it made her heart hurt.

She approached him. He was beautiful also, but in a different manner. She wanted him in a way she couldn't describe, but it wasn't possible. It was not something that could happen. Holding her arms out to embrace him, she stopped, startled. They no longer had claws on her fingers, and there were no feathers. They were, she realized with a start, they were human arms.

How had that happened? She looked down. There were two lumps on her chest that got in the way at first, but then she could see her feet. They were human also. She moved toward him, and he opened his arms to accept her.

Someone was prodding at her breast. "This is a prime example of what I assumed one would look like. Of course, I'll know more when I dissect the specimen. You know, of course, that this represents a scientific advance that is invaluable. How long have you had this creature tied here?"

A man answered, "Not long. We just caught it less than an hour ago. As for the value, as you say, Dr. Wells, it is a scientific first. You will have to pay the price I'm asking for before I will release it to you. After that point, you can dissect it, train it to jump through hoops, whatever. I don't care. You understand, though, that I have a fixed price. No negotiating."

"That's the problem, Passway. I've checked my endowments, and you're asking more than I can pay."

"Perhaps the Russians or Chinese would be able to meet my price, then."

"No! No, don't even think such a thing. Just give me until the end of the week to raise more money. I'll contact some donors who are interested in paleontology, and I'm sure they'll come up with the additional funds. I can't allow this opportunity to slip away. You're a patriot, aren't you? You understand that such a discovery would be the crowning achievement for American paleontology?"

The other man laughed. "Patriot? You're incredibly naive for an educated man, Wells. Patriotism is a fiction for fools. Enlightened self-interest will always outlast any misguided sentiments like that. No, I fear you have misjudged me. I'm not a patriot in any sense of the word unless you're referring to my vision for the world. I'm a patriot if you care to call it that, for that vision."

Wells said, "Sorry. It's just that I can't let this opportunity pass."

Passway continued as if Wells hadn't spoken. "Perhaps I am a patriot to a certain extent. At least enough to give you until Thursday to raise funds. After that, I can't promise anything."

The voices faded. Lola opened her eyes. Her muzzle extended in front of her in its usual fashion. She'd been dreaming, perhaps hallucinating from the drug they had given her. Now her mind was working a little more clearly. She wasn't human. She was who she always was.

They had strapped her wing-arms to her sides. They hadn't been able to figure out a better way to immobilize her. Her joints made it difficult to bind them behind her back and directly in front allowed her access with her teeth.

They had wrapped an elastic bandage around her muzzle. It had some give, but not much. What they had forgotten was that her fingers ended in sharp claws. She thought she could hook a finger into the bindings that secured her arms.

The nylon web belt went entirely around her body, securing her arms to her sides and her body to the table. She twisted, and her hand moved enough to allow a claw to hook the webbing. It popped through easily, but the nylon threads were tough and thick. She strained, and some of the threads broke.

The progress encouraged her. She wiggled her fingers, and a few more threads broke. The belt loosened, then went slack. She had done it! She raised her head a bit and felt something around her neck. She hooked her claws into it and cut it free. Now she could look down.

Her feet were strapped to the table also, but that was all that was holding her. A few slashes and they were free.

Lola rolled over and slid off the edge of the table. Her legs wouldn't hold her. They were limp, and she collapsed on the floor, making a soft thump. She lay there, panting, too weak to raise her head.

The cold from the floor seeped into her bones. She thought she could just go to sleep here. Getting free of her bonds was enough of a triumph; now, she could rest. Her head went flat on the tile, and she shut her eyes.

Cole appeared in her mind. "You're being lazy, Lola. I can't love you if you don't help yourself." He looked upset for a moment, then moved away.

She needed to answer him, but she couldn't get the words out. "You will never understand me. We're too different." That thought hurt. She could never tell him something like that.

He was back. "Lola, get up. You have to get free. I do love you. We're soul-mates."

He had said that once, hadn't he? She couldn't remember clearly.

Nevertheless, if Cole wanted her to do something, she would do it. She took a deep breath and lifted her head, then rolled until she was on her breast and stomach. Now, she had to pull her legs under her. Her tail was tangled up with something behind her, but it would follow along. She hoped she hadn't broken any tail feathers in her struggle. That would impact her balance and maneuverability.

There was a moment of disorientation, and then she was standing, leaning against the table for support. Her balance wasn't good. Whatever they'd given her was still in her system.

She lifted her head. There was a window on the other side of the table. She could see a kind of open lattice structure standing by a river across an intervening stretch of lawn. She needed to get out there, but how?

⸻⸻⸻◈⸻⸻⸻

Cole materialized in his living room. The feathers were still on the floor where they had been. He turned around, alarmed at a faint sound.

His mother and father were standing just inside the front door.

"Cole! What is going on?" Kathleen asked.

"Oh, Mom! It's a huge mess. I think Passway has Lola. Devonette got me free, but she's gone back to talk to him. Lola was here, and I think someone captured her. I've got to do something, but Devonette told me to wait until she called. I screwed up completely."

Cadeyrin put his hand on his son's shoulder. "Everyone makes mistakes. Some people try to avoid responsibility for their errors. They never learn from them. Others accept that they made a mistake, and they're the ones who benefit from the experience. They are the ones who attempt to rectify them. I'm disappointed in you for lying to Lola and us, but we'll talk about that later. Now, where do you think they're holding Lola?"

"I'm sure Passway has her. Look over here. These are some of her feathers, and the chair was knocked over. Besides, there is a smudged footprint by the door. The mud probably came from the planting bed outside. I don't know of anyone else who would know to come here. Lola must have jumped in and been ambushed. They captured her before she realized what was happening. Otherwise, there would be a lot more of a mess."

Cadeyrin inspected the footprint closely. "It was a man, probably around two-hundred pounds." He looked up at Cole. "You read the signs well. Most probably, you're right. Passway is likely to have her. The question now is, what will he do with her?"

Kathleen sounded worried when she spoke. "He won't know how much value we put on her. He definitely wouldn't consider that we'd want her back almost as much as we did Cole. Do you think he'll kill her? She hurt his men before."

Cole was wrought up, and his mother's calm analysis caused his temper to flare. "As much as you did me? I value her more than my life. She's unique. If you don't help me get her, I'm going myself."

His father said, "Calm down, Cole. Rushing into this is going to increase the odds of failure. We need to plan before we do something."

That made sense. He nodded in agreement. "I guess you're right. A plan would be good to have." Something occurred to him then. "Oh, besides, we have plenty of time. We can always jump back to when they took her, can't we?"

Kathleen still looked worried. "We have to be careful. You know we can't afford to come too close to prior versions of ourselves. Time has a way of punishing those who do that, and it doesn't care if it's accidental or not."

He reviewed his actions since getting away from Passway. It seemed to have been a long time. The interlude with Devonette had practically wiped the other events out of his mind. After a little, he said, "No one was here at that time. Lola attacked Devonette's bodyguards in Passway's house. She told me that after she got me into the car. Then I recovered enough to jump us out, but I made a mistake. I think I went way back into the Miocene. We didn't stay there."

He edited the next part. "I brought her back to the lakefront house until I recovered. Then she had me take her to her dad's house. I watched her go in, then came here. When I found Lola's feathers, I went back and asked Logan, then came back here. I don't think I've been gone for more than five minutes. You must have just missed me when you came in."

She said, "Hmm. Yes, we had just come inside when you appeared. We jumped out of Passway's house about..." She looked at her watch. "Thirty-three minutes and twenty seconds ago. We went home, too. Logan was upset. You took off without him and Serensaa."

Cadeyrin took up the story. "I told him to stay there. This rapid jumping gets complicated enough with just the three of us to keep track of. Besides, Lola has figured out how to jump in time, also."

Kathleen said, "Let's assume that Lola jumped here immediately after she left Passway's place. She disappeared while we were still there, so that gives her an additional four minutes or so. I didn't notice precisely when we left ourselves. She could have come directly here. That would mean that we have a thirty-five-minute window in which she could have been grabbed. The problem is that it's too short to be jumping in and out. I've made moves of a second before, but the risk is quite high. A little miscalculation could mean that we lose our memories, or worse."

Cole hadn't realized that there was that kind of problem. "What can we do, then?"

Cadeyrin checked the chamber of the pistol he was carrying and let it close with a click for an answer. "We check out Passway's place first. If she's not there, we'll have to come back here and watch for when they take her out. We can do that from across the street and minimize our risk, but we've got to make sure we get away from the area before we came in a few minutes ago."

It was confusing, but he knew what his dad meant. "Okay. I was in a room that had a window. I couldn't see out, though, so that's not helpful. How do we find her at Passway's? That place must have fifty rooms or more. It's big."

Kathleen said, "We go back to just after we left. I can't cut it too close since I'm not sure when that was exactly. We'll watch from outside. Maybe across the street. We can find a place where we can see their vehicle when they take her through the gate. Then we can jump in and, hopefully, intercept the car on the drive and get her out." She looked at her husband. "That work for you?"

Cadeyrin nodded. "Yes. Do you want to do the jump? You're more accurate than me."

The three held hands, and the room was suddenly vacant. There was only a slight mist in the air where they had been.

———◆◇◆———

There was no good place to watch from across the street. None of the homes there offered any decent cover. As a result, the three took up the watch at a convenience store about a half-mile away. The main road intersected with the road leading to Passway's mansion at that point. It was the obvious route if the car carrying Lola came directly from Cole's home.

They waited inside, one of them pretending to inspect the selection of nuts and chips by the window while the other two looked at other items. A black van came by about ten minutes after they'd placed themselves inside. It made the turn then accelerated quickly down the empty street.

Kathleen had been watching at that point. She called them over. "They just went by. Let's go to the bathroom and jump out."

It took fifteen minutes before the clerk, puzzled about what the three people were doing in the restroom for so long, opened the door. She was expecting almost anything, having interrupted people taking drugs, having sex, and fighting. The room was empty, and that was mildly perplexing. "They must have left when I was doing something, but how?" she asked herself. A group of rowdy young men came in, and her attention immediately switched to them. They looked like the type that always tried to shoplift.

———◆◇◆———

They watched the black van turn into Passway's drive. It halted while the barred gates opened, then it drove through. The gates were swinging shut when Cole asked, "Aren't we going in?"

His father raised his hand in a hunting signal that meant 'Quiet.' Cole paused and listened. He became aware of a high-pitched humming sound.

Cadeyrin looked puzzled. "It sounds like some large insects. What is it?"

Cole was familiar with the sound. "It's a drone or rather several drones." He pointed. "Look over Passway's place."

There was a swarm of quad-copters flying above the mansion. Some circled out over the gate as they watched.

"We can't sneak in there, Dad. Those things will see us," he said.

Cadeyrin, still puzzled, asked, "Do they have eyes? They look mechanical."

Kathleen put her hand on his shoulder. "They are mechanical, Dear. They also have video cameras linked to a central watch station inside the house. If they notice us, someone will set off an alarm. We're going to have trouble with this idea."

Cadeyrin stiffened and pointed silently. A dog-like thing was walking past the inside of the gates, visible through the bars.

Cole swore. "Damn! That's one of those robot dogs. Look! It's got some kind of weapon mounted on it, too."

More of the dog robots were visible back near the house. They were stationary, obviously set in position to guard the approach. It was lucky that there hadn't been any in the back of the house when he brought Devonette home.

Kathleen nodded. "It's as I expected when I saw the copters. Passway has a considerable interest in both AI and military weapons. It looks like he's using some of his products to ensure we don't get in again. Let's go before one of those copters sees us."

She touched them, and they were back in Cole's living room.

He righted the tipped-over chair and sat down. "What do we do now? I haven't a clue. Is there some way to disable those drones? I think I read that there's some kind of transmitter that will interrupt their controlling signals."

She answered, "A spark-gap transmitter should do it, but I'm positive that the copters we saw were autonomous. They have an AI processor and make their own decisions. Interrupting a control signal isn't going to work. Each of them would have to be taken out individually."

Cole considered and discarded several alternatives, then suggested. "Maybe I could phone Devonette and ask her to help."

His parents looked at him. "That's not a bad idea," his mother said. "When you can't surprise your enemy, a direct approach might work. Call her."

He dialed, wondering if she would pick up.

Chapter Twenty-Five

Father and Daughter

S he entered the house, stopped, and looked through the French doors. Cole was gone. He'd followed her orders, at least. He was too independent-minded in some ways. There could be only one dominant person in their relationship, and it was her. She wasn't going to compromise on that.

—◆O◆—

Winston Passway was in his office. The New York financial group was having a melt-down over the cost of petroleum. It impacted his weapons business in several ways, not least of which was the cost of plastics. That was the issue at the moment. They were having difficulty getting materials for a new version of an H-K drone. It was larger and carried either a compact machine gun or a small bomb.

Unfortunately, the production schedule was off due to the inability of the supplier to give them the needed plastic parts. He had directed the NY office to buy more stock in the country's largest pipeline company. That should give him enough leverage to ensure a constant supply of crude oil.

The executive on the other end of the line was trying to explain that it wasn't that simple. The government was planning on shutting down all pipelines in the country under the misapprehension that increased gas prices would force the populace into electric vehicles.

Winston laughed sarcastically. "That's crazy. They must think that there is enough alternate generation capacity to replace gas-fired power plants. It would take years to build enough photo-voltaic generation capacity to do that, and don't suggest wind. It's so cost-inefficient that we'd run out of money and land for the turbines long before we got enough electricity to run the country. I'll tell you what. Call John Wheeling in DC. Tell him that I've got a billion available to donate to key re-election campaigns if they can keep their hands off the pipelines."

Devonette appeared in front of him at that moment. "Don't ask questions, Ed. Just deliver. You know how to do it. Now, I've got to go. Something has come up."

He hung up and raised his eyes to his daughter. She looked pale. She should. "Well. You come slinking back here after what you did? I will give you five minutes to explain why you took that boy out of here. If I'm not satisfied, you're going to regret being born."

"He can travel in time, Daddy. He took me back to prehistoric times. There were monsters back there," she said. She paused dramatically, then continued. "But, the important thing is, he can travel both in time and location. We went from some lake-front house to here in maybe a second or two."

Interested, despite himself, he asked, "What's it like?"

She flinched slightly. "It's not pleasant, but maybe you get used to it. Cole has no trouble doing it. It was so disorienting that I kept my eyes closed when we jumped. I did see him vanish, though. He kind of faded out and disappeared. There was a little misty place in the air where he'd been, but it didn't last. I know that this will be a huge advantage for you. If we can get it, we can easily rule the world."

He tried to suppress a smile. Devonette was definitely his daughter.

"I'm disappointed that you had your eyes closed, but tell me more. How do you propose to get control of the secret?"

She had asked herself the same question repeatedly. It all returned to the fundamental relationship: Cole knew the time-travel secret, and Cole desired her. The equation had become simple in her mind. Cole would have to tell her. That was all.

The problem was getting her father to see it that way.

"Daddy, you know I've always tried to do what you wanted me to do. You said I was to get the secret from him, and I'm working on it." She paused, wrestling a little with having to tell him the details.

"I seduced him. He's already in love with me. Give me a little more time, and I'll have him deliver the secret to us."

Was that the way it had been? She had been every bit as passionate as Cole, but she thought she had been able to keep a little reserve. Sure, he was an amazingly handsome man, and he had aroused both passion and wonderful sensations in her, but she was who she was. She used men. She set them up and dropped them. Wasn't Cole just another victim?

Devonette struggled to justify herself. She could almost feel her mind snap back into old habits. She was the Ice Maiden. She turned that name over in her mind, then giggled. Not a maiden now, that was for sure.

"I can get the secret. You'll see. When I do, we can use it in all sorts of ways. It would be easy to jump in and take everything out of a bank vault, for instance."

Winston frowned. "That's crude and not very profitable. If what you say about this is true, we could go back and buy stocks that would increase in value. We could buy bitcoin at a few dollars each. That's something I missed out on, to my regret. It would be worth billions now."

She nodded eagerly. She hadn't thought of bitcoin. Perhaps she could convince Cole to do that. They could have enough money to live independently. That thought trailed off. No. It would be better if he were out of her life. He made her feel vulnerable, and that was something she detested. Cole had too much power over her. She couldn't be comfortable relying on him. He'd cheat on her, and she'd be just like the dozens of boys she'd destroyed. No. He had to go. Better to do it quickly, too.

"I'll call him and arrange a meeting as soon as I can convince him to give you the secret."

He shook his head. "That may take too long. I want it quickly."

She laughed out loud. "Daddy, that's the best part. It will be quickly. I could take months to convince him and then jump back here tomorrow morning.

You won't have to wait long. You'll see."

He smiled tightly. "Okay. You've convinced me not to punish you. Go ahead and get this for me, and I'll agree that you can drop out of that plebeian university. I'll give you control of the retail group to start. You can't go wrong if you listen to Finch since he's been in retail all his life. You'll learn a lot from him. If you do well, and I know you will, in a year, we'll discuss your taking over the European operation."

He waved her out. "Go on. Get me time-travel. Go."

She stopped a little way down the hall and stared out the window, thinking. How was she going to make this work?

Her phone rang, and she made a face. Probably some solicitor. They had gotten so persistent that cell phones were more of an irritant than anything else. To her satisfaction, it was Cole and not an advertisement for an extended auto warranty. She smiled, her heart speeding. It was showtime. When she answered, her voice was as smooth as honey.

"Hi, Cole. I've got everything arranged. Daddy is going to love meeting you. I told him we were a couple, and he was happy. All we have to do is to help his scientific team with their research."

His answer disrupted her mood.

"Never mind that, Devonette. He is holding Lola somewhere, and I want her freed. Immediately, if not sooner."

A switch flipped in her mind before she could rationally suppress it. He wasn't playing along with the script she'd planned.

"There you go with this Lola thing again! If we're going to be together, Lola is not going to be a part of it. It's just some kind of birdy thing anyway. What's the big deal?"

He was silent for a moment. When he answered, it was as if he were explaining something to a child.

"She is my friend. I grew up with her, and I'm not going to allow her to be held hostage or whatever your father has in mind. I want you to get her out of there like you did me."

"Cole, you listen to me. I've done everything I can to make Daddy happy with the idea of us being together. You'll have to help with the time-travel research, but that's all. I can't just waltz in and get him to release some weird animal because you demand it. It would be different if you had something else to offer – like maybe your Mother's health drug or something. I could use that." Anger flashed through her again. What was he doing valuing some animal above her? Especially when she'd given him what she had.

"Besides, I'm not going to share your affection with a bird," she said, her voice harsh with emotion. She made an effort, and her voice became smooth and seductive again. "You remember how right we are for each other. I've been imagining us in bed again. I can't wait for our next opportunity."

"Devonette, you and I are totally separate from this issue. First, I want you badly. That's a given. Second, I'm not going to divulge any time-travel information or any information about the health drug, as you put it. Both of those things are too easily misused, and someone like your father would be sure to misuse them. The temptation to exploit the power given by either of these would be too much for him."

"Then why you? What do you think you are? Some kind of moralistic superman? You jump through time. Are you exploiting it? Tell me?"

He sighed. "I could exploit it, but I don't see the need. I have everything I want for the most part."

That angered her more. "How about me? You're ignoring me. I need things, and you could help me get them. We could rule the world with just a little work. It'd be easy –"

He interrupted her. "That's just the point. Your father has billions, and he has enough power for any man. Why would I help him get more? I can provide everything you need for a secure, comfortable life if you live with me. We could be happy in the past."

"No, we couldn't. I've got to have everything I'm used to. You know, modern conveniences. I'm not going to be pottying out behind a bush somewhere, fighting off bears, and eating half-cooked moose. I can't live like that."

She was becoming quite impatient with him. It didn't help that she couldn't control herself. Convincing him to release his secrets seemed to be a more and more remote possibility. She drew a shaky breath, then decided to take another tack.

"Cole, I don't want to argue with you. It makes me unhappy." She used her best 'little girl' voice. "Let's meet at my house, and we can discuss it in person. I promise it will be safe. I'll make sure no one interrupts us this time."

She was gratified that he sounded remorseful when he spoke. "I don't want you to be unhappy. I'll come over, but I want you to talk to your dad about Lola. Tell him, if he releases her, I'll see if I can help his scientists with their research. I don't understand Mom's equation well enough to explain it, but there are some things I can tell them that may help."

That was better. She smiled, instantly in a better mood. She hadn't underestimated her appeal. He was hooked like a fish.

"Okay, Darling. I'll talk to him, but I can't make any promises. I don't even know if he has that creature. Besides, he doesn't always do what I ask. He is remarkably stubborn."

"What time do you want me to be there?" he asked.

She looked at her watch. "Let's make it this evening. Say about seven? Okay?"

His voice sounded remote when he answered, "I'll see you then. Tell him not to hurt her, too. Bye."

The phone clicked. She looked at it, trying to control her temper. He had a way of pushing her buttons. He was just too independent. She could...she paused. What was she even thinking? She would dump him as soon as she got what she wanted. Wasn't that her plan?

The memory of their bodies moving together on the bed seemed to say otherwise. She took a deep breath, then said softly, "There are plenty of good-looking men, Devonette. Now that you know what it's like, you can find another one anytime. Mr. Cole can go cool his desire in the past somewhere."

She started toward her suite, then stopped. Maybe it would be better if she knew that Daddy was holding this Lola-bird thingy. She turned and headed toward the room where they had kept Cole captive. Daddy was predictable in one sense. He wouldn't use a different space once he set up a resource, like the detention room. He'd told her that it wasn't economical. He set up systems to be used over and over again. He saw no sense in improvising a new solution when the old one would work.

She stopped in the hall outside the holding room. She'd been thinking over her phone conversation with Cole. It hadn't ended the way she'd wanted. Cole had seemed barely civil. She wanted him to be in love with her. If her plan worked, they'd share her bed tonight, and, she admitted to herself, she really wanted it to work.

She might have been more alluring than she had been. It wouldn't hurt to call him back. It would only take a couple of minutes.

She hit the call-back button and listened to the phone ring. Cole answered after the fifth ring, just as she was beginning to fear he didn't want to talk to her.

"Yes, Devonette?"

"Cole, I'm under a lot of stress. Dealing with my father is almost impossible in the best of times. Losing you made him extremely angry with me."

He made a non-committal sound, so she continued.

"What I'm trying to say is, I'm sorry if I took it out on you. It wasn't something I wanted to do. It just happened. I really, really want to see you. We can have all night. Oh, and just so you know that I'm sorry, I'm checking to see if he has Lola as we speak. I'm outside the room where he had you held. If she's anywhere, she's in here."

His response was excited. "Can you check now? I'd like to know if she's there. If she is, can you get her out?"

Devonette made a disgusted face. He was really boring her with this hang-up on that overgrown chicken. She'd have to do a professional job of acting.

"I'll have to hang up before I go in. There's a guard circuit that won't allow electronics to come through the door. But, I'll call you as soon as I can to let you know if she's there. I'll get her out if I can, too."

His voice was softer now. "Thank you, Devonette. I'm glad you're there and on my side. I'll see you at your place later."

She changed her tone to her most seductive one. "Okay, Cole. I'll do what I can. I can't wait to get you in bed. I'm ready to rip your clothes off right now. I want more of what we did. A lot more. I love you." With that, she clicked off, put her phone in her pocket, and turned to the door.

Inside the room, Lola was trying to decide whether to kill the woman when she came in or just lie back down on the bed and let them kill her or whatever they wanted to do. Her hearing was keen, and she'd listened to the whole conversation with a horrified and sinking feeling in her heart.

It was true. This woman might be Cole's mate in this future time. Maybe this woman was the one he loved, the one who would have his chicks. She had been deceiving herself. He didn't love her. He loved the woman who had just promised to mate with him. Her mind reeled in anguish. She wanted to scream and kill something, preferably the woman on the other side of the door, but Cole loved the woman. She couldn't do that to him.

She looked around frantically. There was nowhere to hide. She wasn't going to let that scientist cut her into pieces either. She closed her eyes and made an effort to overcome the vertigo caused by the drug. After a moment, she saw the pathway and slipped into the spirit world. She'd go back to the Pleistocene but not to the human compound. She would find Aunt Fancy and maybe take one of the unattached males as a mate. She'd never go back to see any of the humans.

That thought hurt, but it also gave her a slight feeling of satisfaction. They'd see that she didn't need them. It was a bitter kind of revenge, but it was all she had.

Somehow she knew precisely where to find Fancy. Perhaps her drugged state allowed her to trace her aunt. Serensaa had spoken of always being able to find Logan in the spirit world. She must have gotten the same ability from the old Sasquatch.

When she arrived back in the real world, she was in a grove of trees, standing beside Fancy, who was obviously hiding in ambush.

Fancy jumped, then said, "Stay still, Chicky. We hunts. Game come soon."

⚫

Devonette opened the door. There was a not-unpleasant smell of something like dry grass in the room, but otherwise, it was empty. She started to leave but noticed the severed restraining straps on the bed.

"God! I hope he doesn't blame me for this, too," she whispered. Her first urge was to get back to her suite and pretend she didn't know anything about it, but then she remembered there would be cameras recording the door and anything that happened in the room.

Devonette sighed in resignation, then called her father. He wasn't going to be happy.

Chapter Twenty-Six

Different Females

Devonette had been right. Her father was definitely unhappy.

"You little idiot! I instructed you to get the time-travel secret for me, not to mention their longevity drug. What do you do? You set that boy free, so I have zero leverage over that Whitby woman. Now you tell me the deinonychus is missing and then act like I'm supposed to believe that you didn't have a hand in that, too?"

He was in one of his negative moods. Normally, she'd have flounced out at that point. He usually got over being mad at her more quickly if left to himself. This time, she couldn't use that ploy.

"Yes, but Daddy, I've got that boy on a string. He's hooked. I'm positive I can get him to tell me what you need. He's already promised to help your research team. He just wanted the dino-thing set free. It couldn't help with the time-travel anyway. It's just a bird."

He looked at her like he couldn't believe she was that stupid. What had she said wrong?

"You said get the formula for you. I'm about to get it, and you're treating me like crap. I didn't do anything with that overgrown chicken. It wasn't there when I opened the door. The restraining straps were torn. It must be stronger than you thought, or maybe it had some help. Someone on the staff, most likely."

He shook his head. "Devonette, now you listen to me. I've got a deal to deliver that overgrown chicken, as you picturesquely put it, in exchange for a quarter-billion dollars. That's not chicken feed, even for me. Did you say that the boy would help us if we let it go free? Now, it is free somewhere, and we've lost that leverage, too. How are you going to make up for those two setbacks?"

That wasn't fair. Neither of those was her fault. "I'm going to convince Cole to give me the formula. That should be worth more than the bird. You can send a team back to where the dinonike came from with the formula and get more. Just don't ask me to go back there. It's too dangerous."

He sighed. "You have a point. The time formula will actually make a quarter-billion seem like chicken feed. So, you think you can get it from him? How do you propose to do that? And, when?"

She could feel her face getting hot. She was probably blushing.

He looked at her and said, "It appears that you do have the ability to feel embarrassed. I didn't think you did. You're going to seduce him and hope that the charms of your body will convince him to spill the secret. It wouldn't work with many men. Not nearly good enough payment for anyone with sense. Let's hope that he's not one of them."

She was so angry that she was shaking. "You don't know! It's wonderful. He's so in love with me, he'll tell me. You'll see!"

He shook his head in amusement. "One woman is much like another for physical purposes. They can all have sex." He smiled grimly. "However, I'll give you this. You're better looking than most of them. Maybe he will tell you, but when? I'm in a hurry."

"Tonight! We're meeting at my place tonight." Belatedly, she thought to add, "And, I don't want any interference. Keep your mercenaries away from us. It will work best if we're left alone."

He nodded, then said, "You had better be correct. Don't come back without the formula." He turned to some papers lying on his desk and began to read them.

She stomped out. He didn't respect her, and he was treating her worse than he'd ever done before. For a penny, she'd... she'd...ohhh! She smiled to herself, a tight, cruel smile. She'd have the formula, and nothing said she had to give it to Mr. Winston Passway. No, indeed. If it was as valuable as he said, she could use the money as well as he could.

She strode down the hall, thinking. She could even keep Cole around for a while, at least, until she grew tired of him. Daddy would just have to earn his money with those irritating drones.

A robot dog was standing in the foyer. She kicked it as she passed. It staggered slightly but recovered and turned its weapon on her.

She faced it, angry that it would even consider a reprisal.

"Don't you recognize me, you pile of cheap plastic parts? Your prime directive says to protect me as well as my father. You know that, so don't point that laser at me again, or I'll have you converted to a kitchen blender."

The AI spoke in a masculine voice. "Yes, Miss Devonette. You are confirmed as a protected individual." It resumed its position, monitoring the front door.

She continued past the front door on her way to one of the garages. She'd take her Lambo even if Daddy forbade her to take it near campus. He didn't want the other students to know that she was rich. That was ridiculous. Besides, she'd park it in her garage and show it to Cole. That would impress him. He'd be more willing to cooperate if he got a glimpse of what money could do for a person.

It wasn't long before she was motoring down the access road, her father's ill humor forgotten. Her mind was exclusively on Cole. She was anticipating their next meeting so much that she was practically quivering. However, she didn't notice the contradiction in her mind. She wanted him badly, but she was planning on betrayal. The thought of reconciling her emotions was far from her mind.

The maid was supposed to have cleaned her house this afternoon. The idea of a student having a house-cleaning service didn't strike her as incongruous. If the stupid woman had forgotten to make the bed again, she was going to be sorry. Everything had to be perfect for Cole. After all, this might be his final night with her.

That wasn't a pleasant thought. She wondered exactly how far she'd fallen. The thought of Cole's body made heat flare in the pit of her stomach and caused her heart to quiver. Maybe she should give up on the ice princess image of herself. It might be good to plan on sharing her wealth-to-come with him. He would have to change some of his attitudes, though, but she could make that happen. He'd be willing to do anything for her, especially after tonight.

———◆○◆———

Lola faded back a few steps from her aunt. Fancy had positioned herself behind a thin brush screen that she could quickly push aside. It was only a fair position for an ambush, although it provided a view across and down the open grassland with the sole exception of some trees that blocked the view down to the right.

Lola's instincts kicked in, and she scanned the grassland. There was a clump of willows out there. It probably marked a small spring.

She scrutinized the willows. There! She'd seen a single eye showing. Fancy had seen it, too. Her aunt moved her feet nervously.

That was one thing about Fancy. She was high-strung. She always seemed on the verge of over-reacting, and sometimes her nerves got the better of her. She'd been known to blow up ambushes by rushing out prematurely. Lola hoped that wouldn't happen this time. Fancy tended to blame others when she screwed up, and Lola didn't want that to fall on her.

Fancy's mate was out there in the willows. He'd have a slightly better view since the treeline faded back in a broad curve that provided cover for anything that approached near the edge of the grassland. The appearance of his eye signified that he'd seen something.

Lola waited, amusing herself by trying to guess the identity of the oncoming prey. Based on the location and how they had structured the ambush, it was probably some herd animals. Deer required a different technique. They were most readily caught by locating terrain that served as a funnel that they used to move from their bedding area to some food source. A deer or even a small herd wouldn't walk calmly along outside the treeline. Camels, on the other hand, would. So would bison.

She heard the sound of the oncoming animals, a drumming of hooves. It was a small herd of bison that were moving quickly. Something must have disturbed them recently. Now they were seeking a more secure place. They'd move farther out onto the grassland, where they could keep a lookout for any predators that might be inclined to go after a calf.

Plenty of predators would take bison calves: Bears, lions, saber-tooth cats, or wolves. Dire wolves, too, although they had been scarce in the area for as long as Lola could remember. She'd only seen one, and that was years ago.

The herd had swerved away from the trees and was trotting in the middle of the space between the willows and Fancy's hiding place. That wasn't ideal. While her kind could sprint quickly, they were more like cheetahs because they had no long-distance endurance. They needed to reach their prey quickly, especially something like bison.

Bison were large, dangerous animals that were difficult to kill, sometimes causing an exhausting struggle. If the herd were out that far, neither Fancy's mate nor Fancy would reach them quickly. If they detected the attack soon enough, the bison might bolt out of reach.

Lola plotted her charge. Fancy would undoubtedly run directly out, hoping to reach the bison before they stampeded. Lola looked around. There was plenty of cover here. She backed up farther, then turned and trotted farther down, anticipating the bison herd's path. There was a spot where the treeline extended farther out into the open space. With any luck, the bison would cut close to that point. Lola was counting on it. She'd be there, waiting.

She was in position. The herd was nearing Fancy's location, and the ambush was about to be sprung. Now, all that had to happen was for Fancy's mate to show himself. The bison wouldn't automatically recognize him as dangerous. That was one thing in the ambusher's favor. There was no in-built fear of anything that looked like a deinonychus. They were out of their proper time, and the prey just didn't recognize them.

However, prey animals specialized in being suspicious. If Fancy's mate showed himself, the bison would swerve away from the willows bringing them closer to Fancy. That would give her aunt the chance to attack.

Lola moved out of the trees into the open, careful to keep a line of the brush screening her from the bison. She now had a clear path to run, which gave her a high probability of success, provided the bison came close enough.

She considered herself, her existence, as she waited. She was far more used to working with humans than Fancy or her mate. Could she use the word civilized to describe her state? Domesticated? No, that word carried the connotation of being a possession. She was definitely not anyone's possession. She belonged to herself. That was a sad thought but realistic. She wanted to belong exclusively to Cole.

That was ludicrous. An independent predator paring up with a human. Ha! Fancy would think she was crazy. Still, that could be wrong. Maybe she'd tell her aunt about her desire. Sometimes Fancy did give good advice, despite her habit of making snap judgments.

The bison were passing the willows. There was a stir on that side of the herd. Fancy's mate was trotting slowly toward them. They stopped and looked at him, their eyes wide.

One of the more experienced cows decided he was a threat. It bellowed and began to move on a course that angled closer to the trees. The rest of the herd bunched together, then broke into a run, following the old cow.

Fancy proved true to her excitable nature. She charged out of the bushes far too soon. The bison swerved away from her and sped up, heading directly for Lola's position. Both Fancy and her mate hit their high gears and converged on the flanks of the herd. If they were lucky, they would reach one of the stragglers before their endurance gave out.

Lola readied herself. The herd would pass her line of bushes within a few meters of her position. She looked at them, trying to spot the one she wanted. There! It was a young bull, but something was wrong with its hind leg. It had a slight limp. Not much of one, but the unevenness of its gait was evident to her. That was the one she would target.

The herd had strung out in an extended formation, the faster animals leading the way. This was better for Lola. Her target was falling back through the herd. He couldn't keep up with their pace, and that meant there would be fewer around to help defend him.

Bison were quirky. Sometimes they would all run away from an attack. At other times, they would cluster around, just watching. What she didn't want was the third choice. That was when some of the herd decided to defend the victim. They had sharp horns and outweighed her by more than ten to one. If they attacked, her best action was to run into the trees and try to lose them in the brush.

The limping bull was close. She waited, tensing and relaxing her thighs. At the right moment, she sprinted out. He saw her coming and swerved, but it was too late. She leaped, partly supported by her wing/arms, struck his flank, and ripped downward with her right killing-claw.

She didn't try to cling, but bounced off, propelled by her left foot. Still in the air, she spun and dashed out of the way of the remainder of the herd. The bull had stopped, his intestines dragging on the ground. He blew heavily and lowed. The lead cows turned, trotting back to surround him.

Lola sighed. It was going to be a long time before they left. The stricken bull's hindquarters collapsed, and then he dropped to his side. He was still breathing heavily. The pain must be intense.

Lola's eyes widened. She'd seen Kathleen kill animals, but Kathleen used a rifle and always made sure they died quickly. She had been caught up in the moment, hunting as a deinonychus was designed for hunting. The other aspect of her personality overtook her. She was responsible for the bull's suffering. It wasn't a pleasant thought. What if something like that happened to her or someone she loved? She didn't dare think about that. It would be horrible.

She couldn't take back her action, and now the herd was surrounding the fallen animal, making it impossible to get close enough to rip its throat. It was going to lie there and suffer for possibly hours. She made a low throaty sound. Without considering what she was doing, she trotted to the nearest tree and pushed her forehead against its trunk.

Fancy came trotting up as she leaned against the tree. "You hurts yourself, Lola? You do good. You gots one."

Lola straightened. "We've got to kill it. It's suffering."

Fancy glanced over her shoulder at the milling herd. "No goods, now. Too many cowses. We gots to wait."

Fancy's mate came up, trotting through the trees. He'd sprinted across the open area, entered the tree line, and stayed within as he caught up to them.

He had no English. Fancy hadn't bothered to teach him, and he'd never been too near the house and barn. Lolita had sent him off along with her own mate. They were too feral to trust around humans.

He was not of a mind to wait for the herd to leave, despite Fancy's objection. He made a series of charges toward one side of the clump of agitated bison. The old herd bull acted as if it would charge, but after the third feint by the male, some of the cows took off. The rest followed their lead.

The stricken bull was still breathing when Fancy's mate began to eat. Lola hissed at him, then kicked her killing claw through the bull's throat. Blood welled out, and its eyes slowly lost the light of life. She felt physically ill. She wasn't hungry, anyway, so she retreated to the trees to wait.

After a while, Fancy came up to her. "What wrong, Chicky? You not hurt. You sick?"

Everything suddenly hit her. She staggered to her aunt and tucked her head under Fancy's wing.

"Fancy, I love Cole. I want him for my mate, but I can't have him. He's human, and I'm a killer animal. I can't even be true to my nature. I killed that bison, and it made me sick. I hate what I am. I hate it!"

Fancy pulled her close and made a comforting sound.

"You good Chick, Lola. I know you love Cole. He love you, too. You not human, true. You got to be good at what you are. Cole want that. He not want you to be sad. If you love him, you gots to tell him. If you want him for mate, tell him. I not say you can't do that. Where you get idea it no good? Maybe you not have chicks. Too bad. I see worse things happen than that. You gots work things out for self. Be happy with self. You not going to change to human. Gots to be what you are. Still, you go get Cole, make work best you can."

Lola lifted her head in amazement. Fancy had never impressed her as having that much insight.

Fancy wasn't through speaking. "There always loss and sorrow. That part of life. How you handle sorrow is what important. Take happy parts and make them biggest part of you life. That what life for."

"I will. I'll do what you say, Aunt. Maybe Cole will want a human mate, but I... I'll be his deinonychus mate. I will let him have a human mate, too. I want him to be happy. He told me once that we were soul-mates. That has to be good enough. I have to be near him, or I won't be able to live."

Fancy nosed along Lola's neck, making a caress out of a grooming action.

"You good Chicky. Cole love you, I know. Maybe you share him with human woman. You gots to love her, too. Love her chicks like you own."

Fancy's mate called. Fancy turned her head and looked at him for a moment, then said, "You go find Cole. Tell him what you want do. Make him understand. I think he feel same."

The male called again. Fancy sighed. "Mans. Impatient. I go now. You go Cole. Love you, Lola."

Lola watched her aunt trot over to her mate. They nuzzled each other, then he picked up a still-warm piece of bison in his jaws and offered it to her. Fancy acted surprised as if she wasn't expecting him to share, then she took it from him and swallowed it whole. The two pressed against each other in affection.

A warm feeling suffused Lola. Her aunt was a remarkable individual, and she'd made Lola's problem seem solvable. Maybe they couldn't physically mate, but she would make sure that Cole knew he was her only choice. They'd figure out their relationship as they went along.

She shut her eyes and slipped into the spirit world. She would find Cole and tell him. She was sure that he'd know what to do.

A belated thought occurred to her. What if he was already at Devonette's house? She had no idea where that was. Perhaps she could find it if she tracked the girl from her father's mansion. That would require a change of her planned destination, but it would be the best chance.

She had a vague idea that there were maps and that houses had some sort of physical address. That only made sense from her prior readings, but how to access such things was knowledge that hadn't been covered in the books she'd read. Humans would know, but no human would be likely to speak to her in this modern time.

The mansion, though. That was a different story. She knew where it was. She'd escaped from it, so she could go back. How she knew its location wasn't precisely clear to her. The place was where it was. She seemed to know how to get there automatically.

The last time she'd been there, she'd been drugged, and Devonette had been outside the door. She'd need to go to the point immediately after she had first left the room in which she was being held. Devonette would still be inside, but she had told Cole to meet her at her own house. It followed from that statement that she would leave and probably take a car to her house. Lola knew she could track the girl's automobile the same way she had before.

She changed direction accordingly, then recoiled in shock. Her action had resulted in the time-storm that she'd encountered before having somehow moved from a remote presence into a threatening maelstrom attempting to suck her in. Maybe the lack of a clear-cut destination held firmly in her mind had brought it closer. She didn't know. The storm was a whirling mass of black, roiling clouds, and it gave off a maleficent aura, one of infinite power with no concern for an entity of her tiny size.

She swerved away instinctively, but that held its danger. She was losing focus on her intended destination. She tried to circumnavigate the storm. It appeared between her and where/when she wanted to go. It wobbled and swung in front of her. She stopped, hanging in the spirit world, wondering how she would get out of this mess.

She backtracked toward the stone house, hoping that the storm would go back to where it had been. It seemed to be farther away one moment and then close to her position the next.

Lola took a deep breath and tried to control her fear. The storm could capture her, and she might not be able to get out without help. How had she gotten into this mess? It occurred to her that she hadn't maintained a strict focus on her destination. Perhaps wandering around or changing one's mind in this strange environment led to problems. That realization made her feel more in control. She would be alright if she could keep her destination firmly in her mental vision. She would find and follow Devonette, then wait until Cole showed up. Then she would tell him what she had concluded. The storm would have to leave her alone. She was determined, and speaking to Cole was the most important thing to her at the moment. She began to look for the path to Passway's mansion. It was there in the middle distance. Abruptly, the path was clear, and she started along it.

The storm was still nearby, and she felt a physical drag pulling her in that direction. Lola wrenched herself back on course with immense effort. She was suddenly free and heading to where she wanted. She materialized a few moments later, next to a house down the street from the mansion.

Shaken, she checked herself. No parts were missing, and her feathers weren't even disarranged. The time-storm was frightening, but it was non-physical. She thought about the Old Sasquatch pulling her back from it. What had he communicated to her? Something about those who go in not coming out, or was it not coming out the same as they were when they had entered?

She mentally shrugged. It wasn't important now. She had to track Devonette. She looked down the street and saw the gates to the estate swing open. Her timing was perfect, despite the storm.

Lola Takes Action

Cadeyrin looked at his son. Cole was as tall as him, and while the boy didn't have the same mature muscle mass, he was well-built and strong. Probably stronger than the majority of modern men.

"Okay. Here's what we're going to do. Your mother will stay here. Cole, you meet with Devonette. See what she knows. While you do that, I will sneak into Passway's house and see if I can find Lola. I can –"

Kathleen interrupted. "No, you don't, Mister. If you're going in there, I'm going too. Just try and stop me. You know you can't."

Cadeyrin looked sheepish. "No, I can't. That's right, but I want you to stay here where it's safe."

She shook her head. "Not going to do it. Besides, I'm better than you at popping in and out of the in-between. We'll go in quickly, fade in and out, and see what we can see. Meanwhile, Cole, you find out what you can, and don't be careless. You let them capture you before. Don't get distracted and do it again. I know she's pretty, but you've got to keep your guard up. Understand?"

Gods, his parents! The next thing Mom would probably tell him was not to get Devonette pregnant or something. It was embarrassing.

"Mom! I'm an adult. I'm smart enough not to get caught again. I'll talk to Devonette and get her to understand that Lola isn't part of any deal."

Kathleen cocked her head and looked at him critically. "You have my permission to tell her that I'll release a new drug we derived from the red paste to her father's scientists. We already have a patent on it, but they can probably modify it without making it ineffective. If they do, they'll have a competing product. Let's hope that's enough for him. But, you understand! Under no circumstances am I going to release the time equation. It's too disruptive and will confer too much power to him."

Without thinking about it, he objected, "We use it, don't we?"

She shook her head. "Yes, but he will misuse it. I've used it to cheat in getting funds. It's easy to do. I don't feel good about that, but we have to have funding. However, I will never use it to gain personal power. Passway will. That's all he wants. He'll make life miserable for everyone on the face of the earth, and he'll enjoy doing it. That's the kind of person he is."

Cole nodded slowly. "Okay. I can do that. I'll be careful."

Inside, he was wondering if he and Devonette could make love again. He'd check her house and make sure that no one would ambush him. No! Better than that. He'd take her to the lake house. That way, they couldn't be ambushed. He could bring her back to her own house within a second of them leaving. He'd have to figure a time when the lake house was vacant before he and Devonette were born. If he took that path, there would be no possibility of a paradox.

"Mom, didn't you once tell me that your lake place was vacant for several years before you bought it?"

She looked at him strangely. "It was, Cole, but why are you asking?"

"Oh, it was just a random thought. I was thinking about it the other day and wondered how you were able to move right in after you bought it."

"It was vacant for over a year before I got it. I suppose I should have sold the place, but it's peaceful, and I like the lake."

Cadeyrin said, "Peaceful, as long as the government leaves us alone."

"Yes. But, it seems that they've decided they can't make any progress with me. They dropped the time research, and I heard they sold some aspects of it." A speculative look came over her face. "Maybe that's why Passway wants the equation. He's got enough money and clout to get the government to give him their research project. I'll bet that's what he's done."

Cadeyrin looked grave. "That might mean that we'll have to deal with Passway before we can be secure. The government was partly successful. Passway could send another strike force to attack us."

Kathleen nodded, "Maybe, but they don't know when we live. We moved back in time thousands of years after their first raid. They'd have to be able to track us."

He nodded and said, "Remember Kenny?"

She made a face. "I was trying to forget. I wasn't happy about his death. He was as much of a victim of our enemies as we were."

"Yes, but he could track us. Who's to say that Passway doesn't have someone else that can do that?"

"If he did, don't you think he would have already come after us?"

Cadeyrin looked thoughtful, then said, "All things are possible given enough time. He might be sending men right now."

She waved her hand negatively. "We can't worry about that right now. Let's concentrate on the problem at hand. Now, Cole, you keep a grip on yourself. Watch for ambushes, and find out where they have Lola. Don't worry about us. Just do your part."

Cadeyrin said, "Before we go, I'm going to take a nap." He stretched and yawned. "There's plenty of time."

Cole shook his head. His father had stated the obvious. They could wait a year in the Pleistocene, and he could still make his appointment with Devonette with no problem.

He said, "You go and nap, Dad. I'm going ahead. I feel like I have to take action, and I wouldn't be able to rest, anyway."

Cadeyrin said, "Be careful."

Cole moved into the in-between world, heading toward his own house in the future.

Devonette drove just above the speed limit, with her foot deliberately light on the accelerator. The Lamborghini always seemed like it wanted to speed. It was an eye-catching vehicle, and she loved to drive it, primarily because of all of the head-turning it drew. Even sitting at a stoplight, it was the center of attention. The engine was loud when driving, but it wasn't much softer when simply idling.

What Devonette did not notice was that she was being trailed. Lola followed her, jumping from one hiding place to the next along the route.

It was easy, except for one section of two miles with no roadside cover and no convenient houses to move behind or beside. Lola paused at the beginning of the space, wondering if she dared jump into the open. She would be easily visible, and perhaps Devonette would look in her rear-view mirror at the wrong time. She wasn't sure if the girl could do anything about her following, but she didn't want to be seen. It would complicate things at the very least.

Inspiration struck her. Her wing/arms and tail weren't adequate for flying. The best she could do was glide for a short distance when she jumped. She looked up. She could glide downward and hold herself in a stable position with enough height. She could glide until her altitude was too low, then she could slip into the spirit world to regain altitude or land somewhere she could not be seen. If she stayed high enough, no human would be likely to notice her. Their eyes weren't designed for distance vision the way hers were.

She blinked and came out ten-thousand feet over the Lamborghini. She wobbled violently for a moment, then regained her balance. She hadn't thought of this trick before, but it was fun. Her wings didn't support her very well, but they sufficed to allow her to glide downward in a controlled descent.

From this height, she could see that the open space would come to an end before she was too low. There were plenty of trees and hedges along the way from that point on. She would be able to resume tracking jumps along the ground.

A few minutes later, the car pulled into a drive, then entered the garage at the back of the house. Lola watched from some overgrown foundation plantings across the street, keeping her head low. This was Devonette's house, then.

The girl exited the garage, then walked across the drive and entered the house as she watched. A glance at the sun indicated that it would be some hours before Cole was due to arrive. Maybe she could find him at his own house, or perhaps he had gone back to the Pleistocene.

It was irritating, not knowing where he was, and it was even worse, not knowing when he was wherever it was that he was. Lola shrank back against the foundation, crouching low. Some students were passing by, talking as they went toward campus. She'd have to be careful not to be seen.

Maybe it would be better to wait in Cole's house, where she'd have a chance to intercept him. She was impatient to tell him what she'd decided. She dreaded how he might respond, but a portion of her heart told her that there was a reason to hope, too.

What if he goes home first, and they're waiting for him there? That was a possibility that hadn't occurred to her until now. If she waited at his house, she could disrupt any attempt by their enemies to capture him again. What if she went there now and ran into them? If Passway had already set an ambush there, would they be able to capture her instead?

She groaned. Thinking through the possibilities made her head hurt. Perhaps it was better to be what she was – a fierce predator. She shut her eyes, slipped between, and came out into Cole's bedroom.

As far as she knew, there was no sound associated with exiting the spirit-world, but she had staggered slightly on entry. It was sometimes difficult to get oriented. Her claws had made a slight clicking sound against the leg of a dresser. She stood still, hoping no one had heard the noise.

Listen. Just quit thinking and listen. You're a predator, so be one, she thought.

She expanded her senses gradually. The human world was full of sounds. How they kept their sanity was a marvel. She was used to the wilderness, where the wind was often the only sound. She could hear the sound of distant music, people talking as they walked down the street, passing automobiles, and then there was something that frightened her.

A horrible thing was coming. It was distant but approached quickly. Judging from the resounding thumping, it was huge, but why it was making that odd sound was beyond her. She quivered, trying to control the instinct to flee. It was outside; then it was past. She suddenly recognized that it was an automobile with some kind of booming music coming from it. How in the world did the human driver avoid injuring his hearing? The deep thumps had practically made her teeth rattle. Humans did so many weird things that she didn't have the background to understand. They must be crazy. That was the only explanation.

No, Cole isn't crazy. None of the people she knew were crazy. They treated her in a loving way and were sensible. They didn't listen to huge, thumping, noisy music. They had sensitive hearing, although it was not as good as hers. They were good hunters. They were people to her, just as her mother and aunt were persons. The problem was that the people of this future human world had separated themselves from the natural world. They lived in an artificial environment and enjoyed that more than the real world. They didn't hunt. She understood they got food from domesticated animals and plants. Most of them barely knew how to prepare their own food.

She didn't do much preparation either. It was her nature to enjoy raw meat. The most preparation she had to do was to kill something. So, maybe it was something different that affected the people.

She could understand houses. Her people had buildings. After all, a house was a sort of human-made cave. Caves were natural, but they were uncomfortable. Houses were designed for comfort and were much nicer than caves. Yet, the modern world had little space for wilderness. The vast stretch she had glided over was the only area she'd seen that wasn't filled with a patchwork of houses.

It struck her that humans might have separated themselves from the natural world because they had no natural weapons. Their teeth weren't good for defense or attack, and their claws were pathetically soft and useless. Their skin was thin and provided only a little protection. Perhaps their separation was because they felt helpless and wanted to be safe. As far as she could determine, humankinds' main advantage was their intelligence.

But, I'm intelligent just like them, she thought. What's the difference? It could be that my kind didn't have to develop language beyond enough signals to coordinate hunting. We didn't have to develop weapons. Our claws allow us to kill just about anything that poses a threat. Maybe it's also because we never learned to cooperate beyond small family groups. Humans have massive and bloody wars. We don't fight on that scale when we do fight each other. We fight mostly over mates, only individually, not in groups. It's odd. What makes them so different? Why do they act crazy when they're living in big groups?

Maybe it was the very density, the crowding of the human population, that made them act in what she considered irrational ways. They probably didn't even think they were irrational. It must be that she simply didn't understand their way of thought. She'd have to do more reading on the subject when she returned home.

That thought led to another. Would she return home? Back to the compound, to the library full of books and knowledge? What if Cole rejected her completely? That idea was terrible. She wouldn't want any of the humans to even look at her if that happened. They might hate her for thinking she could keep his interest, or, worse yet, they might pity her like an animal that tried to rise to their level. She felt frantic inside. If there had been something to attack, she wouldn't have hesitated.

There! An inner voice spoke in criticism. You get depressed, and your only way to cope is by killing. Humans don't do that. She answered her thought with a question: Do they? Do they kill from frustration or depression? She thought they would sometimes do the same thing. That wasn't the difference between them and her.

How about their belief in a spiritual relationship? She'd read about some of the human religions. The members of her species had not thought about anything like that. She knew that her mother felt that the force of nature was a living spirit, that it would help her be successful in the hunt, but Lolita never asked for its help. She just accepted that it was there and acted in harmony with it as best she could.

None of her thoughts offered a solution to the difference between her and a human. There was the physical difference, of course, but mentally or spiritually? It was puzzling.

She thought about the religion issue again. Humans had decided that they were formed in their creator's image, and that was why they were unique. Perhaps it did, but what if the creator created everything? Would that mean that she was also formed in its image? What was its nature? Life was different than inert matter. Maybe that was the creator's nature. It was life and gave birth to life. In that framework, she and Cole were similar. Could it be that the in-between world, the spirit-world through which she and he traveled in time, was the base state of all life? Did it hold the secret to creation?

Such thoughts were alien and frustrating since there seemed to be no clear-cut answer. She wanted to discuss it with Cole, but that would have to wait.

She came back to herself with a jolt. The noisy environment was so distracting for her that she'd allowed her mind to wander in a fugue. If she did that in the wilderness, she'd end up as prey rather than the predator she was. It was dangerous. Here is his house, though. There was nothing that could get at her. She was safe. That very safety had led her into thought patterns that were not normal for her. Perhaps that was the problem with humans. They were so safety-oriented that they didn't take risks and thought odd thoughts out of boredom.

Lola sighed deeply. It was a puzzle to her. She thought she was equal to humans, but she couldn't understand them. Did they understand themselves? She wondered about that. Sometimes it seemed they did not know their nature any better than she.

She was wandering again. Her problem was so consuming that she could barely focus. She shook her head and tried to think about the immediate business.

She had been listening to see if there was anyone in the house. She'd gotten entirely off target and hadn't been paying attention for the past several moments.

After a minute, she felt sure that the place was vacant. There might be a video camera hidden somewhere, though. She scanned the room. Nothing visible. Maybe it's okay.

She moved to the door and peeked down the hall into the living room. There was a tiny reddish spark against the far wall. It was evident to her superior vision. She saw farther into the infrared than humans. The spark was the lens of a camera.

That meant an enemy had been in the house. They were likely watching and would know she was there if she moved around. Given that Passway wanted to sell her for medical experiments or something even worse, she would have to stay in the bedroom to avoid them seeing her.

That was okay. If Cole came home, he would probably come to the bedroom. If he didn't, she could make a slight sound, and he'd come to investigate. When he came in, what would she say?

"Hi, Cole. I was held captive, and I overheard your woman telling you she wanted to meet you tonight for mating." She shuddered. That was a poor way to start.

The clock on the dresser showed that it was late in the afternoon. If Cole didn't come in the next thirty minutes or so, she would go back to Devonette's to watch for him there. Hiding in his bedroom was good, but she'd have to be there to interrupt what she thought would be a mating act. She wanted to have her chance before he took that step.

Humans seemed to pair for life. She didn't know how they became mated and bonded pairs, but she thought the sexual act was a likely starting place. She would never do that with a male until she had entirely accepted him and they had bonded. Cadeyrin and Kathleen gave every indication of being committed to each other, but perhaps modern humans were different.

Her desire protested this thought. Cole isn't. He wouldn't do that before he had decided to stay with a woman for life, would he? She didn't know, and it made her crazy trying to guess. She couldn't understand humans because she wasn't one. That was the only rational thought she had, and it was no comfort at all.

The clock showed that she had waited beyond when she thought she should. She started to go but then stopped, listening intently.

A slight noise had interrupted her thoughts. A lock had clicked somewhere. She hadn't examined the entire house when she'd been here before and didn't know where all of the entrances were, but it hadn't been the front door.

There were footsteps in the kitchen, then a man's voice.

"Let's wait in the living room. He'll most likely come in the front door, and we can grab him then. What do you think, Jax?"

A second man answered. "Suits me, Kang. I don't know why the boss wants this kid, but whatever he says is what we do. I just wish we'd been the ones to head over to his daughter's place. She's worth watching."

The first voice again. "You best be getting your mind off of that one. That Devonette is way above you. Passway would have you killed if he thought you were looking at her for even a second. Besides, she's a mean one."

"What do you mean, a mean one?" Jax asked.

"She eats men for breakfast and spits them out just as fast. She's what you might call a female bully. I've seen it before. She'll pick a victim, then act sweet to him, but when he gets encouraged and makes a play for her, she'll turn total bitch and make him feel like a fool."

"Ugh. Maybe she isn't what I thought, but she's still a nice piece of flesh. Little young for me, though."

"Like I said, get your mind off her. Safer that way."

The men had moved into the living room and were now seated, facing the front door.

Jax was talking again. "What does the boss want with the kid?"

Kang replied, "That's something that we don't need to worry about. He wants him. He gets him." His voice

turned sarcastic. "You may have noticed that he always gets what he wants. No man stands between him and what he wants, and that means nobody, including you and me."

Jax coughed, then said, "Oh, alright, but if that kid puts up a fuss, I might have to clip him a few times. The boss didn't say we couldn't rough him up a little."

Kang grunted. Apparently, he didn't object to that.

Lola had slipped from the bedroom and was in the hall at the entrance to the living room. These men were here to capture Cole. That was enough to make her feathers stand on end.

There was an electronic snapping sound, and a voice came from the camera. "Kang! Lookout."

Someone had seen her, but it was too late.

She leaped, striking the easy chair with her breast as she extended one leg around and kicked Kang. Her killing claw cut through his throat. He cried out, a burbling scream. She careened off the chair at an angle that brought her into the lap of the other man.

He had his pistol out by that time, but she caught his wrist in her teeth and bit down hard. The man screamed as her teeth bit into the joint. The pistol went off close to her ear, nearly deafening her. In a reflexive defensive motion, she slashed at the man's face with her fingers, leaving a trail of ripped flesh and a ruined eye. He groaned and slumped back in shock.

She started to kill him, but something moved in her, and she relented. She jumped to the floor and backed up, wondering if she had absorbed too many of Kathleen's softer ideas.

Jax was holding one hand to his face, covering his eye, but the other eye was looking at her, wide with fear.

"You come here looking for my Cole. Not a good idea. You tell your master that I could have killed you both."

She glanced at the first man. He had fallen forward out of the chair. There was a pool of blood, but it looked like he had already bled out.

The second man was leaning forward, reaching for his pistol again.

"You touch that, and I'll rip your guts out. Your friend is already dead. A slashed throat will do that. You tell Passway that he had better leave Cole alone. I'll get him too if he doesn't."

The man said nothing. His mouth hung limply open. In shock, she guessed. He was still breathing, so he wasn't dead. She didn't think she had damaged him that badly.

"You go out of here now. I know the camera saw me do this. You two were easy targets. When you're hunting, it's best not to send beginners. They often become the prey."

She had retreated into the hallway as she talked. Once far enough back, she slipped into the bedroom again, then vanished into the spirit world. If they were going to try to ambush Cole at Devonette's house, they were in for a surprise. Her only worry was that she was late and couldn't make it up by jumping back in time. Being at the same time twice was not a good idea. She instinctively understood that was bad.

Chapter Twenty-Eight

Passway

Kathleen and Cadeyrin had armed themselves with pistols and extra magazines. He carried a forty-five, but she preferred a nine-millimeter. It kicked less and was easier to control.

She was going to do the jump, so they moved into contact. Cadeyrin took a moment to put his arms around her and bend down for a kiss.

"I can never get enough of you," he said. "I was so desperate for you to love me when we first met. I felt like I'd never earn your trust."

Kathleen smiled up at him. "I wasn't able to trust anyone. It wasn't just you. Besides, you were some kind of primitive caveman. I was frightened half to death by that saber-tooth that was trying to get me, and I was terrified when you attacked it with only a spear. How'd I know you were the most trustworthy, loving man I'd ever imagined?"

He pulled her closer. "I want you to be extremely careful up there in the future. I sometimes think we're too confident in our time-jumping abilities. We can still be hurt by bullets or captured. It's not like it's never happened."

"Yeah, well, you be careful yourself, you big ape. I couldn't live without you. Now, are you ready to go?"

"Almost. Here, take this first." He extended a small capsule to her.

She looked at it curiously. "More of the red drug? Why?"

Her husband smiled tightly. "Let's just say I don't want to risk something happening to you. You haven't had a chance to see the latest research report yet. The more recent the dose, the higher the recovery potential for any injury. If you get hurt, I want to be sure you heal quickly."

She said, "Sounds good to me." She swallowed the pill, then frowned at him. "Aren't you going to take one?"

"Already did. You didn't notice."

Kathleen straightened. "Okay. That's done, then. Are you ready now?"

"Whenever you are. Let's come out across the street from Passway's mansion. Where we saw the drone, remember? We can jump inside as soon as we see what's happening in the yard."

She calmed her mind and began the transition. As she did, something slipped under her arm. Then they were in the in-between space. Kathleen opened her eyes and looked. Everything was different than everyday reality. In fact, she couldn't have precisely explained how she became aware that Lolita had thrust her head under her arm at the beginning of the jump. Now, there were three of them.

They came out precisely where she'd planned. Lolita's presence hadn't made any difference.

"Lolita! What are you doing coming with us?" she asked.

The little deinonychus said, "My Chicky here somewheres. She maybe need protection. Sides' you need help with bad mans, too. You watch, I come 'long to eat their liver."

Cadeyrin shook his head negatively, then reached into his shirt pocket. "Here, Lolita. Swallow this."

She inspected the pill with one eye. "What this?"

"Just swallow it, or we'll have to take you back."

She took it from his palm carefully, then swallowed.

Kathleen said, "Okay. You can stay with us, but be a good team member. Don't go running off where I can't reach you if we need to jump out of here. We're expecting a lot of danger over there in that big house."

Lolita made a chucking sound deep in her throat. "That danger here...it us. They best watches out."

Cadeyrin made a slight hissing sound, and the two stopped talking and looked around.

There was a thin whining, buzzing sound as two drones flew across the drive behind the gate.

He whispered. "See those flying things, Lolita? They have eyes and can see us. We need to be aware that they can be above us at any time."

She hissed back, "They too noisy. No sneak up on me with that noise."

"Yes, but there are other kinds, too. Some on the ground with four legs. That kind has guns, so we have to be careful," Kathleen said.

Lolita said nothing, but her muscles were quivering. Her feathers were beginning to rise. The two humans looked at each other. She was on the verge of attack right now. Controlling her once they were inside the house would be difficult.

Kathleen touched both of her companions, then transitioned into the in-between space. She moved deliberately, searching for the precise location of Passway's office.

The office appeared around them as they came back into the normal world. The room was dark and empty. Passway wasn't there.

Cadeyrin said, "We'll have to search elsewhere. I'll check the hallway. If it's empty, we can try some other rooms. Lolita, smell the chair behind the desk."

She jerked away from the door as he spoke to her. "What? Chair? He sit in it?"

"Yes. It's his chair. See if you can learn his scent. When we're in the hall, it will be partly masked by the other odors in the house, but maybe you can find him."

She looked dubious. "I tries." She trotted to the chair and took several long whiffs.

"Phew! He wear strong perfume. Easy to find, if he still wear it." She blew air from her nostrils in a snort. "Too stinky. Why he do that?"

Kathleen tried to explain. "He thinks that it might make him more attractive."

Cadeyrin shook his head. "No. It's a power thing. He wears a dominant scent to show he's the boss. He doesn't care about attractiveness as long as people defer to his status."

She looked at him. Her husband was a continual wonder. His insight into human behavior was considerable. What made it remarkable was that he understood that even modern men responded in much the same way as they had during the last ice age.

On the other hand, Lolita didn't really care why Passway wore the odor. She was already at the door, trying to figure a way to open it silently.

"I go finds. Open door now."

Cadeyrin opened it enough to scan the immediate area outside. There was nothing there, so he opened it more and looked down the hall.

"It's empty. Let's go. Kathleen, you stay behind me and check behind us often. Lolita, do you smell him anywhere?"

She sniffed twice, walked forward a bit, then said, "He go this way. Smell stronger here."

The hallway opened into a large room with several chairs and two couches. It, too, was empty.

Lolita didn't pause. She trotted directly across to a door on the far wall, then waited for them to open it.

Beyond was another hall with closed doors on both sides. Lolita moved at a steady pace, checking each door as she passed. None of them caught her attention. The hall ended with a closed door.

Cadeyrin hesitated. "I think the foyer is just beyond here. There will be a guard or guards there. We'll have to subdue them quietly."

Kathleen moved forward and placed her hands on both of them. "No. I can jump us to another room. There has to be one directly opposite this door, so we'll go there and look. We shouldn't start a fight that will bring down all his forces on us."

He nodded in agreement. She didn't wait but took them into the in-between immediately. Coming out was slower. She held them just at the transition point, trying to sense what lay beyond. When they materialized, they were in a two-story room with shelves and shelves of linens.

Kathleen's eyes opened wide. "I never dreamed that someone would have this many sheets. Look, they're all different colors, and most of them look new. Oh. There's a press to iron them. This is magnificent."

Cadeyrin took in the room and then whispered impatiently, "We have enough sheets. This is the result of not caring how money is spent." He turned and opened the door.

There was a hall beyond. Spaced along the hall were paintings and sculptures of nude women, some in subservient poses. Kathleen looked at one of the paintings in the dim light. It was quite graphic, and she could feel herself blushing.

There was only one conclusion. They were close to Passway's bedroom. Why else the lavish display?

Lolita came out of the linen room and sniffed loudly, then said quietly, "Sheets'es tickle nose. Strong scent in there." Immediately after that observation, she stiffened in much the manner of a bird dog that had picked up the scent of a pheasant. She took two steps one way, then turned and went back.

"He this direction. Smell stronger. Must be close."

The hall turned a corner. Beyond was a wider area with ornate double doors. Cadeyrin moved forward and listened, one ear pressed against a door panel. "Some man is talking in there. He is probably speaking on the phone since I can only hear one person. Let's wait until he stops. No sense giving him the chance to alert someone else on the phone."

He put his head against the door again. After thirty seconds, he nodded, then jerked the door open and jumped through.

———— ◆◇◆ ————

The room beyond was a bedroom that also served as a private office. Passway was sitting at a desk, inspecting a spreadsheet on a computer screen. He turned as Cadeyrin burst through the door.

He didn't seem too surprised. "Mr. Caveman. I was expecting you." His eyes widened as Kathleen came in, followed by Lolita.

"You, too, Ms. Whitby, but not this little feathered creature. A deinonychus, I presume?"

Kathleen was put off by his calmness. "I thought you knew that, but, yes, she's a deinonychus. She's quite dangerous and also very impatient, so it would be better if you answered our questions without dissembling."

Passway nodded. "I see. However, you haven't asked any questions, at least not yet. On the other hand, I have many requests to make, and I'm not planning to be reticent. First, tell me the time formula. I'll also want your signature on some papers that I've conveniently drawn up. They're nothing that should worry you too much. They give me control of your holding corporation, but you don't actually need that. I believe that will lead to control of the medical research company. Once you do those two things, you will be free to leave. You see, I'm not unreasonable. I won't bother to have you killed as long as you go back to your primitive location and stay there. I'm not interested in anything that far back. I like modern conveniences and comfort too much to have a fascination with living in a cave."

She opened her mouth, then snapped it shut in anger. "You've got a fine way of greeting people. If you haven't noticed, we're both armed. We came to talk, not to fight, though. We want Lolita's daughter freed. She's an important member of our group. As for the two things you want, I'm not disposed to make those concessions, and you aren't in a strong negotiating position. If Lolita doesn't get her chick, she may decide to bite, and that's something you won't enjoy."

He laughed dryly. "You think I didn't know you were coming? I have a state-of-the-art surveillance system in this house. My men know you are in here, and they're waiting for my signal to act. In addition, I have my own special enforcers." He snapped his fingers. In response, there was the sound of servo motors as a robot dog appeared from the far side of the bed.

Passway made an expansive motion as if to introduce the robot. "This is Duke. He's got numerous brothers, but they're not here at the moment. You will notice that his sister, Daisy, is present, though."

A second robot came around the bed. This one had a laser mounted on its back.

Passway continued, "Duke's bite is much worse than his bark, but Daisy disdains such primitive methods. She has a fifty-megawatt laser mounted on her back. It is somewhat limited due to battery technology, but it will fire four times before the batteries are fully discharged. Since there are only three of you, I believe that will be enough. Daisy is quite accurate. In fact, she never misses."

Kathleen was standing beside Cadeyrin, and she thought about jumping them out of the room, but Lolita was beyond her reach. She called to her. "Lolita, come here. This man is too well protected for you to attack."

Passway lifted his hand negatively. "No. Stay still. Duke is now alerted. He will attack anyone who moves. You see, I have the upper hand, and I will have your secrets shortly. Otherwise, your caveman and your dinosaur won't make it out of here alive. That might not be a total waste, though. I have a scientific group that is willing to pay me a significant sum for the chance to dissect one of your deinonychus friends. They might even pay for the opportunity to study the physiology of a prehistoric human. Now, the time formula, please."

Lolita screamed her battle cry and leaped at Passway. The robot dog shot forward and collided with her, throwing her spring off. She landed beside Passway's chair and scrabbled wildly on the tile floor as she reoriented herself.

Duke moved forward and snapped at her wing/arm. He was armed with teeth that looked like spikes. His mouth closed on her wrist, and she screamed again, this time in pain. The scream was instantly followed by a violent front kick with her killing claw.

It caught the robot's neck and dug into a seam between the plastic plates. The machine was flung violently into the air and landed on its back. Lolita jumped behind Passway's chair as a flash of coherent green light came from Daisy's laser. The light struck the wall beyond the chair, leaving a smoking spot.

Lolita shot out from the other side of the chair and leaped into the air, flapping her wing/arms. A second green flash was accompanied by a cloud of smoke that smelled like burning feathers. The little raptor fell, off-balance on the bed. She regained her feet, hopping mad.

"You burns my wing. I kill you!" She jumped off the bed, landing behind Daisy. The robot dog began to turn around, but it wasn't as maneuverable as Lolita. She turned with it, keeping out of the direct line of fire. There was a third flash, and the bedspread blazed up in flame.

Cadeyrin had his forty-five out and was emptying the magazine into Duke. The robot dog leaped forward, but one of the heavy slugs struck an unarmored spot. Duke's legs folded, and its body dropped to the floor.

Cadeyrin moved the barrel of his pistol to cover Passway.

Daisy saw the motion. The robot appeared to be programmed to protect its master at all costs. It turned away from Lolita and fired the laser the fourth time.

Cadeyrin grunted, and his pistol arm dropped. Kathleen saw a smoking hole in her husband's shirt where the laser had struck his upper right chest to her horror. He hadn't dropped the pistol, though. He carefully took it out of his right hand with his left and raised it at Passway again.

Daisy leaped forward, jaws open. Lolita leaped as quickly and landed on the robot's back. The mechanical dog went down, and there was a flurry of action on the floor. It resolved quickly with a metallic snapping sound, followed by an electric spark.

Lolita lay still, her neck held in the robot's jaws, her right killing claw hooked in the underside of the robot where it had shorted out some vital circuit.

Kathleen screamed in horror. Lolita had been like her first child in some respects. She lifted her pistol to cover Passway, her hand shaking so violently that Passway simply smiled.

"You see, my robots are equal to your dinosaur. The best part is I have many of them. They're coming now." He waved at the computer screen where there was a floor plan of the mansion. Flashing spots were converging on the bedroom area from all over the house.

Cadeyrin grunted in pain, then spoke, "You intend evil. If you had the time equation, you would make the world into hell for everyone else. You cannot have it, nor can you have the secret of life."

Passway's eyes widened. As he watched, Cadeyrin lifted his right arm and ripped his shirt away. The laser burn had faded to only a spot.

Cadeyrin said, "When taken at full strength, the drug makes you heal almost immediately." He casually aimed and shot Passway's leg. The man screamed hoarsely and grabbed at the wound.

Cadeyrin continued. "Sorry. You won't heal that quickly. Now, where is Lola?"

Passway looked confused. "Who?"

"Lolita's daughter. We want her back."

"She-she escaped. I don't have her now. She was in the same room that your son was, but she escaped on her own. He had Devonette's help."

Kathleen shouted, "You miserable beast! You strike at my children and me! Your creature killed Lolita, you--" Her finger tightened in her emotion. Her nine-millimeter pistol made a sharp sound, more like a snap than the boom of Cadeyrin's forty-five. Passway's eyes rolled up, and he slumped out of the chair. He landed on his back, with blood pooling from the hole in his head.

Kathleen grabbed for Cadeyrin. "I didn't mean to shoot. I had my finger on the trigger, and I pulled it by accident, but he deserved it!" She dropped the pistol, then went to her knees beside Lolita, tears streaming down her face. "She was so sweet. Why do we have to lose the ones we love? First Belle, now Lolita. They'd have been better off if we'd never brought them forward."

Kathleen pressed her cheek to the feathered breast and started to gather the still form into her arms. She stopped and looked at him, eyes wide. "I heard a heartbeat! She's still alive."

Cadeyrin answered, "Hold on to her. We have to leave before the robots get here. Try to keep her neck in the same position. I'll put us in Dr. Wolf's old bedroom. She can recover there."

His hand touched Kathleen's shoulder. She started to ask, "Are you sure she'll recover?" They were moving through time before she finished the sentence.

◆

When the first robot came careening through the open bedroom door, it found Passway's body and nothing else.

Chapter Twenty-Nine

Devonette and Death

Cole was conscious of his heart rate as he moved through time to their appointment. It was pounding – much faster than average. The thought of meeting Devonette had a definite effect on him. He tried to clear his mind, but the memory of her body beneath his and her arms around him made his rationality disappear.

Cole was taking his time in the in-between dimension. Time disappeared when one was in the spirit world. He could have been there for a second or hours. He wasn't sure. However, he felt no sense of urgency other than the rising desire making his blood grow hot.

Did she love him? At times, she acted as if she did, but she could change instantly. Devonette was so erratic that it made him crazy. First, she blew hot, then cold. What if she had set him up? She denied doing it before, and her rescue seemed to be evidence of her innocence.

He had to remember that she was under the control of her father. She was used to her lifestyle, and he held the purse strings. Passway wanted Cole. No, he wanted the time-equation and the red paste. Devonette wasn't stupid. Far from it. She could see the benefit of controlling both of those things. She might decide to help her father.

He made a disparaging sound. At least it was intended that way. His hearing was distorted in the in-between, along with his other senses. He was realistic enough to know that she could easily find another man. He wasn't that unique. Others had the same equipment that he did. Devonette could be content with someone else, especially if she could live the life to which she was accustomed.

It would be better if he arrived early. That way, he could watch the place and make sure that he wasn't being set up. With that thought, he visualized exiting into the modern world beside her garage. There was a tree there, and he could take cover behind it.

As he formed and held the image of his destination, he was suddenly there. The tree trunk materialized as if he were standing in a fog that dissipated quickly. It was in front of him, and then the fog was gone. He was back in the everyday world.

⸺◆⸺

Devonette parked her car and climbed out. She had done nothing but think about Cole's body since she'd started driving. As a result, she had become so aroused that it felt like her skin was on fire. The cooler air in the garage raised goosebumps on her arms, and she shivered. The texture of her clothes seemed rough and abrasive, nothing like Cole's smooth skin. She couldn't wait for him to arrive.

She locked the garage and strode to the house, then fumbled the keys as she tried to unlock the door. She was shaking so much. Damn him! No one should have that degree of control over her. She'd make him regret it the instant she saw him.

She entered the kitchen and there he was! Cole rose from the dinette table where he'd been sitting. Her pique was forgotten instantly. She darted forward and threw herself in his arms, her lips seeking his.

"Oh, my god, Cole. I'm so glad to see you. I've been dreaming about us tonight." She pulled him close and pressed her hips against his with a wriggling motion.

His senses were screaming at him to hurry, that Devonette was a wonderful thing, and she wanted him. Every aspect of him was focused on her. It took an immense act of will to push her away.

"Let's talk for a bit. Where is Lola?"

It wasn't what she wanted to hear. That was obvious. She made a disgusted face as she answered, "I don't know! Can you get that through your head? The birdy-thingy disappeared somewhere. Daddy's mad about it, but no one knows where it went. How can you ask about that when we're here together now?" She finished by stamping her foot.

He considered her overall demeanor. She didn't appear to be lying and, even though she seemed petulant, he knew he was going to ignore it.

"Come here, you!" He pulled her close again. Their lips met, and she made an inarticulate sound, then her hand slipped between them, and he lost his ability to focus on anything but getting her clothes off.

⸻⬦⸻

There was a trail of clothing leading from the kitchen to the bedroom. They had discarded every garment without thought. Now they were lying on the coverlet in a pool of sweat. He rolled to prop himself on his elbow and look at her.

There was reddish sunlight filtering through the blinds, and it highlighted her flushed face and closed eyelids. She looked happy and calm. Her eyes opened, and she smiled radiantly.

"You're what I've always wanted and, yet, I didn't know how much I really needed you," she whispered.

He tried to analyze the statement. It betrayed a self-focus that he wasn't sure he liked, but maybe he should interpret it in the spirit of the moment. He replied, "You're exactly right for me. I'll prove it to you."

She made a soft laugh, then said, "Again? So soon?"

He moved over her and pressed his lips against her neck.

"Aren't you interested?"

She groaned and moved her legs, offering him access. "Don't make me wait like this. I want you now."

This time was less rushed. Cole took his time, moving slowly and concentrating on her reactions. He controlled himself until they reached a point where everything lit up and exploded in a blinding flash of passion.

Afterward, they drowsed in each other's arms.

Cole snapped awake with a sense that there was something wrong. The room was dark. The sun had set while they were asleep. Despite the darkness, he felt a sense of presence. There was someone nearby, perhaps not in the room, at least not yet, but definitely in the house. He slid to the side of the bed and rolled silently to the floor.

There was no chance to dress. He had a brief flash of amusement. The first thing he thought about was pulling on his pants. Something about fighting while naked bothered him. It was silly, he supposed, but he felt more vulnerable exposed as he was.

Devonette made a slight sound. Her breathing was still regular, so she hadn't awakened. He stayed low and slid to the foot of the bed. The bedroom door was on his side, and he wanted some cover before whoever was out there entered.

From the foot of the bed, he moved to the side of a dresser, then along the wall toward the door. He was standing by now, and the movement had gotten the blood flowing in his arms and legs. He controlled his breath. Slow and soft was the way he wanted it. Gasping or panting would only tell his opponent where he was.

The bedroom door was half-open. Cole hadn't paid attention to it when they had come in. There were more urgent things on his mind at that point. He must have bumped the door to swing it partly closed as they rushed for the bed.

His eyes had adapted to the darkness. It wasn't as black as he'd initially thought. There was a slant of faint light coming through the door. That was in his favor since it would cast a shadow when someone prepared to come in.

The light dimmed briefly, and then the door swung slowly open. Cole tensed as someone moved through the opening. There was the soft sound of shoes crushing the carpet. He gauged the distance then struck as hard as he could.

His fist caught the intruder on the temple, and the man went down with a cry and a thump. Cole jumped forward for a follow-up strike, but something hit him on the neck just above his shoulders. He saw a flash of red as the blow jolted him. It knocked him to his knees, one hand landing on the prone attacker.

He had the presence of mind to lean forward and kick with his left foot. It caught the man behind him on a leg and the second man went down with a curse.

By now, Devonette was awake. She screamed a curse, then shouted, "Not again!"

Cole slammed his fist down at the prone man's head, but his enemy blocked the strike. The guy was muscular, and he knew how to wrestle. He caught Cole's arm and tried to lock it up. Cole knew some judo, but not enough to be very effective against an expert. His primary defense was his strength. He yanked his arm out of the other man's grip and slammed his fist into the man's midsection. The guy grunted with pain, then slapped at Cole's face.

The blow caught him on the nose. It was painful and made his eyes water. He knew he had to get clear. The second man would be on him any time.

Devonette clicked on the overhead light, and he squinted, trying to clear his watering eyes.

She swore again. "What the hell are you two doing in my bedroom? I told you the last time to get out. Stop it! Stop it right now!"

Cole recognized the two bodyguards, Randy and James. James was on the floor, still gasping and holding his solar plexus. Randy had regained his feet and now was pointing a pistol at Devonette. He immediately realized that she wasn't the threat. He swung the gun, trying to cover Cole, but Cole was already moving laterally.

Cole jumped high, one leg landing on the mattress. He bounced off and crashed into Randy. The gun went off, sending a flash of light by Cole's side but missing him. The sound of the shot emphasized how serious the fight was. Cole hadn't mentally made the transition to kill or be killed, but the shot pushed him over that edge.

He slammed the edge of his hand into Randy's throat. There was a crunch, and he knew he'd broken the hyoid bone. The bodyguard staggered back, grabbing his throat. He'd be lucky if he didn't strangle. Breaking that bone often sent the larynx into a spasm that closed the airway.

Cole looked for the pistol, but it had skittered away somewhere. James was climbing to his feet now, and he had a pistol, too. It looked odd. Cole suddenly recognized it as a taser.

The bodyguard lifted it and fired, but again Cole was moving fast. One of the prongs struck him in the chest, but the other one missed and went under his outstretched arm. James cursed and swung the taser for its second shot. By this time, Cole had gotten close.

He struck the bodyguard's arm, knocking the taser up as it fired and the second set of barbs lodged in the ceiling.

James immediately shoved the weapon into Cole's chest and triggered it again. There was a paralyzing jolt that locked all his muscles painfully for an instant.

He fell back away from the weapon. He hadn't realized that it also acted as a stun weapon. It had electrodes mounted on the barrel in addition to the darts it shot.

James laughed cruelly. "Don't like that, do you?"

The man advanced, and Cole backpedaled, trying to keep out of reach of the weapon.

James lunged forward and struck him a glancing blow on his forearm. Again the weapon jolted him. Cole's arm went numb for an instant, and he staggered.

James leaped forward, jabbing the taser at Cole's chest, but he swung his left arm and struck the leaping man a resounding slap on the right ear. It made a loud pop. James fell to his knees, stunned.

He clapped his hand to his ear but kept the taser pointing at Cole.

This time, when he spoke, he didn't laugh. "I'll kill you for that, you stupid caveman." His eyes strayed to Randy for a moment. The other man was lying on his back, his eyes staring at the ceiling.

"And for Randy, too. I'm going to make it slow and painful." He pulled something from his belt. He held it up, and it clicked as a double-sided blade popped out.

"Maybe you don't know much about knife-fighting, but I do. I've cut more men than you can imagine. I'm going to give you a hint, boy. When you're in a fight with a man who knows how to use a knife, you're going to get cut. The only thing you can do is pray that it isn't too deep." He paused, shaking his head. "Damn, I think you ruptured my eardrum. I'm going to cut you bad, and I'm going to make it slow. Passway'll have to live with not getting his way. He wants you alive. That's not going to happen."

Cole looked to the side, searching for something to hold or throw. He caught up a perfume bottle from Devonette's dresser.

"That won't help, kid. Unless you're going to spray it on her." James motioned at the naked girl. He turned his head to look at her as if he'd only now noticed that she was nude.

"Maybe that'd be a good idea," he said slowly, his eyes lingering on her breasts. "I think when I'm done killing you, I'll take some time to show her what a real man is like. Passway and I have just parted company. I don't need any more of his BS orders."

Cole lunged forward and squirted the perfume directly in Jame's eyes as he turned back. It must have burned. James yelled and slashed with the knife.

Cole felt a burn that crossed his chest. He looked down at a thin line that began leaking blood. He backed up. James was still trying to see, but the knife was in continual motion, and he didn't want to get too close.

———◇———

Devonette watched in a kind of stunned horror. She'd been overwhelmed by the sensations Cole elicited in her, but now she was angry. Those two shouldn't be here. Her father had sent them. Daddy didn't trust her to get the information he wanted. Now James was threatening her, and he'd turned on her father. That was too much!

It all came from her falling for Cole. He had too much influence over her, and she couldn't--no, she wouldn't stand for it. No man could gain the upper hand over her, not through force or pleasure. She was so angry that she was shaking, and a red hue tinged her vision.

Her foot struck something by the bed frame. It was Randy's pistol. She bent and picked it up, holding it the way she'd seen in numerous movies.

James had recovered enough of his vision to see a little. He moved cautiously forward, trying to catch Cole in the corner of the room.

Cole threw the perfume bottle as hard as he could. It struck the bodyguard on the cheek with a thud. It was a heavy bottle, and James staggered from the blow. Cole leaped in, catching the muscular man's knife arm with both his hands.

James struck with his left hand, striking the back of Cole's head. It hurt, but Cole kept his focus on the knife. He wrenched at the wrist, then grabbed the man's fingers, twisting the knife out of his grip.

James struck him again, this time hitting his temple. Cole's vision flashed, and he shoved the knife out hard in a counter-strike. James grunted loudly.

Cole released James' arm and backed up. The bodyguard held his hand near the center of his chest, and blood was flowing around his fingers. He opened his mouth to say something, and a gush of blood came out, splashing over the nearby chair and saturating Irwin, the unfortunate stuffed tiger.

Devonette had been paralyzed, watching the fight. Now her anger peaked. She lifted the pistol and shot. The bullet struck James in the back, and he fell.

That wasn't enough. She screamed, "You ruined Irwin! You can't do this to me! I won't have it." She shot James twice more, then turned the weapon toward Cole in a fury.

Cole lifted his hand in a calming motion as she aimed at him. The pistol fired a fourth time, and the window beside him broke. The crazy girl was trying to kill him now.

She aimed again, a glint of madness in her eyes.

There was a rushing sound, and a colorful streak of feathers flew through the door. Lola's wing/arm struck Devonette's arm as she sailed by, knocking the pistol out of line.

Lola bounced off the bed and turned to spring at the girl. There was another shot, and the deinonychus faltered but then rushed forward, enveloping Devonette in her wing/arms. Devonette shot again, and Lola screamed, then the two faded into the in-between world, leaving a fading mist and some feathers drifting to the carpet.

Cole stared in shock. Both the bodyguards were dead. Lola had taken two bullets protecting him, and Devonette might be dead. All it would take was one kick, and she'd be ripped open.

He moved forward and sat on the bed. There was no tracking the two as they moved through time. Serensaa might be able to do it, but he didn't have that ability.

The enormity of what had happened seeped through him. In one moment, he had lost the two women who were essential to him. Devonette was crazy. He saw that now, but he still loved her, or maybe it was simply lust that he felt. He couldn't differentiate.

Lola was kind and sweet, and he knew he loved her. They'd been together so long. His heart made a pounding throb and felt as if it would leap out of his chest with pain. What would he do without her?

⸺◆⸺

There was a soft sound, and he looked up. His father had materialized in the room.

"Are you alright?" Cadeyrin asked. Then his eyes narrowed as he moved forward and pulled Cole's shirt away from the slash. He looked at it then said, "Not too bad. You'll scar from it, but that will heal. What happened here?"

Cole waved his hand at the two dead men. "Devonette and I were in bed, and they came in. Passway sent them to catch me again. We fought. I was winning, then Devonette got one of their guns and started trying to kill me. Lola got shot. Then she took Devonette in between. I don't know where they went, and I want Lola back!" His eyes were watering again. He wiped at them, then realized that tears were flooding over his cheeks.

Cadeyrin put his hand on his son's shoulder. "We have to get out of here. I can hear sirens. Someone must have heard the shots and called the police."

Cole sniffed. His nose was running. He shrugged. "I don't care. They can throw me in prison. My life is over without her."

His father shook his head. "You got in a real mess, but don't say that. I lost my first wife to a saber-tooth. I loved her. Then I lost my father and my tribe. My life was truly over, but then I found your mother. There's always another chance. There was for me, and there will be for you."

There was a pounding at the front door. Both men looked, then Cadeyrin shut his eyes and took them through time.

Chapter Thirty

No Use Running Away

Lola knew she was struck hard. Her lungs were filling, making it difficult to breathe, but the human girl would kill Cole if she didn't do something. She grabbed Devonette, yanking the naked woman close. The gun went off again, burning a painful trail through her guts. She screamed in pain but continued to hold the woman.

She was falling. It hurt, and she couldn't feel her legs, but she couldn't leave Devonette here to shoot Cole. She strained to clear her mind, then began to pull them both into the spirit world. She hadn't chosen a destination when she entered. Her only goal was to get away. Panic made her try to run from the specter of death that was rapidly approaching. Her thoughts were blurry moments interspersed with bolts of lightning-like clarity. A wave of remorse, so strong that it almost overpowered the physical pain, struck. She'd never see Cole again. He would live out his life, and she wouldn't be part of it. The thought was so filled with anguish that she screamed again. This time blood came from her mouth and splattered over Devonette's face. She shuddered and forced herself to focus.

The in-between world was different. A terrible roiling blackness surrounded her. Devonette was forgotten, although she held her close enough for the blood from her lungs to flow down the woman's torso. She couldn't hold a destination in her mind with enough clarity. The pain was so intense that it seemed as if a terrible wind was blowing her in random directions.

The storm! Lola suddenly recognized the clouds. She'd jumped into the middle of it, or her lack of destination had attracted it. She couldn't tell which. What she did know was that she couldn't focus on getting out of it because her guts pained her so, and it was so hard to get a breath.

She felt more than saw a black mass of clouds envelope the two. A massive force tossed them in a direction that might have been high if there had been dimensions that sentient minds could understand. The winds tore violently at them, and they were thrown with incredible speed through clouds of gibbering lost souls. She saw deformed monsters, creatures that had never existed, things mutated by the time storm's ferocity. They howled and loomed over her, threatening to pull her soul away from her.

Disembodied fingers clawed at her, trying to rip her apart, trying to steal her life, to take it away to some horrendous destination that was beyond her imagination. Lola clung tight, but her mind was fading. She was so tired. It would be good just to let go and sleep.

Everything grew tight and then tighter as if time itself was stretched to a breaking point. There was a moment where she felt incredibly compressed, as if she was being pushed through a tight opening by forces beyond her control. The lightning flared, once, twice, and then it struck Lola with a flashing explosion of multi-colored lights. It might have been death striking; it was so brutal. She could see nothing except intermittent flashes in the gathering darkness. Then she could hold on no longer. A sensation of infinite relief washed over her, and she relaxed into total blackness.

⸻◆⸻

The bright morning air suddenly formed a misty cloud, and two bodies fell on the damp ground with a thud. They lay still, facing each other, eyes open but unseeing.

⸻◆⸻

The Cretaceous morning was sunny and bright. It had rained the night before, making scents easy to pick up in the high humidity. The huge yellow-feathered Acrocanthosaur pushed through the grove of small trees, drawn by curiosity. Something had made a thumping sound over this way. It sniffed, drawing air across the roof of its mouth and over the sensitive olfactory nerves.

The giant predator inhaled deeply. The light breeze carried the distinct scent of a small raptor along with something else. It was something that smelled edible but different from anything it had ever smelled before. Hunger was always on its mind, and it hadn't eaten this morning.

The barrier of trees parted with a crash and a drag on the beast's legs. There, on the verge of the lake! Two animals lay still, near each other. The Acro's salivary glands began to flow. It was time for breakfast. It halted for a moment to check out the area. There was no other animal in sight. It had this find to itself, and that was a good thing. It was still suffering from a serious bite from another Acrocanthosaur that it had received in a dispute over a rotten carcass.

It approached cautiously. It was the dominant carnivore of the area, but it was still careful about strange things. It peered with one eye at the two prone creatures. They were staring at each other, ignoring its presence.

As it watched, the raptor stretched out its claws to touch the curiously blunt fingers of the other creature. The two held that position, touching, then the raptor made a strangled cry, and blood poured from its jaws.

The smell of fresh blood made the Acro's hunger overcome caution. The colossal head dropped, jaws open. A glob of saliva dripped out, and then the jaws snapped shut on the small raptor's body, making a crunching sound as the teeth penetrated. The Acro shifted its bite to get a better grip, then raised its head to swallow.

A few loose feathers blew away on the wind, catching the Acro's eye. It swallowed once hard, then again as the mass moved down its throat. It was satisfying, but not enough. It bent to pick up the other creature, but that one had disappeared. There was a cloud of mist in the air but no sign of the creature, other than the fading remnant of the strange scent.

That was odd. Creatures usually didn't simply disappear. The predator was puzzled for a moment but then turned away. It was still hungry, and there was food somewhere. It just had to find it. That was what was important. It quacked once plaintively as it strode off.

The damp ground showed the outlines of a human and a deinonychus, the Acro's footprints, and a few colorful feathers that were suddenly caught again by the breeze. The feathers drifted out over the lake and landed on the water, then the gust died, and the water was still.

Chapter Thirty-One

The Front Porch

The afternoon was warm, and BW was lying on the top step, gazing into the distance. There might be something to hunt out there, but it was too much work right now, and besides, he thought that Kathleen might feed him something. She was fixing food in the kitchen for Lolita. She needed to eat. He understood that she was hurt. He was concerned about her but figured she didn't need every bit of what Kathleen was preparing. There would be a bite or two for him.

He leaped up, surprised. There had been a thumping sound behind him and a gust of strange scent. It was a strange human scent. Before he finished turning, he knew it was a woman who had recently been having sex and who had been in contact with his friend Lola. His face wrinkled, displaying his fangs as he growled at the nude form lying sprawled on the porch.

The woman moved feebly, her fingers twitched, and one leg moved slightly. Other than that, she did not respond to his warning. He walked stiff-legged to inspect her. She appeared to be unconscious. He sniffed suspiciously, then decided she wasn't a threat. She was too small in stature to be dangerous. He sniffed delicately at her, then wagged his tail. His nose told him that she had been intimate with Cole, which made her acceptable.

He nosed at the woman, trying to get a response. She took a deeper breath but otherwise lay still. He left her and scratched on the closed door to the house. This situation wasn't something that he could deal with alone. It wasn't normal, and he figured that one of the humans needed to address the problem. He scratched again, then heard Gridley's footsteps approaching the door.

He sat expectantly, waiting for praise. He knew he'd done a good thing.

The door swung back, and Grid asked, "What's the problem, BW?" Then he saw the woman's foot. "Ah! Where did she come from?" The man leaned over the woman and placed a finger on her throat. After a moment, he straightened and went inside yelling for Kathleen. BW sighed. Maybe she'd reward him with something good to eat.

Meanwhile, he thought he'd better protect the strange woman since she was a friend of Cole's. He lay down beside her. Nothing would dare to bother her while he was on watch.

Kathleen and Annie came running out. Annie took one look and asked Gridley, "She's still alive?"

"Yes. Faint pulse, but she hasn't moved. Who is she, and how did she get here?"

Kathleen put her hand on the girl's forehead. "She's Devonette Passway. She is the one who has been causing Cole all sorts of trouble. As to how she got here, I haven't a reasonable idea. She must have projected herself through time, but why here? Cole isn't here. Cadeyrin went off to collect him. There's no one here who could have brought her."

He looked around. "She's the only one here. Could she be a natural time-traveler like Serensaa?"

"Perhaps. But I'm not sure. There's no way to tell. The first thing is to get her inside and see if she regains consciousness."

Kathleen patted the girl's smooth cheek. There was a slight flutter of eyelashes in response.

Gridley said, "She's awake. She just doesn't want to face her situation yet. You saw her eyelashes move? I've seen that before. People shut down when faced with too much stress. She'll come out of it on her own. She has to reach the point where she recognizes she has no alternative except to open her eyes."

BW jumped to his feet and ran into the house at that point, his tail wagging. Then they heard Cadeyrin calling, "Kathleen?"

She answered, "Out here. Devonette's here."

Cole strode through the door first, his face white and set. He knelt by his mother and slapped the cheek that Kathleen had just patted. The closed eyes opened wide, and the girl screamed. She drew a ragged breath, then screamed again, a despairing cry that spoke of anguish and incredible loss.

BW nearly knocked Gridley over as he charged back out of the house in response to the screams. He seemed to have appointed himself as Devonette's guardian. He stood by her side, teeth slightly barred, ready to defend her.

Cole pushed at the wolf. "Make some room, BW. She doesn't need your help."

The girl's eyes focused on Cole. She made a tentative motion with her lips, then said, "Cole?" She slurred his name, but he could tell she recognized him.

"Yes. It's me, you murderous bitch. You shot Lola. Where is she? What did you do with her, and how did you get here?" He raised his hand to strike her again, but the swing was stopped by Cadeyrin, who caught his wrist.

"No hitting defenseless women. Let her have time to recover. Then we'll get her story." The big man released his son, then extended his hand to Kathleen.

She took it and pulled herself up. "Let's take her inside. The porch is no place for an injured girl."

Cole was furious, but he tried to control himself. "Yeah. Let her recover, and then she'd better tell me where to find Lola."

The girl moved her hands, extending them toward him. "Cole? You're here?" Her voice was more understandable this time.

Cole looked at her. The rhythm of the phrasing wasn't that of Devonette. It sounded different, softer maybe, and the tonality wasn't the same. He bent to look directly in her eyes, a position, he reminded himself, he'd been in just a short time prior.

He jumped, startled. She was humming softly deep in her chest, and the sound was vaguely familiar. Her eyes and face looked contented, and she was looking at him with an expression of love, something that Devonette had not previously done. Devonette looked at him with lust, certainly, but he hadn't seen this degree of love and trust in her face before.

He bent and lifted her carefully. She clung to him as he raised her to her feet. She immediately fell when he released her, forcing him to catch her in his arms.

"Balance is bad," she said, speaking clearly for the first time. "How can you stand this way?"

He shook his head. "I don't know what you mean."

She moved her feet experimentally, relying on his embrace to support her. "Maybe with practice, it will work." She wobbled a little, then took more of her weight on her legs. She seemed to gain stability quickly. After a moment, she quit looking at her feet and raised her eyes to his. "I've always loved you, Cole."

"Loved me? You just tried to kill me? And, what have you done with Lola?" He caught her upper arms and shook her.

She leaned close to him and nipped at his neck in response, then drew back, startled, holding a hand over her mouth.

"Ow! That hurts. Lips are in the way. I've got to be careful."

Cole's anger exploded. "Only Lola nips at me that way. What the hell do you think you're doing?" He shook her again.

She answered, "Lola? Don't you know me, Cole? I am Lola."

His mouth dropped open then snapped shut. A puzzled expression slowly appeared on his face.

Serensaa had come out during the exchange. She moved close and looked at the girl, then made a sweeping gesture toward the heavens. "The body is different, but the spirit is Lola," she said.

Cole stared at the Clovis woman, wondering if she'd lost her mind.

Cadeyrin moved close and looked into the girl's eyes. After a moment, he drew back. "That's not a human gaze. It's too direct."

Kathleen asked, "So, is it Lola, like Serensaa says?"

He looked again. "I can't tell. Serensaa is more sensitive than me in some ways. Perhaps she's correct."

The girl said, "This body is hard to use. Human balance is tricky." She looked behind her, then added in surprise, "No wonder! No tail makes it difficult."

She abruptly staggered again, then went down on one knee. "No breath either. I can't breathe the way I used to." She panted for a moment, then added, "She shot me, and I jumped us into the spirit world. The time-storm was there." She abruptly looked panic-stricken, then wailed, "It caught us. It was awful!"

Cole instinctively bent and caught her close, then asked, "What did it do?"

"The old Sasquatch told me that no one who entered it escaped the same as they were when they went in." She paused, remembering. "It was horrible. I was squeezed down a tight tunnel, and then we fell out into the world. We were in front of a big yellow, and it ate me. My beautiful body! My poor body. I saw it happen from her eyes. We changed bodies in the storm when the lightning hit us. Now, I--I'm dead. Oh, Cole, can you love me if I'm dead?" She slipped from his arms and dropped to all fours on the stone, gasping for breath as tears streamed from her eyes to the stone porch.

She wasn't making sense. Cole shook his head, trying to understand, then knelt and pulled her close to smooth her hair. She sighed and rested her head on his shoulder. She kept her eyes squeezed tight and clung to his arm as if she were fearful he would disappear if she opened them. "I've loved you forever, you know, but we couldn't be mates."

He tightened his embrace, and she opened her eyes to look up at him coyly. "I have some of her memories, you know. They are in this body, and I can remember things she did. They're mixed with my own memories, too. You were mating with her. Will you mate with me now? I want to do it myself, not just have a memory." She pulled him tightly against her body. "Right now?"

He looked at his mother in confusion. She shook her head and shrugged. "You're an adult, Cole. I don't pretend to understand what has happened, but if you are going to mate with her, please have the decency to go somewhere private."

He looked down at the girl's beautiful, glowing eyes. There was a different element in them now, and he realized he couldn't recognize Devonette in their depths. Instead, he was looking into Lola's far-sighted and direct gaze. He wanted to believe, but there was still doubt in his mind. It was too much to accept easily.

"How do you kill a bear?" he asked.

"I grab its side, then kick my claw between its ribs. I jump up to kick downward and rip it open. Then I get away fast before it hits me."

"What about a big yellow, an Acro?"

"I wouldn't try alone unless I had no choice. They're dangerous." She sounded distressed. "An Acro! It ate me. I saw it swallow my body." She paused as a wondering expression crossed her face. "But, she was in it, not me. Now I'm in hers." She looked down at herself as if starting to realize exactly what that meant.

She looked at her hand as if seeing the flat nails for the first time, then added in a calmer voice, "An Acro? I'd want a rifle. These fingers are useless for that kind of stuff." She looked up at him with a smile. "You're testing me, aren't you?"

He glanced at his father. Cadeyrin held a neutral expression on his face. Cole received the distinct impression that his father was judging his actions as well as hers. After a moment, Cadeyrin responded to the implied question. "She identifies as Lola. She knows things a modern woman wouldn't. Who is to say that she's wrong? She should know better than anyone else who she is."

Cole stuttered. "Umm. Maybe. The Devonette I know is devious." He turned to look at the girl. "You could be pretending."

She shook her head urgently. "No. I'm me. Lola. Did she know about Ulfsaa?"

He tried to remember. "I didn't tell her. I'm sure I didn't speak of him to her. She didn't want to know anything about my life here. She wasn't interested. She only wanted me, and I kind of think it was because her father wanted to use me as leverage."

The girl put her hand to her temple as she searched the memories in the brain in which she found herself. "It was her father. He wants the red paste formula for his company. They intend to make everyone ill, so the common people have shorter lives, but they will keep the paste for themselves and live forever. They want to be gods with human servants. He wants the time-travel secret even more. He thinks it will give him unlimited power."

She shook her head and again touched her temple with her fingers. "I remember what she did. Oh, Cole. She wasn't a nice person. She did a lot of bad stuff." She shuddered. "Nasty things to other people."

He nodded. "She was out to add me to her list of canceled people. I think she wanted me to love her so that she could hurt me even more."

Lola leaned close, her eyes searching his. "She did other things, too." She hesitantly asked, "Can you love me? I mean, this body isn't mine. I'm not human, I'm--" She felt her breasts. "It's worse now. Every new moment I discover a difference. I feel so strange. It must be true that I'm in her body, but I'm -- I'm still me inside!" She began to sob again. "Is that important? Tell me it isn't. I love you. I've wanted to have a chick with you since forever." She gasped for breath, then cried, "You mated with her. Why not with me?"

Cole couldn't stand the sadness in her voice. He tentatively kissed her.

Lola found herself lost in the feeling from the lips that she had never had before. She floated on a sea of sensation that was so far beyond her imagination that she would have fallen if he hadn't supported her.

He pulled back and asked, "Are you really Lola?"

She nodded in response, her eyes fixed on his.

He pulled her close again and kissed her deeply. She drifted in the warm sensation. It was like nothing she'd ever dreamed. Her mouth parted, and, to her excitement, his did also. Their breaths mingled, and she unconsciously made a humming sound from deep in her chest.

Cole pulled back, his eyes wide. "You did it again! That sound."

"I...did I make a sound? I don't know. I was happy. I didn't mean to make a sound." She searched his face, alarmed. Did this mean he didn't believe her?

He gripped her shoulders, and she looked down. Having human shoulders was different. Her wing/arms had come from a narrow shoulder girdle. This body had distinct shoulders. She'd have to get used to that. She leaned forward as he pulled her close again.

He held her face close to his as he searched her eyes.

"Your idea of having a chick mostly convinced me. No human would say that, but that sound you made...it was Lola's sound. You did it before. It's her happy sound. It is really you, isn't it?"

Content, she gazed deeply into his eyes. "It's always been me. This body is new for me, but I've loved you forever."

Chapter Thirty-Two

Wintertime

The weather had turned cold during the last week. The leaves of the trees on the hilltop had been a brilliant mix of red and gold. Now they had faded and were dropping to blow in the gusty wind.

Gridley and Annie were visiting their daughter in 1962. She had gotten married six months ago and was happily engaged in homemaking for her aerospace engineer husband.

Serensaa and Logan were somewhere off at the back of the house or possibly in their suite.

Kathleen's family relaxed in the great room, watching the flames dance in the fireplace. She and Cadeyrin were sitting on the long couch across the room. She was snugly wrapped in a quilted throw, and his arm was around her shoulders. Lolita had come in late, and, seeing how things were, she had settled down quietly on the carpeted floor by Cadeyrin's legs and was now resting her head on his thigh.

Cole and Lola sat on another couch, a throw over their legs. Their eyes kept moving away from the fire to each other. Lola looked up at Cole. He was looking back with so much tenderness in his expression that she felt her heart would burst. She snuggled closer to him, secure in his arms and enjoying the heat of the fire.

Her baby suddenly kicked, causing the comforter they had wrapped around both of them to bounce up. She laughed and put her hand on the spot, feeling the little one move inside her. It was strange, having a child in her belly instead of laying a precious egg, but she still felt a strong maternal bond growing with the baby.

A moment of disorientation passed over her. Such feelings were gradually fading, but she sometimes missed her old body. Her human body was very different from her old one. Her nails and teeth were useless compared to her old fangs and claws. The advantage was that she could fit closer to Cole than before. She didn't need defensive weapons anyway. He'd protect her.

The disorientation faded. A question occurred to her: She knew who she was, but what was she? She'd inherited Devonette's memories, but the human brain was so impressionable that it had stored all of her own with no problem. She remembered everything she'd done in her prior existence. It seemed obvious that a particular body did not determine her identity. She was still Lola despite the change. There was something beyond the physical aspect of life, and that something contained her essence. Human books spoke of the soul. She'd known the word before, but now it took on a new significance.

She looked up at Cole again, and he tightened his arms in response, pulling her closer.

"You know I'm still me, your life-long soul-mate, don't you?"

His answer was physical. He bent, and their lips touched. Once again, she was lost in a wave of sensation. She could feel the passion rising in her, but the child kicked again at that precise moment. They both laughed.

———◄O►———

A slight smokey odor filtered into the room when the wind blew strongly and curled down the chimney. Despite its size, the great room was a comfortable and cozy haven. BW and one of the other wolves were toasting their sides near the hearth. It was a wonder they didn't catch on fire. They lay so near that their fur grew hot to the touch.

Kathleen leaned back in her husband's embrace and looked fondly at her son and the beautiful, black-haired woman at his side. Lola was eight months pregnant, and it looked as if the baby would be there by the turn of the year. The two kissed as she watched. The sight caused her to feel deep satisfaction. In her previous life at the university, she had never thought about having a son. She had never even imagined finding a love of her own. Now her heart was powerfully drawn to her grandchild resting securely in Lola's body.

Cadeyrin asked softly, "Does it make you feel old to think you're going to be a grandmother?"

She looked at him. He was as handsome as ever despite the years they'd been together. The red paste was a miracle drug. They hadn't aged at all since they'd first taken it. The old Sasquatch had given them a miracle that conferred the ability to regenerate damaged tissues, heal wounds, and at least promised to extend their lives indefinitely.

She shook her head in bemusement, who could say they would live forever until they reached the end of time. And time, she thought, had no end.

Cadeyrin moved closer and whispered in her ear. "Well? Does it?"

She leaned to kiss his cheek. "No. I'm not old physically, and I'm not bored with you, at least not yet, so I don't feel old."

They laughed softly, then he said, "Make sure you never get bored with me, please."

Lolita lifted her head to comment. "I going to be a gramma too. You gots share the chicky with me."

Kathleen nodded in agreement, then asked, "Are you sad that Lola has changed?"

The small raptor turned to look at the younger couple. The girl's complexion was rosy, and her hair was thick and glossy. She was the picture of health. The two lovers were again looking deeply into each other's eyes with a warm glow of passion.

"Sad, maybe, but Lola makes up for it. She may look like you, but inside she is still my baby chicky. I think I'm happy." She looked back at Kathleen with her eyes sparkling in amusement. "But then, I'm just a deinonychus from the Cretaceous Period, so what do I know?"

Before Kathleen could answer, Lolita added, "You better watch out, human woman. If you go die, I take your mate." She was back to speaking in her usual mode.

Cadeyrin scratched her neck affectionately as she spoke. She stretched her neck out, so he could reach an itchy spot better, then added, "He be good mate for me, just like Cole be good for Lola."

Cadeyrin nodded. It was a warm feeling, having a family, even if it included wolves and raptors. He felt he should say something profound in his role as the elder male. After a moment, he said, "In all of time, there is a time for all things, no matter how improbable."

Kathleen looked at her man with pride. She'd initially thought he was a primitive, a caveman with only a rudimentary understanding of the world. He was far from that. He was, she thought, the perfect mate for me. I just had to travel thirteen-thousand years into the past to find him. He was amazingly insightful.

She smiled at the thought. His statement was correct. Time stretched out infinitely before them, and all things were possible.

The End

About the Author

Eric S. Martell set out to become a scientist when he was five. He has a PhD. in experimental psychology. When personal computers came along (way back in prehistory), he became adept with them and spent years in software design, working on projects that ranged from early childhood learning software to military training. He has been trained in various types of energy healing, is an expert in real estate investing and sales, and holds a black belt in Tae-Kwon-Do. He is also a pilot, scuba diver, guitar player, outdoorsman, and is addicted to both science and science fiction.

Eric's science fiction books offer both believable science and compelling characters set against realistic action. They are carefully researched, and, while his fictional science sometimes strains against the bounds of current knowledge, it is always plausible. His stories cover alien invasion in an apocalyptic setting, political structure, space travel, advanced weapons, quantum physics, hunting, war, romance, time travel, and alien worlds.

He's been published in a series of anthologies and has published many full-length science fiction novels. His writing goal is to provide his readers with stories they cannot put down and he takes readers' suggestions seriously.

Notices about new books, free short stories, opinion posts, and preview pages for many of his books can be found on his author blog at
EricMartellAuthor.com

A request for you:

I make every effort to ensure your reading experience is enjoyable. This involves multiple editing steps, interior book layout, design, and using a professional cover artist/designer. Even so, it is becoming more difficult to generate sales. Please leave a review and tell your friends if you liked this story. That would help me immensely.

Reviews may be left on the platform of your choice or emailed directly to me through my blog.

Thank you,

Eric Martell

Venice, 2021

Also By Eric S. Martell

The Time Equation Series

Heart of Fire Time of Ice

Paradox: On the Sharp Edge of the Blade

All the Moments in Forever

Time Enough to Live

All Things in Time

The Belter Series

The Pirates of the Asteroids

The Belter Revolution

Cyber-Magic Series

CyberWitch

Nano-Magic

The Gaia Ascendant Trilogy

The Time of The Cat

Second Wave

Confederation

Other Books

Dustfall

Asterats and Other Stories